STRANGERS AND PILGRIMS SERIES
BOOK ONE

THE BEGINNING

THE LAST OF THE WAGON PIONEERS

By
John and Patty Probst

The Last of the Wagon Pioneers
by John and Patty Probst

Printed in the United States of America

ISBN 1-59781-638-8

Unless otherwise indicated, Bible quotations are taken from the King James Version.

Cover illustration by Yakovetic

www.xulonpress.com

Dedicated with love to our friend Ru Diaz,
who long before we put pencil to paper
encouraged us to write novels

. . . and especially to our daughters . . .
Marla, Joni and Jessica,
whose loving support and insight
were most valuable
to the outcome of this story.

CONTENTS

FOREWORD

These confessed that they were strangers and pilgrims on the earth. Hebrews 11:13 (KJV)

By faith Abraham, when he was called to go out into a place which he should after receive for an inheritance, obeyed; and he went out, not knowing whither he went.

By faith he sojourned in the land of promise, as in a strange country, dwelling in tabernacles with Isaac and Jacob, the heirs with him of the same promise. Hebrews 11: 8, 9 (KJV)

CHAPTER 1
FARMER

The glory of the Old West had long since faded, the war to end all wars was history, and the restlessness Farmer felt today was stronger than it had ever been!

Farmer was restless for as long as he could remember. "You was restless in my womb, son," his mama often reminded him. "Why your feet was on the run from the minute you was born." How many times Farmer had heard mama say that!

And the story had been told around the town of Holt, Texas, for years, that on the night Farmer Trevor was born—a most strange thing happened. A destructive tornado defied the laws of nature by angling west. It passed near Holt after hitting Chandler, Oklahoma.

Well, the story had evolved several times, so the last version Farmer heard went like this. 'The very hour that Farmer Trevor was being born—'twas the exact same time that terrible bad tornado was bearin' down on the Trevor farm. And the exact moment the cry of the Trevors' first child was heard in their farmhouse—'twas the exact same time that tornado ripped across the north section—strong enough to tear parts of the roof from the farmhouse. Surely, that tornado passed on its restless spirit to the Trevor boy as it swept by on its trek west!

Farmer sadly shook his head. He remembered when he was very young, a wagon train passed through Holt headed west. They camped outside of town where they found some water. Farmer's father had taken him to Holt and they swung by the camp.

Farmer hung wide eyed on every word as settlers told of mountains covered by tall pine and fir trees, clear running water, land farther than the eye could see! Just for the taking! As Farmer and his dad sat by the campfire and listened to stories of a true promised land, Farmer for the first time felt his restless feet point west.

From that time on the slogan, 'Go West Young Man,' was Farmer's battle cry for change and adventure. He remembered one spring morning when he was eight; the longing to go west was so strong that he could not stand another minute on the farm. He determined that morning to be like the settlers he had listened to three years before, and leave home for a new land. He put some clothes and food he found in the kitchen in a satchel—scribbled a note, and slipped out the door while his mama was tending to his two little brothers.

Farmer walked steadily into the afternoon—the sun now in his face. He had never been this far out of Holt before— except for last fall when his papa took their whole family to Abilene.

"Is Abilene west?" Farmer had queried.

"No, son, it's a fer piece to the southeast."

It was the biggest, busiest place Farmer had ever seen, beyond anything he could have imagined. Years later, Farmer had come to realize how that trip had changed the direction of his life.

He saw the cattle pens. He heard ranchers talkin' cattle talk. He watched the cowboys riding into town. The sights and sounds filled his mind—and he knew that day! "I'm going west and get me a ranch and raise me some cattle!" That was what he was doing the day he ran away.

"Wonder where I woulda ended up if Reverend Tunnell hadn't found me and brought me home?" Farmer mused out loud.

Farmer's head drooped, and that familiar longing unfulfilled weighed heavy on his heart. It was 1925 and everyone who was going west had already left. Farmer was married now to his childhood sweetheart Emile, and they had two boys of their own. With each event—the wedding, the birth of each child, Farmer's dream of going west grew more and more distant. It seemed that he would never get off his father's farm.

Wasn't that what was expected of him? The farm had been in the family three generations. In fact, his papa so much figured that farming was in the boy's blood, and he would help till the land, and plant crops, and gather harvest—that he named his first son, Farmer.

Painfully, an ugly confrontation that occurred last winter between he and his papa pushed its way into his thoughts. It happened during a church potluck after a Sunday morning service. A rancher from up around Amarillo visiting a relative in Holt, attended the morning service, and he stayed to eat. Word spread around quickly about the visitor, and Farmer cornered this rancher at the tables. "My name is Farmer Trevor, and we air right pleased ta have ya visiting us!"

"How do, Thomas Redkin," a burley man accepted Farmer's handshake.

"I hear tell ya raise cattle."

"That's true, son. Are you runnin' some cattle?"

"Oh no, sir, but I reckon I want ta do thet more'n anything!" Farmer could barely contain himself. "Tell me 'bout yer ranch, what breed of cattle have ya, how'd ya get started?" His questions shot out in rapid fire.

"Hey, slow down, son!" and with that Mr. Redkin painted a wonderful picture of his ranch and cattle as he told of buying 6400 acres of lush grassland, of his first herd of Longhorns, the excitement of calving and branding. He drew his brand on a piece of paper for Farmer.

Farmer was still caught in that excitement and the reviving of his distant dream, when he took his place at a table next to Emile. He retold to her everything that rancher Redkin had said. "He told me thet we could have a decent cattle ranch with a half section of land, ifen we have good feed and water! And not only thet…"

"Get this fool notion outa your head!" his father loudly interrupted from behind. "You been thinking and wastin' most your life dreamin' 'bout something that ain't a happenin'. This is your place right here!"

Farmer felt anger burn hot in his chest!

"No Papa! This isn't my place! It ain't never has been my place," he retorted. Everyone at the potluck grew still.

"I thought you had forgotten that fool notion—then, then someone like rancher Redkin comes along and fills your head with silly ideas."

"Papa, ranchin' ain't a silly idea!"

"'Tis for you. You ain't got no money. How are you to buy land? Your home is here! You've worked the farm since you were a boy. When I'm gone, the farm goes to you and your brothers."

"That's just it, Papa. I don't want ta be a farmer!"

"Well you are—and that's all you'll be. That's what the Good Lord made you. An' don't you forget it." With that crushing blow, Farmer was put to silence.

Everyone went back to their eating and visiting, but the hot words left the air tense over the gathering.

Farmer felt Emile slip her hand in his—turning to look in her face, her moist eyes told of the hurt and embarrassment she felt for him. Farmer attempted a half smile, but his mind was full of the angry words with his father—and words he wished he could have said.

When the potluck was over and all were saying their good-byes, Thomas Redkin lingered. At an appropriate moment he approached Farmer. His eyes and his voice conveyed kind understanding.

"You ever get up around Amarillo come see me and I'll show you my spread. Just ask around as most folks know where my place is." A firm handshake, a warm smile and Redkin was gone.

Farmer had thought about making the trip north and accept Redkin's hospitality, then winter set in. Now March had arrived, time to think about getting into the fields and planting spring crops. That thought brought Farmer rudely back to reality and he became conscious of the slow clomping of his team of horses, and the jolt of the wagon.

Farmer had made this trip into the town of Holt more times than he cared to remember. The sun glistened on the wet fields, and he was passing the property line of his father's land. Behind him—two miles west, and one mile south set the home that family and friends helped raise for Farmer and Emile when they married. Farmer laughed out loud, "Ha, thet was the most papa did ta help my dreamin' come true. He gave me the most western section of land to live on!"

But this was just another trip to town. Even the horses seemed to sense the dreary routine of one more trip into Holt as they slowly made their way down the dirt road.

"Dear God," Farmer breathed a prayer, "I surely need a change. Please don't make me plant another crop!" Then he thought, "What a senseless prayer. What else am I gonna do but plant a crop!"

CHAPTER 2

OFFICIAL LETTER

Farmer pulled his team up alongside the entrance to Hatchet's Mercantile. Hatchet was one of the first storeowners in Holt and built a successful business. Sadly, he contacted the fever the year it swept through their area, and he and several others died. His wife, Margaret stubbornly continued their business. Another general store recently opened down the street that boasted of newer—better—lower priced—and more stock than the older Hatchets. In spite of the pull to the newer establishment, Farmer had remained loyal to Margaret Hatchet.

"Well howdy, Farmer," the elderly Mrs. Hatchet greeted him with a broad smile. "You didn't bring Emile and the boys?"

"Not this time, Margaret. The boys' air huntin' rabbits, and Emile is busy with some Saturday cookin' and sewin' she said she had ta get done. Ya got anything new?"

Mrs. Hatchet eyed him for a moment then laughed, "Farmer Trevor, you don't fool me one minute. I've known you for years! Me and my man came calling the first Sunday after you was born—seen those legs and arms of yours a going. Why you would a been headed west right then if you'd known how to run." She had a twinkle in her eyes.

"Now you tell me that it's new goods I got on my shelves you are interested in," she went on teasing Farmer and making the most of withholding from him what he really was after. "Or is it new news you are looking for—especially from out west, hummm?"

Farmer wanted to appear calm, but the curiosity he felt he knew betrayed him. His face flushed hot. "Well yes," he coughed, "I like ta know what's going on." Farmer looked away, picking up a work shirt.

"Well, one of those automobiles come through town 'bout two months ago. It was a newer one. It had glass all 'round, two seats, four doors—it was a dandy!" replied Margaret.

Farmer put the shirt down and began gathering the supplies he needed.

"Farmer," Mrs. Hatchet went on, "do you think those things will catch on? I mean they make such a noise—and stink to high heaven, belchin' smoke out."

"I hear tell Margaret, thet there air lots of automobiles in the big cities, but they have ta stay close ta where they can get—um—I think they call it gasoline."

"That's it. I heard that the General Store is talkin' 'bout layin' some of that gasoline by for when travelers come through."

Farmer placed the items he had gathered on the counter, and looking Mrs. Hatchet firmly in the eye, he asked the question he had been dying to ask. "Was those travelers comin' from out west?"

"Farmer, I was just gettin' to that," Margaret went on—more serious now. "This fellow and his wife pulled up in front and both come in. They was dusty and tired—lookin' for some of that gasoline. They had come a far piece,

Arizona I think they said. It wasn't funny, but I thought it funny, 'cause that automobile was out of that gasoline," Mrs. Hatchet chuckled. "I told them if they had a horse— could just take it out back for feed and they'd be ready to go again in the morning." She started adding up Farmer's bill.

"What about the roads, Margaret, did ya ask them 'bout the roads. Air there roads going west?"

"Well don't know if I did ask, Farmer."

Farmer groaned! How could she not ask something so important, he thought.

"But they did tell me there were long stretches that were very rough," she added, looking up with a smile. "Said some places in Arizona and New Mexico was barely more than wagon trails. Said that trip 'bout beat them and the automobile to pieces. And I'll tell you, Farmer, from the looks of those two all covered in dust and that there rig of theirs— well…I just don't think automobiles will ever catch on in these parts."

Farmer shook his head.

"What, Farmer?" Margaret asked.

"How can ya believe that?" Farmer said, "Haven't ya seen newspapers thet pass through town? Sure they may be weeks old, but they have stories and pictures and everything. A man named Henry Ford few years ago invented a way they can make these automobiles in two hours—they call them Model T's."

"Wagons can be built that quick and cost a whole lot less," Margaret was defensive, "Horse and wagon been just fine around here as long as I can remember, Farmer Trevor."

"It's not fine when the rest of the country has found something better!" Farmer felt a surge of anger starting to take over.

"There's automobiles every where in the cities, and they air buildin' roads and people air travelin' those roads goin' places. But we air such a backwards town—no one comes here. Can't even buy a can of gasoline," the words poured out as Farmer vented feelings held inside.

Margaret Hatchet's eyes showed surprise—Farmer stepped closer to her. "Who owns an automobile in Holt— Who? No one! We're still holdin' onto our horse and buggies while the rest of the United States rides in automobiles. And you know what else? Last year I read they started carryin' mail in airplanes. That means airplanes air flyin' all over the place like birds flyin' in the sky—and in all my life I ain't never seen one. Folks on the move and here I sit in Holt!"

Farmer's voice cracked and he felt tears well up in his eyes. He became conscious that his fists were clenched—his face hot with the anger he displayed.

Margaret blinked, then spoke, "Now Farmer, you don't speak to me in that tone and wipe that look off your face or I'll be tellin' your Pa."

Farmer glared at Margaret, then softened. He laughed out loud as he remembered she used to say that to him as a boy.

Just then Emile's older sister Susan opened the door.

"Just got in from Fort Worth, Farmer," she called, "I saw your wagon outside. Is Emile with you?"

"You don't want to talk to ol' restless Farmer here," Margaret injected before Farmer could answer. "He's all upset 'cause he ain't never seen no airplanes flyin' round his head in the sky and we ain't got these automobile contraptions poppin' and bangin' up and down our main street."

Susan's bewildered look revealed she wasn't sure if Mrs. Hatchet was joking or serious.

"We're just talkin', Susan," Farmer dropped his eyes. "Emile's at home—doin' some woman chores she wanted ta get done."

"Yes, just a talkin', Susan," Margaret went on, not willing to let up on Farmer. "We was talkin' 'bout his restless feet gettin' restless all over again. But seems to me ever time those feet takes off—he just ends up back here."

"Oh Farmer, we thought you had gotten over wanting to travel west," Susan touched his arm.

"It's not thet at all, Susan, I was just sayin' how far we air behind," Farmer felt the anger begin to rise again. "In the cities they have automobiles and airplanes, and electricity, and telephones and trains," the words flowed as fast as Farmer could speak. "In some places they has water in the houses with baths an' johns; we just sit here in our outhouses!" Farmer saw the shock on Susan and Margaret's faces but he couldn't stop now. "The whole country's on the move—progessin' faster 'en we can wink—an' we got none of it here in Holt. It ain't no sin ta want ta change in my thinkin'," Farmer spoke with deep conviction.

"Oh Farmer! Don't be angry," Susan implored.

"What's me to do when folks here 'bouts is content ta live just the same as they has for a hundred years."

"Well ifen Holt ain't good enough for—" Margaret checked herself and tended to totaling up Farmer's purchases.

Susan took Farmer's hand. "Oh Farmer, please come and visit us. I know you and father don't get along that well…"

"Lota folks Farmer don't get on with," Margaret mumbled under her breath.

"We all want to see you along with Emile and the boys," Susan went on ignoring Margaret's remark. "It has been a long time."

"Possible—soon," Farmer attempted a smile. He had no reason to be angry with his sister-in-law. His eyes and manner softened, he squeezed her hand. "I means thet."

Farmer made three trips to his buckboard, carrying the items he had bought from Margaret. She thanked him; Farmer said his good-byes and climbed up onto the seat of his wagon. As he 'giddieuped' his team on down the main street of Holt, he recognized Clem and Ann Harrison in their one seat buggy headed towards him. Clem was Postmaster of Holt's post office.

Farmer pulled his horses in as Clem pulled alongside and stopped.

"Howdy Clem, Ann,"

"Morning Farmer, Where you headed?"

"Been ta Hatchets—thought I'd step into the café fer a cup o' coffee, see who's there," farmer replied.

"You know there's plenty of farm neighbors and their help in this morning. Getting close to planting."

Farmer sighed!

"Say," Clem went on, "You check your box?"

"Hadn't even thought about it, Clem. Seems 'bout all we ever get is some mail order catalogs—we already have the spring one."

"Well, you got an official letter, came in four days ago. I'd thought to deliver it to your place if you didn't come to town soon."

"I'd a thanked ya kindly, Clem. I'll pick it up now."

Farmer moved on down the street. As he came to the café, he went on by. Talk of spring planting left him empty—then he felt guilty because he knew the importance of a good crop for his families' survival.

He halted his team at the post office, climbed down and walked in. Clem was good to leave the door unlocked on Saturdays so those coming into town could check mail. His box did indeed contain a letter. Looking at the return address, it read Bureau of Land Management and came from Washington, D.C.

"Hummph," Farmer grunted. He had received several such letters before. The same year he and Emile married, Farmer had sent numerous requests for homesteading land to raise cattle. One was denied—several declined as no available land left. Now it had been two years since any word—Farmer felt he could not take another disappointment. He tucked the letter in his pocket, unopened, and returned to his wagon.

Farmer felt gloomier than ever. He dreaded opening the letter. Being denied again seemed a mockery of his restlessness—and a final attempt to completely snuff out the last flicker of Farmer's dream.

How many times had he begged and pleaded and bargained with God to help him. God apparently was unmoved by Farmer's pleas—answering other prayers but not this one. 'Maybe He doesn't want me anywhere else,' Farmer had reasoned; yet when he tried to surrender to God's will to stay in Holt and farm the land, he encountered such resistance from inside himself. Even the thought now brought revolt, and old feelings of the pain of disappointment filled his heart.

Farmer was now well beyond the end of town, the team moving at a slow pace, when Farmer mustered the fortitude to open the official government letter.

His hands trembled as he unfolded the letter and read:

Dear Mr. Farmer Trevor,

In keeping with a policy of encouraging the increased raising of cattle in the Pacific Northwest implemented by former President Theodore Roosevelt, President Calvin Coolidge has authorized the opening of twelve sections of public land in the state of Oregon for the purpose of homesteading. The land was dispersed by lottery from a list of applicants who had requested land for the purpose of raising cattle.

We are pleased to inform you that your name was ninth in the draft. Based on survey records, section 9 has stands of timber, ample grassland and running water. Please note the exact location of your section on the enclosed map.

We request an immediate reply as to your intentions. You have until December 31, 1925 to physically settle on your land, and two years to complete a house and out buildings. The third year will require cattle on the land. Under our short term policy you will be deeded your homesteaded land in five years.

Farmer sat stunned! His mind began to spin. Could this be true! He read the letter over and over again—covering every inch of the letter—picking at every word—looking for the part that would crush his dream—renew the sting of disappointment! But it wasn't there! The letter said what he read.

The wagon jostled over a rock, and suddenly it hit Farmer what had just happened. Like rushing water in a dry creek bed after a huge thunderstorm—the reality flooded all over Farmer. All of his restlessness, his dreams, days of disappointment and waiting was changed in an instant—with the opening of an official letter! God hadn't ignored his prayer or said 'No.' He had been at work!

Farmer stood up! Excitement burst inside him. With the letter raised in one hand—reins in the other, Farmer went to shouting and whooping the likes of which he had never done in his life.

The noise startled the team, which bolted, throwing Farmer backwards over the seat. An instant later Farmer popped up behind the seat—letter in his teeth—hat pulled down hard on his head. He quickly grabbed the letter from his teeth shoving it into his overalls. Struggling to regain control, he gripped the reins in both hands.

"Run Sunset—Run Wind! Run like you've never run before!" Farmer shouted. His excitement exploded them into a race, as they felt Farmer give them full rein.

"Go Sunset—Go Wind!" Farmer urged the horses faster. "Get me home! Have I got news for Emile! We got us a trip a comin'!"

The wagon swerved from side to side, the wind rushing in Farmer's face, now wet from tears. He took no mind whether the old wagon might fall apart—He was going to Oregon!

Seeing Walter and Clifton coming out of a grove of trees near the creek bottom, Farmer went to shoutin and screamin' again. The boys stopped—then broke into a run towards the house.

Farmer kept on whoopin' and hollerin' all the way to the house! He was well ahead of his sons and almost home when he saw Emile come out the door—a look of fear on her face.

Farmer pulled the team hard—the horses turned quickly almost turning the wagon over—coming to a halt at the barn.

Emile came running, "Dear God, what has happened, Farmer?"

Chapter 3
EMILE

Farmer's boots hit the ground even before the wagon had come to a complete halt. Remembering he had the government letter shoved in his pocket, he pulled it out, proudly holding it high as he ran towards Emile. When they met, Farmer scooped her up laughing, crying all at once as he swung her in circles! He kissed her over and over!

"Farmer, please, I can't breathe!" Emile tried to free herself. "What is it?" she gasped for breath as Farmer set her down. "What happened?" she asked again as her eyes searched his.

"Oh Emile, the Lord done answered our prayers! It's a dream come powerful true—Everything's changed. Lookee at this letter—it's official from the government. They had this drawing in Washington fer some land, an-an-we got picked! There's a whole section of prime land in Oregon, just waitin' for us ta come settle it. Here, look what it says!" Farmer unfolded the letter for her to read.

"Oregon?" Emile replied, her face somber as she read. She stood motionless for a long time.

"Ain't this the most wonderful news, Emile?" Farmer wanted to go to whoopin' again.

"I suppose," Emile said quietly.

"Whatcha makin' all that noise fer?" Walter and Clifton had reached them. They were panting from their run.

"Pa, yer face is all wet. You been cryin'?" asked Walter.

"Ya bet yer britches I have, son, we got us a journey to make."

"Will we make it home for dark?" Clifton wanted to know.

"Heck yeah," Walter looked at him." We be back by supper time?"

Farmer laughed, "I think it will take-"

"I have lunch about ready," Emile cut in before Farmer could finish what he was saying. "You boys get washed up and to the table."

Farmer stood confused and puzzled as he watched Emile herd the boys towards the house. He busied himself with tending the horses. He unhitched them from the wagon, let them water and shut them in the corral.

"I'll never understand women," Farmer muttered as he threw some hay over the top board of the corral. What was supposed to be one of the happiest days of his life was suddenly clouded.

Emile didn't look up at him as he entered the kitchen. She had set the table, and was dishing some soup. Farmer hung his hat on the peg by the door, and walked to the basin to wash.

"Pa, we saw us some rabbits in the field by the creek," Walter was going on.

"Ya get one?"

"Heck no, Pa,—I ain't got no gun."

"We throwed rocks at it!" Clifton chimed in.

"Pa, when can I have me a gun so's I can really hunt me some rabbits?"

"Walter, you are only five and much too young for a rifle," Emile sharply cut in.

"But Emile, I was his age when I first got a gun. . ."

Emile's glare made it clear to Farmer that this conversation was over.

Farmer sat down and they bowed their heads to say grace. "Thank ya, Father fer this food, an Emile a fixin' it, and fer answering our prayer 'bout the land—in Jesus' Name, Amen." Farmer looked up in time to catch Emile wipe her cheek.

"What land you talkin 'bout, Pa?" Walter asked as he and Clifton dove into their soup.

"Well, the Government is giving us this land in the state of Oregon. All we gotta do is move on it, and build a house, an-"

"An' plant us some cotton," Clifton added happily.

"No, boys, we's gonna raise us some cattle."

Walter and Clifton's eyes got big. "Cows?" they said in unison. "Like our Ol' Babe?"

"No, we'll raise Herefords in Oregon." Farmer could feel the excitement back.

Both boys jumped up! "Can we leave tomorrow?" they squealed as they bounced around the table.

Emile who had been silent to this point fled to the bedroom and slammed the door.

The three of them just stared at the closed door—then looked at each other. Clifton's lip began to quiver, "Mama," he spoke faintly on the verge of tears.

"Come on boys, let's finish our soup," Farmer said helping them both back into their chairs. Lunch was eaten in silence.

"Can we see Ma?" Walter asked when they were finished. Farmer nodded. Walter took Clifton's hand and they both walked to the bedroom door and knocked. Farmer could hear Emile beckon them—they disappeared inside and closed the door.

It was apparent that Emile did not share his excitement over this move. Farmer felt an awful ache in his heart. She had not reacted at all the way he thought she would—and this bewildered him to the point his mind was whirling in confused circles. He replayed scenes and rehearsed what to say over and over in his thoughts. He had his face in his hands—still sitting at the table, when he heard the bedroom door open. Looking up, he saw Walter and Clifton come out. He could tell they had been crying.

"Can we go outside and play?" Walter choked out. Farmer nodded, and the boys went out.

Emile came out of the bedroom as soon as they were outside and slumped in the chair across the table from Farmer. Her eyes were red and her cheeks wet from tears.

"Emile, I don't get it," Farmer got right to the point. "This is our prayers answered—our dream come true! I thought a move—a change would make ya happy."

"That's just it!" Emile blazed. "It's your dream—your prayers, not mine. You never asked me about it!"

"But Emile," Farmer sputtered in shock, "we talked about it. I showed ya every letter I sent off ta the government—you agreed!"

"I never thought anything would come of it!" she wailed. "What's wrong with here? We have land here—our home's here—our family—we have friends—our church. Walter starts his school this fall. And crops need planting soon-"

Farmer exploded as he stood up! "Why does everone want me ta be a farmer? I hate farming! I hate this place! I've dreamed of a chance like this all my life—an—an . ." Farmer was pacing around the kitchen, talking with his hands! "An' ya just want ta stay here doin' the same ol' thing! Why, Emile?"

"We have a good life here, Farmer," Emile retorted, "why throw it away?"

"Throw away! We's betterin' ourselves!"

"How will we get there?" Emile argued. "We have no wagon for a trip like that. Oregon is primitive—the army still fights Indian uprising, and I read the winters are harsh in the mountains. How will you protect us against—" Emile's voice broke as she sobbed, "the—the cold and wild animals and Indians—desolate—to raise a few dumb cows. Oh Farmer, how can you be so foolhardy?"

"God gave us this chance, Emile," Farmer felt his temper flash, "an' by golly, we air gonna take it!"

"You'll take it by yourself, Farmer Trevor," Emile shouted at him as she stood up. "Me and the boys will not be any part of your foolish dreams—and we'll not make this trip!" Emile's eyes blazed at Farmer. "You want to go—GO! And leave us be." With that Emile stormed off to the bedroom and slammed the door behind her.

Farmer stood in shocked disbelief. How could she feel this way? How could she crush his excitement in one quick swoop? How could she talk to him like this? Farmer's anger waxed hot as he paced back and forth in front of the kitchen stove.

"Not fair, Emile," Farmer yelled as he sent a chair from the table crashing into the wall. He could hear Emile crying loudly in their bedroom.

Farmer stomped out of the house and went to the barn. He tried to do chores, but his heart wasn't in it. His chest felt like it was squeezed in a vice and his boots were heavy as lead.

Walter and Clifton joined him in the barn from their play and tried to help. Clifton pulled on his pants leg, "Is mama sad?" Looking down in Clifton's eyes, then in Walter's, he saw a look of fear.

"We don't want you to go away, Pa," Walter began to cry.

Farmer squatted down and drew his boys to his chest and held them close. "Pa's not going anywhere unless we all go," Farmer consoled them. "Ok? So's let's get these chores done so we can go in. It's gettin' mighty cold."

By the time the three returned to the house, it was nearly dark. The fire had died out, and Farmer noted that Emile had not been out of the bedroom. Lighting a lamp, the fleeting thought that electricity still had not reached Holt crossed his mind; maybe it never would.

"Pa, I'm hungry. Where's Ma?" Walter asked.

"She's in the bedroom. We still have soup from lunch. Let's butter us some bread."

"Aw, Pa! Soup again," Walter complained.

"Be thankful ya have something ta eat," snapped Farmer.

The usually talkative youngsters ate quietly that night, and didn't make excuse when told to get ready for bed. Farmer tucked them in and listened as they both prayed that mama would feel better.

"Make her smile," Clifton prayed, "aaamen."

Farmer carried the lamp and ventured into the bedroom. Emile's, "Go away—leave me alone," cut him like a knife, and he retreated from the room closing the door.

He donned his heavy coat and taking his hat from the peg went outside into the night. The moon was bright and shimmered across the fields. Farmer had no trouble seeing his way to the corral. He could hear the horses snort as he approached. Wind stuck her nose through the opening in the corral boards for attention.

"Ya be ready ta go ta Oregon ain't ya girl? Ya an' Sunset been ready a mite long time, 'bout as long as me. But I don't know what I'm a doin'."

Farmer angrily struck the corral sending the horses running to the other side. "Lord, I reckon I don't understand this—not a tall! It's like ya give me the desire o' my heart and then 'for I can enjoy it, ya snatch it away! I just don't understand!"

Farmer put one boot up on the bottom board, and rested his chin on his folded arms on the top board. He looked at the vast expanse of stars. "Those stars air shining on my land in Oregon," he thought. He went over the events of the day in his mind. Of the letter, the excitement, he wondered how Oregon looked, and then—Emile.

He reached back in his memory to the first time he saw her. It was the first day of his fourth grade in school. Emile started school that day as a first grader. If he had seen her before he hadn't noticed. She attended church in town and Farmer went to a rural church near the Trevor farm.

Farmer had sort of fallen in love with Emile that first day of school. They grew up together and seemed to know they would share their lives forever.

Emile was the younger of two daughters in the Holt family. She came from a long line of distinguished ancestors. The Holts had started the town named after them and were well respected.

Farmer was a visionary—but only average in school, while Emile excelled—with top grades. Hirum Holt had plans to send both his daughters on to higher education in distant big cities, but Emile had already given her heart to Farmer. She would not leave him—even under severe pressure from her father and mother.

Farmer shivered as he recalled the first times he called on Emile to court her. Hirum forbid Emile from seeing him. "He's just a poor dirt farmer, Emile," Hirum told his daughter. "You deserve better than that." And Emile had stood up to her father with the same stubborn resolve that Farmer had experienced tonight. "I love Farmer Trevor, and I want to marry him," she told her father. That was before they had even courted. Farmer smiled. Then shook his head. He felt that the Holts had never really accepted him into the family. Well, Emile's sister Susan had, but not Hirum and Vivian.

Farmer's love for Emile flooded his heart and soul, and no matter how angry he was at her—he knew she was the only girl for him. His love for her ran deep.

"She's right," Farmer thought. "Why should I rip her up from everthing she has known and loved?" He remembered a part of a message delivered by Preacher Tunnell. In Peter, husbands are told to dwell with understanding with their wives as the weaker vessel—or it was something like that. Farmer just knew he wanted to understand Emile—and to have her and the boys' close was far more important than going to Oregon. He knew that! Hot tears filled his eyes as he gave it up, and surrendered to just being a farmer and work the land, and staying where they were.

He buried his face in his arms; the tears freely flowed as he saw his dream dying a final death. So near—yet so distant.

As Farmer looked up into the heavens to a God he loved, he felt Emile's hand slip around his arm and her body draw close to his. She was looking up into his face with a smile.

"It's ok, Farmer, I'm ready to go. God told me He will take care of us," Emile whispered.

"No, Emile, you're right. We should sta-"

Emile put her fingers to his lips to stop him.

"It's ok, Farmer. I was afraid. Not of change—or leaving family—but the long ordeal of the trip—because, I think I am with child."

Chapter 4

FIRST DECISIONS

Farmer and Emile stood by the corral talking into the night. The realization that a dream was coming true; soon they would take a long journey; there was land that would belong to them made them immune to the cold or to sleep. They would build a new home in the west! A dream beginning into reality fanned their excitement into a rush of plans, thoughts and questions. It seemed they could not talk fast enough. It thrilled Farmer to see Emile's child-like, playful approach to this adventure. Yet as he looked at her and listened to her, he was keenly aware that she was very much a woman—a mother, concerned about her children. In that special time by the corral, the two of them made decisions that would affect the future of their family and their lives. Farmer felt the love he had for his wife deepen. He sensed the same was happening to Emile. The hot words that had been exchanged in anger faded from thought, and the two were one heart, mind and soul.

It wasn't until their nose and ears began to sting, did they become conscious of how cold it had grown. Their breaths showing in the crisp air, Farmer and Emile walked arm and arm back to the house.

Once inside, Farmer stoked wood into the kitchen stove. Emile went in to check on the boys and kiss them. When she returned she put on a pot of coffee. Farmer went outside for more wood, and when the coffee was poured they sat at the table talking. "We have so much to do," Emile said, "how will we travel? Are there roads? What about our house here? Our things? Is there a town in Oregon, a school?"

"I don't reckon I know those things just yet, Emile, but ya said yerself thet God would take care of us, an' He will!"

It was three in the morning when they gave up and went to bed. There was so much planning and deciding to do; however, they were in agreement of the first steps they knew had to be taken. First thing in the morning they would talk to the boys. Walter was five and Clifton only three, so they both knew that their sons would not fully understand what all of this meant. But they knew they must prepare them for the move. Then it was decided that right after Sunday morning church they would ride to the Trevors to tell them of their good fortune. They would leave from there and go into town to share the news of their move to Oregon with Emile's folks.

"Maybe it be best we not tell...well at least 'till ya air sure yer havin' a baby," Farmer suggested.

"Uh-huh," Emile agreed as she snuggled up against Farmer in the warm bed. He kissed her good night and soon her breathing grew heavy and Farmer knew she was sleeping peacefully.

Farmer was exhausted, but sleep far away. His mind raced over the events of the day. A hundred details kept intruding his thoughts—'till he wished he could get up and start packing now! He wondered about transportation. He hadn't mentioned this part to Emile, but he knew their ol' wagon would never make that long and rough a trip. Why, he'd buy them one of those automobiles—Nope! Can't do that—don't have enough money, not even if they sold what little they owned. What to do! We have to make it to Oregon!

Then the dread of facing their fathers settled heavily into his thoughts like a thick, black cloud. He wasn't too worried about his Papa. Sure he would be upset—stomp around the house and yell a mite. But he'd come around. Franklin Trevor placed high value on land ownership. When Farmer showed him that he and Emile had a whole section of land—given to them free and clear—just for settling on it, his Papa would change his mind in a hurry. Farmer smiled.

It was Hirum Holt that Farmer dreaded facing. Emile's father had never really accepted Farmer. He wouldn't let Farmer court his daughter, even tried to take her away to the big city—enrolling her in the same college as her sister Susan, and set her up in the women's dormitory. By the next spring Emile got so homesick she came home—to Farmer. They got married shortly after that. Emile's mother, Vivian tried her best to talk Emile out of marrying that soon, but conceded defeat when she saw that stubborn Holt determination had a strong hold on her daughter.

Hirum on the other hand never gave his consent or blessing on the marriage. He sourly tolerated it, but always blamed Farmer for robbing his Emile of a "higher education" and sticking her on a farm to be a poor dry land farmer's wife and bare babies.

Now in a few hours he must face this outspoken man and tell him that he was taking his daughter and grandsons 1400 miles away to a wild and untamed land. Farmer could not even imagine how Mr. Holt would react. "And he doesn't even know that Emile may be pregnant. Thet will fer sure make matters worse," Farmer thought. He could see Emile's face in the moonlight coming through the window. How content and beautiful she looked. As he watched her, he became upset with himself for being in such turmoil. "This be the most excitin' day o' my life," he reasoned, "and I'm lettin' these fears muddy up my joy—like throwin' dirt in a clear pond."

No matter how hard Farmer tried to think of other things and regain the excitement he had felt, the dread of the meeting with old man Holt kept coming back to grip his heart. Finally, sleep came and freed him of his struggle.

CHAPTER 5
WALTER AND CLIFTON

From a place that seemed far away, Farmer slowly began to be aware of the voices and sounds of Walter and Clifton talking, laughing, and playing somewhere in the house. Smells of fresh brewed coffee and bacon frying filled the bedroom, reaching farther into Farmer's consciousness. He stirred, raising his head. Emile was not by his side; he could hear her in the kitchen. His eyes felt full of gravel as he tried to focus on their clock that sat on the dresser.

"Dang, I slept late," Farmer mumbled. "Musta died ta the world. Too late fer church now…"

He pulled his trousers on, poured water from the pitcher into the basin, and proceeded to wash his hands and face. "This pitcher an' basin gotta go with us," he thought as he remembered it was one of their wedding gifts.

The boys raced to Farmer when they saw him open the bedroom door.

"Pa! Ma says you got somethin' to tell us!" Walter threw his arms around his Pa's neck.

"Yeah, tell us!" Clifton squealed as he wrapped his little arms around Farmer's leg. Both boys were laughing and holding on so tight that Farmer had to drag them into the kitchen where Emile was pouring two cups of coffee.

"Good morning," she smiled looking up at her husband with their two wiggly, noisy boys.

"Mornin'! Now boys, let me set ya at the table. Yer mother has breakfast waitin', and we'll tell ya our surprise whilst we eat."

Walter and Clifton were so excited it seemed impossible for them to settle down. As Farmer led in prayer—Clifton giggled, then Walter couldn't hold back and burst out with a kind of snort, which tickled Emile and she muffled a laugh. At some other time, Farmer might have reacted in anger, and called the boys down, but today he also felt the excitement and even though he didn't laugh out loud his heart was laughing with his family!

"Lord, this is just all so wonderful, an'," Farmer continued the prayer, "we air so happy 'bout your blessings. Thank ya, Lord, Amen."

"Tell us Pa!" Both boys chimed in together.

"Well," Farmer smiled at Emile who was dishing out the boys' breakfast, "we be moving ta Oregon and start us a cattle ranch."

The boys' eyes got big.

"We'll travel fer a long time in the wagon. We can camp along the way, and build campfires and hunt game," Farmer explained. Walter's breath made a whistle sound as he took a deep breath.

"Hot ding!" Clifton said in his squeaky voice.

"I hear tell," Farmer had their complete attention, "hear tell thet our land has lots o' tall trees and mountain streams runnin' clear, cold water. We'll build us a house, and start raisin' cattle."

"We're gonna be cowboys!" Walter shouted.

"Yes," Emile laughed, "and you'll be good ones!"

Both boys clapped their hands as they yelled, "Wahoo!"

Then Walter got serious, "they better have some rabbits for huntin' there in, uh, where we goin', Pa?"

"An' some huntin' skunks too," Clifton added.

"Boys, better 'en that! In Oregon, on our place there's deer to hunt, an' in the fall, ducks and geese flock in by the zillions!"

"Bust my boots!" Walter breathed in awe.

"Where did you get that, Walter?" Emile asked.

"Pa says it, Ma," Walter gave her a look of disgust for breaking his train of thought.

Farmer snarled up his face, "and there may be mean mountain lions roamin' 'bout!"

"Oh Farmer, don't scare us." Emile interrupted with a laugh.

"I'll shoot 'em with a arrow," piped up Clifton, acting like he had his bow and pulling back an imaginary arrow.

Walter grew thoughtful and serious. "Will we have to fight off Injuns, Pa?" he asked.

All eyes turned on Farmer.

"Yes, Husband, shall we build a house or a fort?" Emile teased.

"I think," Farmer responded thoughtfully, "thet coyotes will be more problem than Indians."

The excited chatter continued until breakfast was concluded.

"Missed church this morning," Emile spoke softly as she cleared dishes from the table. "Folks will be wondering what happened to us..."

"True, Emile, it seems as ifen our life done be changin' overnight! One time don't hurt us none—hey, ya boys wanta help do chores? Then we air a goin' ta Papa and Mama Trevor's, then ta town ta see Grandfather and Grandmother Holt."

Farmer shuddered as he thought again of the visit to the Holts.

Chapter 6
TELLING PAPA

Sunset and Wind wanted to run! It was a windy March day and black clouds were forming to the north. It was still early enough that a northerner blowing in could bring cold rain, or even ice.

"Clouds look ugly," Farmer observed as they pulled in front of the Trevor house. The wind whistled in the trees that lined the lane, and rippled across the yellow grass left from the fall before.

The Trevor dogs ran to greet them as they entered the lane, and to the delight of the boys, jumped up and down along side the wagon.

Farmer's father stepped out onto the porch, and from behind him bolted Farmer's brothers Jacob and William running to meet them at the wagon.

"Howdy," Farmer grabbed them both in a bear hug.

"Might proud to see you," Jacob grinned.

"Sure a glad sight, Farmer," William patted Farmer's back. "Let me put up yer horses."

"Now leave em be, William. We can only stay a mite 'cause we air also goin' ta see the Holts."

"Aw, visiting day is it?" laughed Jacob.

They helped Emile from the wagon as the boys ran towards the house. They threw their arms around their grand-father, and as they disappeared into the house, Farmer could make out one of them saying, "We's goin' to Oregon!"

Farmer and his father met in a strong handshake. "Missed seeing you all 'round here as late," the old man spoke as he motioned them into the house.

Inside, Farmers' mother was holding the boys on her lap.

"Well hello, strangers!" Farmer's little sister Stella came from her bedroom. "Missed you in church today."

"Farmer, do tell, what are these boys all goin' on about? What stories you been tellin' 'em?" Farmer's mother asked trying to keep track of what her grandsons were saying. "My lands, you're both a talkin' at once and so fast about Oregon an' huntin' an' coyotes. What do they mean?" she looked at Farmer and Emile.

Farmer swallowed hard. "We got us some wonderful news!" he started. Old man Trevor pulled up some chairs and motioned for everyone to have seats.

"Ya all know how I been writin' ta the government fer some homestead land. Well, I'd all but given up. Yesterday I got this letter in the mail, see here it is. It seems thet the President wants more cattle raisin', so's they are given away whole sections of land just fer cattle ranchin', and they had this drawing in Washington fer the land, an we was number 9, an we have 'till end o' this year ta claim the land…" Farmer took a deep breath. He felt Emile slip her hand inside his arm and squeeze. "And we'll be movin' ta Oregon-directly," he finished.

The room was silent.

"And make a house," Clifton offered in his squeaky voice.

All eyes turned toward Franklin Trevor who was studying the official letter. Farmer could see his face redden and the veins on his neck stand out. The old man stood to his feet.

"Just couldn't leave well enough alone, could you boy?"

"Sir?" Farmer responded.

"After all we've done for you. Raised you, fed you, gave you a warm bed, sent you to school!"

"An' I'm grateful," Farmer dropped his head.

"It was me that kept you and Jacob out o' the war—you was needed here, on the farm!"

"I wanted to serve. I was willin' to go."

"And most likely you'd be dead!" the old man thundered.

Farmer rose to face his father.

"I thought you was over this fool notion," Franklin went on. "But you couldn't be satisfied with what you have, could you?"

"But Papa, they air givin' us a whole section of land free and clear."

"You have land here—it's free an' clear. You want more, I'll give you more!" He wadded up the letter and threw it in Farmer's face.

"I don't want more!" Farmer retorted, picking up the crumpled paper.

"You are a Trevor! We have been farmers for generations—right here! Workin' the land. Why can't you accept that?"

"Can't you see!" Farmer exploded. "I don't want ta farm. I'm gonna raise cattle!"

"Y'all starve or freeze to death; want that for Emile an' the boys?" Franklin shouted, waving his fist.

Walter and Clifton started to cry and Stella fled to her room.

"Franklin Trevor!"

"Hush! Allison!" Franklin snapped. "This be between me and Farmer."

"Our mind's made up." Farmer tried to calm himself.

"You don't have to claim this land. Let someone else have it. This is your place!"

'No, it's not my place. I want ta move on!"

"It's always 'bout you, isn't it? What you want? Think about your wife and babies. How you gonna get there, boy? You think that rickety ol wagon will make the trip? Huh! An' 'bout the time you arrive, snow will come. An' it snows deep in those mountains, Boy! You thought about all that?" Then it seemed as though Franklin appeared to plead. "Your home is here, your family, friends, the church you growed up in. How can you leave everything you ever know'd—for, for a wild and hard land that can't grow nuttin but trees and bushes. How can you do that, Farmer?"

Farmer sat back down. "I'll never know what could a been if I don't try," he dropped his head again.

William took the children out to play around the house. Muffled crying could be heard from Stella's room.

Jacob broke the silence, "Papa, William and I are still here to work the..."

"Jacob! Shut your mouth. You'll be gettin' the same fool notion as your brother, and I've had me a stomach full here today. Now Farmer, tomorrow mornin' you write you a letter back to the government an' tell them you ain't comin' to no Oregon."

"I'll write, yes, ta tell 'em I'm a comin fer my land," Farmer replied quietly as he smoothed the letter and placed it in his pocket.

"What you say!" Franklin yelled.

"I say thet we be going ta Oregon, Papa. This has been my dream all my life."

Franklin got in Farmer's face growling, "Then you ain't no son of mine!"

"Franklin, you can't mean that!" Allison cried.

"I told you to hush, woman!" With a swift movement Franklin grabbed Farmer by the neck and arm jerking him up from his chair. "I want you off my place! You ain't welcome here no more!"

"No Papa, please!" the words cut into Farmer's heart like a sharp knife.

As Franklin pulled Farmer towards the door both Allison and Jacob grabbed him, but he tossed them aside like an ol' rag. Allison fell back to her chair and Jacob was sent flying across the room.

Stella came out of her room crying and screaming, "Stop it! Stop it!"

Farmer tried to free himself and hold his father's arms, but Franklin was too strong. The next thing Farmer knew, he was thrown out the door, landing on his side, sliding across the porch.

About this time William and the boys came running up, fear on their faces.

"William,—get them—in the—wagon!" Farmer managed to choke out the words.

By now Emile was at his side. "Are you hurt?" she questioned feeling his arms and legs.

"I be alright Emile," Farmer struggled to get up.

Sounds could be heard inside—the slamming of doors, crying.

Then Franklin appeared in the doorway, an ominous figure, red faced, holding his rifle. "I want you off my land, an' don't come back 'till you get over this crazy idea of runnin' off! You hear, Boy!"

"Franklin, he's our son," Allison's sobs come from inside the house.

Emile faced Franklin, "We are all Christians, and we have acted like heathens this afternoon. I am ashamed, and" her voice broke as tears streamed down her face, "I'm ashamed that Farmer has you for a father."

"An' I, that I have a foolish boy that knows nothin' but chasin' a dream that keeps flyin' away like a frightened bird, Emile." Franklin retorted.

"At least he has a dream!" Emile snapped back.

Farmer took Emile's hand, pulling her away. "We need ta leave now."

CHAPTER 7
HIRUM HOLT

Farmer ran the horses fast as they could pull the wagon until Emile's pleas to slow down brought him to his senses. He pulled the horses in. "I'm sorry, Emile, all I could think ta do was get away. I can't member anything ta hurt me so bad as what my Papa just done."

The boys who had been holding on for dear life in the back of the wagon scrambled to climb up between Farmer and Emile on the seat.

"Why was Papa so loud?" Walter wanted to know.

"Had a gun," Clifton added.

"He just doesn't want to see us move away," Emile said softly, and held the boys close to her.

They rode on, slower now, for some distance. They suddenly heard a rider coming' hard behind them. Farmer turned to look. "Is that Jacob?" Farmer asked. He halted the team.

Jacob was up to them in a few minutes throwing chunks of damp dirt in the air as he reined his horse in hard.

"What happened?" Farmer looked into Jacob's smeared, dirty face.

Jacob rode his horse near the wagon on Farmer's side. "Couldn't let you leave that a way. 'Twas not right, what Papa said and done. He was yellin' and kickin' things in the house, went outside an emptied his rifle into the air..."

"Did he hurt Ma?" Farmer interrupted.

"Naw, he'd not do that, but scared heck outa us. Then Papa and me got into an argument, an', well, I left out. I had to tell you that I'm right proud—you know, strikin' out on your own. Want you to know I'm for what you an' Emile and your boys are doing. I'll miss you powerful, but Farmer, you just gotta do this!" Jacob wiped his eyes.

Farmer sat numb, but was deeply touched by his brother's words. "We thank you Jacob," Farmer heard Emile say.

"Yes, ya have helped ease the hurt," Farmer added. Then after a moment of thought; he went on, "the house and all we leave is yours, Jacob."

Jacob raised his hand—"Have no need of it. I may just move somewhere else myself. Then William can have it!"

Farmer smiled, "But you been courtin' Dorothy Shipley. I'm thinkin' ya might need thet house soon."

Jacob's horse stomped its hoof, and Jacob settled her down tryin' to hide his reddened face.

"I know ya like workin' the land. I see it in you, Jacob. Now ya best get on back an' not rile papa more'n need be. This ain't your battle." Jacob nodded in agreement, and turned his horse towards home.

"Just had to tell you I was for you," Jacob shouted as he urged his stead into a gallop.

Farmer and Emile looked at each other. "You want to wait to tell my father and mother?" Emile asked searching his face for an answer.

"I'd sure be tempted ta wait. Twice ta get throwed out in one day ain't ta my likin'."

"I'll tell them, Farmer," Emile replied as she touched his arm.

Farmer thought on that for a moment then started the team down the road again. "No, I should be the one—I'm the head of our home."

"We can wait—till, uh, you are better," she offered.

Farmer thought on that for a while. Everything in him wanted to put this off. "No!" he finally said with resolve. "Your folks should hear it first from us—not Margaret Hatchet." Emile smiled and nodded.

Too quickly they rode into town and halted the wagon in front of the Holt's residence. Farmer's heart sunk as he could see in the window the Holts had quests.

Susan answered the door, and let out a squeal of delight when she saw Emile. They hugged, then she wrapped her arms around the boys making them squirm and fuss. Smiling at Farmer her mouth silently worded, "Thank you!"

"Come in, come in," Vivian Holt motioned them to the parlor. "What a surprise," Emile's mother went on. "My, how you boys have grown. You look well, Emile. It is so nice to see you and Farmer," she never even glanced at Farmer.

"Well, Emile, what brings about this visit? It has been sometime since you have been home," Hirum Holt entered the room followed by an elderly and distinguished couple. Hirum approached Emile and kissed her on the cheek, patted the boys on their heads, glanced at Farmer and turned to his guests. "Ira and Doris, Vivian and I would like to present our daughter Emile, her husband Farmer, and their sons, Walter and Clifton." Turning towards Farmer and Emile, "This is Judge Ira Garrison and his lovely wife Doris. Ira is presiding judge in Burgess County."

Farmer had said many times that the bland formality of the Holts would drive him raving mad. 'This might just do it!' Farmer thought as greetings were exchanged.

When everyone was seated, Susan brought in tea. Emile slid her hand inside Farmer's arm and got right to their reason for being there. "Father, Mother, we have good news! We have come to tell you-."

Susan started laughing and clapping her hand, "Oh Emile! You're pregnant!"

Hirum frowned as he looked at Susan, "For goodness sakes, calm yourself and let your sister tell it."

"Well, I don't know about that, but that's not our news," Emile went on.

"Ya know how all my life, far back as I can remember, how I dreamed a goin' west?" Farmer took over.

"I heard that rumor," Hirum spoke gruffly.

'Dear God, Mr. Holt is our town's attorney and I'm a simple farm boy. If you don't help me, he's gonna have me carried off ta jail right now. He even has the judge here!' Farmer felt on the verge of panic and ready to run out the door as he breathed this prayer. Everyone was waiting for him to go on. His mouth was dry; he felt hot!

"Tell em, Pa," Walter burst out."

"Well," Farmer proceeded, "I wrote, seemed like hundreds of letters ta Washington 'bout homestead lands. Some came back tellin' the land was already taken, and most didn't answer at all."

"I believe homesteading was fairly well finished by 1910," Hirum injected. Judge Garrison nodded his agreement.

"But thet's the good news. On Saturday I got this official government letter from Washington. Here it is, Mr. Holt. It seems our President Calvin Coolidge wants more cattle raisin' an' since I had written thet's what I've dreamed all my life a doin—so's they put my name in a hat with a multitude of others, and, well ya can read right there in the letter. We were the ninth, and they is givin' us a whole section of land, in Oregon.

"Oh!" Vivian Holt put her hand to her mouth. "That is so far away."

Hirum studied the letter for a long time. It seemed that no one wanted to speak until they saw his reaction. He was the attorney in court, preparing his case. Farmer's heart sunk.

Walter and Clifton got off their chairs and climbed in their aunt Susan's lap, she bounced them around and made faces. When they laughed—she hushed them with her finger to her lips.

It was Judge Garrison who broke the silence, "I've heard of good things happening in Oregon. They are raising potatoes in the southern part, pears mid state, and delicious apples in the north. Most of all they have a booming lumber industry.

Hirum Holt stood up. His commanding presence seemed to fill the room. Then he began to pace—back and forth.

Farmer braced himself.

Hirum would pace—stop and gaze at Farmer. Then he paced some more, head down. Farmer could see the muscles in his neck tighten. He stopped, looking intently at Emile. He resumed his pacing back and forth.

"I think it time we retire for the night," Doris Garrison spoke.

"Yes," her husband quickly agreed, both sensing the evening had become awkward. "Hirum, I believe you and Vivian have matters to discuss with your family. We bid you all a goodnight."

Farmer wanted to cry out, "Please don't leave me alone with this man!" He felt like a steer waiting for the slaughter.

The Garrisons quietly retreated to the guest room. Farmer noticed that Clifton had fallen asleep. Walter was playing with a toy Susan had gotten.

Hirum continued his pacing—stopping every so often to look at Farmer—then Emile, then his two grandsons. His actions spoke of a man used to the courtroom.

"Farmer," Holt spoke roughly.

"Sir!" Farmer stiffened.

"You've dreamed of going west and raising cattle since you were a boy?"

"Yes sir," Farmer felt like he was on the stand.

"You persisted in your letter writing to Washington, D.C.?"

"Yes sir, but the last two years, I was a mite discouraged and didn't write none then."

"They are giving you a section of land with timber and water?"

"Yes sir."

"You for this Emile, or just going because Farmer wants to?"

"Oh no, Father, I have prayed and the Lord has told me it's His doing. I want it as much as—as my husband!"

Hirum eyed her keenly. Then his face and voice seemed to soften.

"How will you get there?"

"It being so new—haven't had the time to think on that yet, but we'll get there."

"You're determined to go to Oregon are you? And be a rancher are you?"

Farmer braced for the verbal onslaught.

"I think this is the smartest thing I've known you to do, Farmer."

Farmer couldn't believe the words he just heard from Hirum Holt.

The women gasped!

"This country is changing. It's on the move, never to be the same. I've always had the adventurous blood running through my veins—and I've always admired a man with vision." Hirum leveled his eyes on Farmer. "I did some hard serious thinking tonight, and had to come to some conclusions. I'll admit Farmer, I never accepted you as good enough for my daughter. All I ever saw from you was working your Pa's land—scratching out a meager living on a dry land farm. But, I was wrong. You had a vision long before any of the rest of us could see it. It takes a man to pick up and move to a strange land and make a new life." Hirum's face broke into a broad grin. "I've been to the big city looking—and next year I'm buying us a grand automobile. We'll have a gasoline station here in Holt by then. Roads are being built, and by golly, I've been looking for a good reason to travel to the Northwest and take a look around."

"Oh Father!" Emile flew up into his arms, and Vivian joined them as they hugged and laughed.

"Will there be room in that automobile for me?" Susan teased, "to visit my favorite sister?"

"Your only sister!" Emile laughed.

Suddenly all of the dammed up emotion of the day broke, flooding Farmer's heart and soul. He began to sob! He tried to turn his head and hide the tears—he felt ashamed for being such a baby.

"What's wrong, Farmer?" Susan saw him. The room grew quiet.

Emile sat down beside her broken mate and put her arm around him.

Farmer buried his face in his hands.

"His father ordered him off his land—never to come back. Said he was ashamed of him, and Farmer was so afraid you all would be as mean and hateful. Thank you for—for," Emile's voice broke and she started to cry as well. "Thank you for understanding and accepting."

"You let me talk to Franklin Trevor," Hirum snorted. "Come Vivian, Susan, prepare rooms. Emile, you and Farmer and the boys must spend the night. It is too dark to make your way home. Besides we have much planning to do in the morning."

There was excited chatter, as beds were made ready. Hirum joked, and Farmer thought it to be the first time he had ever heard the man laugh.

"What a difference from my family," he pondered, and sadly, painfully remembered scenes from that afternoon. He continued deep in thought, and later that night as he looked out on to the moonlit street of Holt, he remarked to Emile, "as long as I live I for sure will never figure people out."

CHAPTER 8

GOOD NEWS—
BAD NEWS

F armer was up early—eager to get into the day, and
there were chores needing done at home.

"You get your chores done Farmer, leave Emile and the
youngsters here," Hirum suggested during breakfast. "Leave
me your letter from the government, so by the time you
return I'll have drafted a confirmation letter for you. I'll ask
Susan to type it up so it looks respectful. That way, it can go
to the post office today."

Farmer was only too happy to comply. Sunset and Wind
were anxious to return to their familiar farm and ran as
swiftly as Farmer would allow.

Arriving back at the Holts, Susan presented Farmer with
an official looking letter, which gave his acceptance of the
terms and land concerning the property in Oregon. It
concluded that the Trevor family would be taking posses-
sion by December 31, 1925.

"You sign right here, Farmer," Susan instructed, her face
breaking into a warm smile. She handed him a pen she had
just dipped in an ink well.

"Here's an addressed envelope all stamped and ready for mail," she continued, "and Farmer, I am very happy for you; you've yearned to go west for so long. But, I am most on the verge of tears missing Emile and those boys—and you already, and you haven't even left yet!"

Just then Emile walked into the room and Susan hugged her. Farmer could see both women's eyes get misty, and decided he best go and mail the letter before they talked themselves outa goin' to Oregon.

"I hear tell a Holt town family is pickin' up stakes and headin' to Oregon," Clem Harrison greeted Farmer with a grin as he entered the Post Office.

"Now where'd ya hear thet?" laughed Farmer.

"News is spreadin' like a grass fire. Whole town is talkin'! And that letter in your hand would be your reply?"

"Sure nuff, Clem. Have ya heard from Benjamin?"

"No, but I expect him to call on the telephone directly. He is still in Fort Worth last we heard."

"I would sure like ta see him before we leave Holt," Farmer said hopefully.

"Oh, he'll burn him a trail home when he hears the news, you can bet on that, Farmer. Meanwhile, I'll get your letter on its way. Now tell me 'bout the land you're homesteading in Oregon."

Farmer relayed to Clem all he knew—which wasn't much. "It's so new, Clem, thet's 'bout all I can tell ya right now."

Emile was ready to return home when Farmer walked into the Holts. They lifted the boys into the back of the wagon and decided to stop at Hatchets Mercantile for a few supplies on their way out of town.

"Well, Farmer, you done gone and did it!" Margaret shouted—catching the attention of the few customers in the store.

"I declare, I never would of believed it had William not stopped in earlier this morning tellin' me the good news himself!"

Margaret approached Emile and Farmer, grabbed them both at the same time in a bear hug.

"Tell me Emile, I bet those itchy feet of your man's been doin' a dance!"

Emile laughed and nodded.

"We're going to Oregon and hunt us some coyotes," Walter piped up.

"Well slap me on the fanny if you ain't!" Margaret's eyes twinkled as she scooped Walter and Clifton up in her arms.

While two women in the store whom Emile was acquainted with excitedly asked her questions about the soon coming journey, Margaret drew Farmer to the side.

Sending the boys on to explore, Margaret lowered her voice, "William says your Pa's as mad as a hornet that's been swatted at!"

Farmer dropped his eyes.

"An' your ma's been cryin' a heap!" Margaret went on. "It's hard for a ma and pa to let their youngens' move off a thousand miles away. But William and Jacob are a mite happy about your good fortune. Give your pa some time, he'll come around, ya hear!"

"It'll have ta be pretty dang quick, 'cause we gotta leave soon as possible," Farmer spoke thoughtfully.

"Well, I hate to be the one to tell this, but William also told me your pa was so spittin' mean an' ugly and yellen' all this morning that ifen it wasn't for Emile an' the boys, he'd run you outa your home today. That's what William said."

Farmer glanced to see if Emile had heard, but she was talking and laughing with her friends as she gathered the items they had need of. The pain of what Margaret just said struck deep into Farmer's heart. Words failed him, so he picked up a pair of boots—looking them over attempting to hide his hurt. "I'll need a pair of these," he mumbled, "before we leave."

Margaret, who had been eyeing him keenly, ignored his remark about the boots. "How'd ol' man Holt take it?" she asked, "seein' as how Emile will be leavin'."

"That's the good news, I suppose," Farmer attempted a smile.

The ride home was in silence. Even the boys sat still in the wagon. Emile sensed that Farmer was troubled.

"What is it Farmer?" she finally ventured.

Farmer thought awhile before he answered. "Emile, God has blessed us with a chance fer change, an' adventure, an' ta better ourselves. But, it has heaped up a whole bunch of good news an' bad news. My pa has been like a black cloud on a sunny day. I don't want us ta leave Holt with our families so split apart. But, I don't know how ta fix it, except we stay put." Emile started to speak, but Farmer stopped her as he continued. "I don't believe down deep in my heart thet God wills us ta stay here. He has made a miracle in giving us this chance. I jus' seem ta know it's Him sendin' us, not just 'cause I want ta go, Emile. You have ta trust that I wouldn't be careless 'bout God's will and ya an' our sons', er children's welfare."

"Then we must go, Farmer, to Oregon to start a new life, whether our families approve or not," Emile murmured with firm resolve.

CHAPTER 9

MOUNTAINS
AND PRAYERS

The week was full of preparations for Farmer and Emile. There seemed countless things that needed to be done, and their anxiousness to begin the long journey grew more intense with each passing day.

Emile busied herself with decisions of what they would take, and what they might sell, or give away. Some things just to be left in the house for Jacob, William or Stella. She took it for granted that they would travel in their wagon, and that was a concern for Farmer.

Each time he took the wagon into Holt, he paid closer attention to how it traveled, now in light of a trip of over one thousand miles, rather than five miles to town. Granted, his wagon was larger than a standard buckboard, good for hauling grain or hay. He had rigged it so that two horses could be hitched up making it an easier pull.

Emile had asked several times if Farmer was going to attach hoops and if he wanted her to begin sewing canvas to make it into a small covered wagon for protection from the elements.

Farmer was torn in what to do. Age had taken its toll on the wagon. The sides needed repair. Some of the spokes were splitting and Farmer questioned that even if they were new wheels, if they would be heavy enough to make that rugged a trip. And two of the hubs had worn so much that the wheels wobbled. Finding parts appeared improbable.

Farmer spent the following days making the rounds to every farm to inquire about a suitable wagon for such a long journey. The only one that was even a consideration was an old freight wagon with high sides that had set idle by the Pollards' farm for some years.

"Darn, Son," Jake Pollard exclaimed, "that freighter takes least 8 mule just to pull it empty."

Then it began to dawn on Farmer, he resembled a steer kept in a corral. He had no earthly idea of what lay beyond the fourth hill out from Holt. All he had ever known was the farm. Get up early to tend chores, work the land, and go to school, always, every waking moment, the farm. Only time he had ever been out of Holt was when the family traveled to Abilene, and he was just a kid of ten.

Suddenly, what had seemed a distant hill now loomed as an insurmountable mountain. Farmer didn't know how they were to travel to Oregon, and he felt his faith waver.

Then, if possible, the black cloud that had been hanging over his head got blacker. The following Sunday in church, Franklin Trevor refused to look at Farmer or speak to him. When pastor proudly announced the news of Farmer and Emile's good fortune and move to Oregon, Franklin took Allison's hand, and they walked out of the service. "Best be prayin' the boy gets some of the Lord's good sense to stay home!" Franklin rudely remarked as they made their exit.

That afternoon Emile tried to make excuses to Walter and Clifton when they wanted to know whey grandpa and grandma had left church and gone to their house, and why couldn't they go see them. "Maybe yer ma can take you,"

Farmer offered, but Emile's look told him they would go together or not at all.

"Is my head full of cotton, or was some of the folks at church cold towards us?" Farmer pondered that night as he and Emile lay in bed.

"They were cold," Emile replied softly.

"Why they be actin' thata way?" Farmer flashed.

"I think they are envious, dear," Emile sighed, snuggling close to him to go to sleep.

On this night, sleep proved fretful for Farmer. Thoughts of a ranch in a new land, the work of building a house, starting a herd of cattle, were now overshadowed by the questions of the unknown. Then a replay of events with his Pa and the scene in church just that morning made escaping to sleep impossible.

As the next week progressed, Farmer found himself giving more and more time and attention to prayer. His prayers narrowed down to two areas—what to travel in and where do we go from here to arrive in Oregon. No answer was forthcoming, placing Farmer in a state of near panic. By the time Friday arrived, Farmer was irritable and frustrated. He felt driven to get ready for their travel, but he clearly didn't know what to do. "Lord, you'll have ta piece everything in place, 'cause I'm flat stumped," Farmer prayed.

It was well into the afternoon when he turned the horses and their milk cow into a field to feed. He caught a reflected flash from a wagon traveling down the road. Soon he recognized the Harrison buggy and his good friend Benjamin.

CHAPTER 10

BENJAMIN HARRISON

B enjamin Harrison, born to Clem and Ann Harrison one month apart from Farmer Trevor. Named after former President of the United States, Benjamin Harrison, the 23rd President.

There was a tale about Benjamin that had circulated around town for years. It became apparent that Benjamin was as restless as Farmer, who was the elder. It was told that on the very day that Benjamin was born was the exact day that the Stanley twins drove their new invention out of their shop—the Stanley Steamer. So folks would laugh and say, "That Farmer Trevor will no doubt run all the way to the Pacific Ocean and stop 'cause he can't go no further, and that Benjamin Harrison will drive an automobile wherever he goes.

The two boys entered school together and a strong unshakable friendship formed. One day in their fifth year of school, a group of older boys ganged up on Benjamin, whose mouth had the habit a gettin' him in trouble. Farmer jumped into the fight to defend his friend and with their backs to each other they fought with all their might, outweighed and outnumbered. They limped to their homes beaten up that day, but they had won.

Yes, both boys were of the restless sort, but while Farmer had gotten stuck on the farm, married and had a family, Benjamin had left Holt for Dallas and lived and worked there.

Farmer felt joy to see his dear friend roll into the yard. His heart was warmed by Benjamin's wide grin. Their hands locked in a hearty handshake, then they were locked in a manly hug.

"I came as soon's I heard, Farmer. You're finally gonna do it! I'm so proud I could just. . ." Words just seemed to fail him. "Well, anyways, it's 'bout time. Why you ain't never been outa Holt in your whole dang life!"

"Been ta Abilene," Farmer corrected.

"Shoot fire, Farmer, that ain't nothin'," then they both laughed.

Farmer helped Benjamin unhitch the horse from the buggy and he led it into the corral. Farmer brought hay from the barn and carried some water.

"I'm figuring ya ta spend the night," Farmer looked at Benjamin and smiled. Benjamin started to object. Farmer went on sternly now. "Haven't seen ya fer a dang long time and I plan on talkin' yer head off 'till the sun's back up; won't hear no argument!"

Benjamin laughed. The two men propped their arms on the top rail of the corral and began eager conversation.

"The world's gettin' smaller and going faster. I've been places and seen things that would jus' fry yer ears off with my tellin' it all. You know what I did?"

"What?" Farmer was eager to hear.

"I bought me one of those Model T Fords."

"Naw, you're foolin' me! Where is it?" Farmer's eyes got big with excitement.

"Couldn't bring it to Holt. Still too early in the year an' roads are impassible in some places. So, I took the train and hitched a ride with a family. But, I'll tell you the truth, Pa's buggy goes like a turtle compared to my T Model. Think on this!" Benjamin stepped away from the corral to use his hands to talk with. Farmer hung on every word.

"You run yer team at full gallop—fer how long, Farmer? Will they make it all the way to Holt runnin' hard?"

"Just barely," Farmer acknowledged.

"Well my Ford Model T would pass you by and keep right on goin' for hours."

"Glory be," Farmer shook his head in wonder.

"An' there's some new models just out that goes even faster than mine. Jus' as soon as I can save me some money I'm a tradin' fer one of them."

Then Benjamin got a silly look on his face and he playfully pushed Farmer. "An' I met me this cute little Dallas girl. We been goin' to these dancin' parties an' livin' fast."

"You gonna get hitched up with a little filly? I'd say it's about time!" Farmer exclaimed ignoring the parties and fast livin' remark.

"Whoa—Whoa, didn't say nothing 'bout marryin'," Benjamin held both hands up.

Farmer felt a twinge of sadness as he recalled that the two of them had also taken two different spiritual paths.

Benjamin's face brightened up, "My Pa got on the telephone to the office where I work. 'The government has done given Farmer and Emile a section of land in Oregon for homesteadin',' he was tellin' me on the telephone." Benjamin's face grew sad and his voice softened, "and you all have to leave soon's as possible to get there 'fore winter. An' I'm thinkin' I've got to get here 'fore you leave. 'Cause it might be a mighty long time before. . ."

"An' I'm sure glad you came," Farmer felt his throat tighten and his eyes water up. Both men put their arms back up on the corral and watched the Harrison horse for a long time.

Farmer broke the silence, "I've found out 'bout myself, Ben, thet I'm like a steer kept in this corral all my life. I have no idea what's over the next hill. I don't know nothing 'bout it. I've been prayin' lots."

"Ha!" Benjamin broke in with a laugh and slapped Farmer on the shoulder. "When Pa tol' me you all was leavin' for Oregon—I says to myself. I says, 'I know Farmer Trevor. He's my best friend so I know him like a book I've read, and I know right now he's walkin' 'round in circles 'cause he's never been outa Holt his whole life' . . ." Benjamin paused to get Farmer's reaction. "Abilene's the wrong darn way," Benjamin teased, "and my friend Farmer's a thinkin', 'I can't take off on a road and jus' see where it takes me. Why, they might as well end up in New York.' So, I says to myself, 'my friend Farmer is in a heap o' trouble with a place to be an' not knowin' the way,' right?"

"Dang right!"

"Well, I says to myself, thinkin', 'how can I help my friend?' So's here what I done." Benjamin went to the buggy and gathered a bunch of papers.

"I did some studying 'fore I came—and I found maps of roads an' everything. I've got it all figured out for you."

Farmer was speechless.

"Now ifen you'll take me inside yer house we can go over how you can go. Anyhow, I'm ready to see Emile 'cause she's a whole lot prettier to look at than you."

"Thet's why ya need ta get a wife, 'cause I sore get tired of yer face as well," Farmer laughed as they walked to the house.

The boys leaped into Ben Harrison's big arms as he walked in, and Emile's smile and look told Farmer she had kept the boys in the house to give him time alone with Benjamin.

"Howdy Mrs. Emile," Benjamin removed his hat and took her hand, "you sure will grace the mountains of Oregon with beauty."

Farmer saw Emile's face flush.

"You both must be famished. Come, I have supper ready," Emile motioned to the table.

Farmer, for the first time since Benjamin had arrived became conscious of how long they had been at the corral. It was near dark.

As supper meal was eaten, it seemed everybody wanted to talk at once. The conversation was happy and light-hearted. Farmer made a mental note that when Benjamin was alone with him, he was plain ol' Ben, Holt bred and born. But in Emile's presence he displayed an eloquence and refinement he must have learned in the big city.

"Benjamin, I think you're 'bout ta drive me plum frantic," Farmer broke into the conversation.

Benjamin was surprised!

"Emile, our dear friend Benjamin here," Farmer was savoring his upper hand, "he has done a heap o' study in Dallas 'bout where we're goin', an' he brought us all these maps he gathered."

"Oh my!" Emile clapped her hands in girlish glee.

"What's a map?" the boys questioned.

"We'll see ifen we can ever get Ben ta finish eatin' and talkin'. Never seen him eat so dang slow. Why December will be here shore nuff 'fore we ever lay eyes on one."

The boys looked puzzled and Emile covered a giggle with her hand.

Benjamin stared at Farmer a moment, and then broke into a long, from the heart laugh. They all laughed untill tears ran down their faces. Walter and Clifton got down out of their chairs, not sure what was goin' on, and Emile cleared the table.

Benjamin showed the boys a map and pointed out a few things, and Emile herded them off to clean up and get to bed.

"Ben, if ya don't stop this torture you're a doin' me by draggin' on—I'm gonna wrestle ya down right here in my kitchen!"

"Ha! Won't get nothin' from me but a whippen' doin that," Benjamin started spreading paper and maps across the table.

"Farmer, our country is growin' big and changin' fast. Folks all over is on the move!" Benjamin got serious and sat down.

Farmer took a chair across the table from him. "Go on!" he pleaded.

"Well, here's what's comin' to pass," Benjamin's eyes were charged with electric excitement. "Fer two years going on, there's been talk of connecting some existing roads and trails an' makin' what they call an interstate highway from Chicago to Los Angeles. I read in an Oklahoma City newspaper last year that a big crowd met in Tulsa with all their automobiles to promote this highway."

"Ah ha! I seen it comin' years ago! Ya know, in my head. I jus' didn't know how exactly, or where."

"An hear this, Farmer! I's just read an article in our Dallas newspaper where the Secretary of Agriculture appointed this Oklahoma fella name Avery to figure out the route this very year."

"But, we're goin ta Oregon, not California way."

"That's just what I'm tryin' to get to, Farmer. The automobile is changin' our nation. The way we think and do things—will do it even here in Holt."

"You joke!" Farmer laughed.

"Listen Farmer. The automobile is bringin' change. There's better roads' being built. There are gasoline stations and repair shops springin' up! Folks can now travel farther and faster—and travel they will."

"Wish I had me an automobile," he now spoke wistfully. Farmer needed to reassure himself.

"There will be some long stretches of rough trail and no gasoline. But a good thing the automobile has brung to ya is maps!"

Benjamin had been piecing maps and papers together on the table. Some were printed maps, others he had drawn.

"What you think o' this route, Farmer?" Farmer stood up to get a better view.

"Here's Holt—right here. You go out the west end of town like goin to ol' man Pollard's place. Keep on that wagon trail to Flag. See here on this map—this shows that at Flag there is a road to Plainview. Then north outa Plainview is a better road to Amarillo.

Now at Amarillo is the road there talkin' 'bout bein' part of this long highway to the Pacific. You'll follow that road to New Mexico.

"Now we change maps. First town o' any size in New Mexico is –ah- Tu-cum-cari, don't know how they say it. You see here, the map shows some road and these markings show a wagon or stage trail. Looks like mountains, long 'bout Santa Rosa to Albuquerque. Now goin' on west, I heard a fella tell me who had been there that you follow a river valley through a mining camp town, an' Gallup is in a desert with lots of Indians. The Arizona map shows a bad road to Holbrook—only wagon trail through Winslow. When you get to Flagstaff you'll be on top of the world."

"How be thet?" queried Farmer.

"Look at the altitude printed there. Horses and automobiles have a heck of a time breathin' there in that city," Benjamin said with a laugh.

"At Flagstaff is where ya turn north, and this may be where the goin' gets a heap harder. This is mostly wagon trail and not much water stops shown. Make your way to Grey Rock, and you'll be crossin' the Colorado River here at Marble Rock. Now following into the Utah map, it looks like dry desolate travel to a town called Hurricane. Now, what the map tells me is that you'll hit a pretty dog gone good road to Salt Lake City." At this juncture, Benjamin looked up and paused until their eyes met. "Farmer, here's where you gotta make a hard decision, and you have to think long and careful on it. You're aimin' at the ol' Applegate Trail. At Salt Lake City you can keep on due north into Idaho and pick it up here, an' follow the trail down into Nevada or, you can cross the Great Salt Flats, carvin' days off your travel. But, you'll have ta be considerin' Emile, your boys and your horses. I read in a book that the Salt Flats are whiter 'an white snow and blindin' on sunny days. Shows a road across, but no water. Now, I had to draw out the rest from a book I found in a library, which showed me the Applegate Trail route. You gotta reach the Humbolt River at Winnemucca, Nevada. The trail from Idaho a coming 'cross the flats seem to merge together somewhere here. Leavin' the Humbolt, you'll head northwest across Black Rock Desert. The book said this was a dangerous and most discouragin' part of the journey. Once you reach Surprise Valley, the goin' gets easier. Pass around Goose Lake an' on to Tule Lake in California. In this area Farmer, you'll cross over into Oregon. It shows a natural stone bridge to cross Lost River. Passin' lower Klamath Lake, the trail crosses over a mountain pass named Greensprings and drops down to a small town called Ashland on Emigrant Lake. Now you're almost home, my friend. Head your wagon northeast into this river valley, follow that, and your place is here!" Benjamin marked the spot with his finger and looked up at Farmer with a satisfied grin. "What you think?"

Farmer collapsed into his chair, "God has answered one of my prayers," he exclaimed.

"Well, you can thank Him ifen you want, but I'm the one who read the books and gathered maps, an—!"

"Yes! Of course, Ben!" Farmer exclaimed as he stood up and placed a hand on Ben's shoulder. "How can I ever thank ya for what's ya done?"

The look between them conveyed the strong friendship they had shared since childhood.

Benjamin smiled, "Hot cup o' coffee might jus' do it! An' yer promise that you'll finish yer dream."

CHAPTER 11

A TRIP TO AMARILLO

It was the early morning hours Wednesday. Farmer woke with a start—he thought he had heard something or someone. He quietly got out of bed. Emile was sleeping peacefully. He made his way to the bedroom window and looked over the yard to the out buildings. Was it a polecat tryin' to get the chickens? He listened. . .silence.

He softly opened the bedroom door and went to check on the boys. Both were asleep—there was enough moonlight to make out their faces. Walking to the kitchen window he peered out to the barn and corral. He listened . . .the faint whooo of a distant owl.

'I miss ol' Badger soundin' off if there was trouble,' Farmer thought and a sense of sadness swept through his mind.

Badger had shown up on the Trevor's porch years ago when Farmer was reaching his teens and the two sorta adopted each other. The dog had a vague appearance of a badger, and certainly dug holes like one. He had proven himself a good watchdog. He was there when Farmer and

Emile married—and loved the boys with endless devotion. He just up and died in the winter of old age.

Farmer shook off the sadness and went back to bed. He lay awake for a short while, then started to drift off to sleep.

"Farmer!"

"Wha!" Farmer sat straight up in bed.

"Farmer, get up. You must travel to Amarillo to see Thomas Redkin."

Farmer knew the Lord was speaking to him. It had happened once before—so strong on his heart and mind, clear as a speaking voice—yet it was on his heart, like when prayin'.

Then he began to question. 'Was it really from the Lord? Amarillo is a long trip, an' I hardly know rancher Redkin.' Besides, in March the weather can turn bad . . .'

"Farmer! Get up! You must leave quickly. Go to Thomas Redkin!"

"But Emile and the boys?" Farmer prayed softly.

"I will watch over them."

"I'm not sure of the wagon," Farmer implored.

"I will get you there."

"I don't understand why I'm a going there," Farmer was confused. Was he to arrive and announce to Redkin—"Well, I'm here!"

"You will understand in time."

Farmer lay back in his pillow thinking of all he would have to do in preparation.

"Farmer! Go quickly! As the sun rises!"

Farmer's feet hit the floor.

"What is it, Farmer?" Emile was awake.

"The Lord told me ta go right now ta Amarillo ta see Thomas Redkin."

"Who is Thomas Redkin?" she questioned.

"Remember the rancher who was at church and potluck months ago?"

"Oh yes," she put her hand to her mouth. "That's when your father became loud and upset."

"Yes, Emile please pack me some food. I suspect it might be a two day journey up there and two back."

"You're leaving right now?" her voice revealed concern.

"Yes, God promised ta take care of all of us. Ifen we can't trust Him ta get me ta Amarillo an' protect ya here—how can we figure Him ta get us all the way ta Oregon?"

Emile laughed and playfully kissed him. Farmer knew then that she was all right. He lit a lamp and built a fire in the kitchen. Completing that, he went outside to hitch Sunset and Wind to the wagon. His hands and face stung from the cold. He could see grey forming on the eastern horizon.

Inside, Emile had coffee on and breakfast cooking. Farmer took the Texas map that Benjamin had left. He dug out a bedroll, and took his rifle off the pegs on the wall. He filled his pocket with extra cartridges.

Breakfast was eaten with little conversation while they both tried to take in all the meaning of what was happening.

"Why are you going, Farmer? What are you to do?" Emile wanted to know.

"I have no idea on God's green earth! I just know I'm ta go—by sunrise!"

They looked over the open map.

"I'm guessin' distance, but I reckon I should be around Plainview—maybe beyond, by sundown. Depends on how the horses hold up."

"Oh do be careful, Farmer. I will miss you so!" Emile cried as she kissed and hugged him goodbye.

Farmer placed some clothes, the bedroll, and the food Emile had packed in the back of the wagon. He slid his rifle in the sheave and climbed onto the seat.

Sunset and Wind were anxious to go, and turned out of the yard onto the lane headed towards Holt. Farmer turned to wave to Emile. He could barely see her in the grey light of dawn, but knew he carried her smile and her heart in prayer as he left.

The ride to Holt was routine. Farmer could see a few homes lit up as occupants were beginning to stir. As he neared the Pollards, he suddenly became unsure. A sense of fear gripped him. It was fear of the unknown. He was going somewhere he had never been before—alone! No, not alone! God had promised to get him to Redkin's!

A mile past Pollard's farm, the golden light of the sun caught up to Farmer then spilled beyond him to make brilliant every hill and ravine on the trail that lay before him.

Now an incredible excitement filled his whole being dispelling any fears he might have felt. He was finally doing the very thing he had been destined to do from his birth. He was headed west, and Farmer had a deep sense that he was doin' exactly what he was suppose' to be a doin!

Sunset and Wind must have sensed the excitement of travel to a new destination, as they wanted to pick up their gait. Farmer let them, keeping an eye on the trail for rocks or rough spots, while at the same time drinkin' in all he could see of the landscape.

Eventually the horses tired, so Farmer slowed them to a walk. He could see a line of trees ahead, which might indicate water. He took advantage of the slow pace to look over his wagon as it rolled along. It appeared to be holdin' up well.

The trees lined a creek bed, which was still running a little water. Farmer scooped water in his hat and gave the horses only a little water at first—so as not to make them sick.

He let Sunset and Wind feed, rest and drink from the creek freely. A rider on a horse appeared on the trail comin' from the west.

"Howdy," Farmer greeted him.

"How do yerself, fella. Where you comin' from?"

"Holt."

"Well do tell. Don't reckon I been there," the rider let his horse drink from the creek.

"Where ya hail from?" Farmer asked.

"Got me a farm the other side a Flag."

"Do tell, how far ta Flag?" Farmer queried.

"Well, I'd say you got 'bout an hour o' easy riden'. You got business in Flag?"

"Goin' on further ta Amarillo ta see a rancher, Thomas Redkin. Ya know him?"

"Seems I heard the name—'bout all. You a rancher?"

"I'm gonna be!"

"Fer this Redkin fella?"

"Na, I've got me some land in Oregon."

"Goin' on to Oregon then," the rider brought up his horse into the grassy spot where Farmer was sitting.

"Na, gotta go back ta Holt ta get my wife an' boys."

The rider laughed and shook his head. "Seems we both be runnin' from our wives," he said sadly.

"Ain't runnin'. God tol' me ta go see Redkin—is all I know." Farmer stood up.

"Name's Timothy," the rider said extending his hand to Farmer.

Farmer shook Timothy's hand, "Farmer Trevor," he exclaimed.

The two men sat on a log while the animals grazed.

"I'm a church goin' man, but life has handed me a deal I don't know if even God can fix it right."

"Ya runnin' from yer wife?" Farmer remembered the remark Timothy had made.

"It's my Karen!" he started pouring out his heart. "I love her so much. People tol' me she was loose. She seemed to get angry over my church goin' after we tied the knot. This mornin' I was s'pose to work south corner, but my harness broke so's I went home early. An-an- I caught her in bed with a no good,—" Timothy wailed.

Farmer didn't know what to do or say.

"I grabbed my rifle, an'—an' I tried to kill him—an' I'm not the killin' type. Maybe hit him once 'cause he sure hollered. Then I was so hurt and angry at my Karen I—I coulda shot her too! So I got on my horse and been a ride'n. If the folks in Flag hear tell, the women folk will tar and feather her, an'—an' I don't know what I should do."

Timothy tried to wipe his wet face with his hands. "I'm sorry to put all this offen on you, but I'm mighty glad you were here to talk to."

"Well, I recall our preacher tellin' 'bout a prophet in a sermon long time ago," Farmer began slowly. "God tol' him ta marry a whore. This prophet wanted ta do as God tol' him so he married this loose woman and loved her. Now as I recall, God maybe wanted ta teach town folks a lesson of sorts, or maybe God figured this woman needed someone ta love and care for her. Well, this woman done run off with some fella who only wanted her body—an' God tol' her husband ta go find her and take her back an' love her."

Timothy sat thinking. "Is that story really in the Bible," he asked.

"Shore is," Farmer grinned, "or else the preacher was foolin' us. Come on and help me hitch up my team. I'm taken ya home ta make up ta yer wife. No one in town has ta know what went on 'bout the matter."

The pair rode together on to the town of Flag. They spoke of things concerning the Lord, love and marriage, and lots about forgiving, and healing. On the outskirts of Flag, Timothy turned Farmer onto a more traveled road to Plainview. He thanked Farmer, and headed his horse towards home, determined to love and forgive his Karen.

CHAPTER 12

REDKIN RANCH

F armer made good time on the road to Plainview. Parts were hard packed from travel, and in low places that he figured would tend to get muddy, a thin layer of small rocks was spread for a mile or so. It was the same rock put down the main street of Holt that Benjamin called gravel, but Farmer argued that a gravel was the little hammer used to call to order meetin's and such. He felt again the flush of embarrassment he had when he found out he was thinking gavel.

Farmhouses became more frequent the closer he got to Plainview. Farmers in fields would wave as he rolled by in his wagon. He passed several men on horseback heading the way he'd just come, a man and a woman in a buggy came up behind and went around him—in a hurry to get to Plainview.

As he curved around a bend in the road, the setting sun blinded his sight. Pulling his hat brim lower, he made out what appeared a small carriage coming fast towards him. To Farmer's amazement, he saw it had no horses. Soon he could hear a popping sound that hurt his ears—and Sunset and Wind began pulling on the reins wanting to move out of the way. Farmer pulled his team to a halt trying to calm them down.

The horseless carriage rolled to a stop next to Farmer's wagon midst a flurry of dust.

"Top o' the evenin', neighbor," the driver tipped his hat. "Nice team of horses you have ye there."

Farmer eyed the carriage without speaking. As the dust settled he could make out what looked like a horse drawn buggy, but no horse. Noise and smoke came from a box compartment behind the seat. From that, there were gears and chains attached to the rear wheels. The driver's hand was on a bent stick coming up out of the floorboard.

"So this is one of those new fangled automobiles," Farmer was fascinated, but ashamed to admit this the first one he had actually seen in his whole life.

"Ha! An' nary so new lad! This be a 1910 Chevrolet. I ordered it meself from the Sears Roebuck catalogue. Came on a train to Amarillo she did. Now, I'm thinkin' I may sell this contraption and purchase me a new model. I seen me a Dodge touring car that strikes me fancy. Ya seen that one yerself?"

"No, I haven't. Ya say ya go ta Amarillo?"

"Aye—and often for business."

"Then maybe ya can help me. I'm needing to locate Thomas Redkin."

"Aye, I know Redkin by golly!" The man's face lit up. "But you needn't be goin' to Amarillo. Redkin's ranch is some miles southeast of Amarillo."

Farmer was relieved to find someone who knew Redkin. "Can ya tell me how ta find his ranch?"

"That be easy, lad. You take this road into Plainview. It crosses a main traveling road goin' to Amarillo. There be signs and you go right like you was goin' to Amarillo. Keep headin' north on that road. There it be when you come on a place on the road named Katie's Stop—ye stop!"

The man waited for Farmer to catch the joke—then laughed.

"She be a eaten place, with gasoline pumps, some shops, an' cabins for overnight travelers. By golly, lad, yer not makin' much time by wagon—dark be on ya before ye make Katie's. May think on stayin' in Plainview tonight. Don't want to be makin' yer journey after the sun goes down."

"Is Redkin's Ranch at Katie's Stop?" Farmer asked beginning to feel annoyed.

"Nay, and be knowin' ye got nearly a half day's travel left when you leave Katie's a goin' by wagon as ye are. But listen now, lad, by Katie's Stop is a small road that points towards the settin' sun. A sign there reads, Cottonmouth. Ye follow that road 'till you come to a high up in the sky gate. On it says T bar R Ranch. Well, by golly, that be it. Go through the gate an' that trail will lead you to Mr. Thomas Redkin. When ye see him would ye say, 'Robert Riley sends his regards!' Best o' luck to ye lad. Take care o' those fine horses ye got ya."

With that, Robert Riley bolted off before Farmer could answer—or thank him for the directions and advice he had given. "Thank ya fer yer help. . ." Farmer's voice trailed off, unheard. He watched the automobile disappear around the curve.

Farmer knew it would be dark soon, but to seek out a room in Plainview as Mr. Riley had suggested was outa the question, seen as Farmer's pockets were near empty of cash.

Coming to a rough hand painted sign, he read 'White Salt Fork & the Brazos'. Long about another hundred feet the road joined a sizable stream of water and ran alongside—possibly on into Plainview. In a few minutes Farmer located an open grove of scrub trees and decided to make camp there.

Farmer had to re-acquaint himself with camp life. He tied the horses with enough rope to fed and water. Next he gathered wood and built a fire. He was so hungry he could have eaten his provisions raw. Right now, not only did he miss Emile's companionship, but her good cooking.

After his hurried supper, he warmed himself by the fire and looked up into the sky that sparkled with a million stars. He wondered how it would be in Oregon. Would it be as beautiful and peaceful as where he was at that moment?

Sleep soon overtook him, so he crawled under the wagon where he had laid out his bedroll. The sound of the water sang him to sleep, and he didn't stir until the chill of the dawn air cut through his skin to the bone. He fumbled with shaky hands to rebuild the fire.

"Dang!" he fumed, "Ifen I can't handle this, how'm I gonna be a pioneer ta Oregon?" he laughed at himself.

Sunset and Wind were alert and eager to be on the road. Breakfast and coffee finished, Farmer broke camp, and was soon urging the horses back up on the road. The wagon creaked and groaned as if trying to stretch and wake up.

The sun just topped the trees behind him when they rolled into Plainview. It was like coming into another world. Shops and houses lined the street, which was some kind of hard surface now. The horses' hooves rang sharply as they nearly pranced at a quick gait.

Not many folks were out and doing yet, but Farmer could tell it would be a busy place soon—especially as they turned onto the Amarillo road. This curved away from the river and appeared to be the main part of Plainview. Some shops and houses were already active as the day was beginning. Numerous automobiles sat parked along sidewalks. Farmer felt like a young boy seeing something exciting for the first time—It was more than he could take in and felt a tug to stop at a lit up café and have coffee and just listen to the folks already inside. But he was anxious to get to the Redkin Ranch, so he passed on through Plainview.

Farmer was pleased to discover such a good road heading towards Amarillo. The team pulled the wagon with ease and seemed delighted at the sounds they made on the road.

The number of travelers increased as the morning wore on. Farmer was amazed at how many automobiles there were. He believed they must outnumber horses and wagons three to one. He kept track for a while and found the ratio more like eight to one.

"Ol' Margaret Hatchet would plumb have a fit seein' all this!" Farmer mused out loud.

However, more amazing to Farmer was how fast these automobiles traveled. At first they were very frightening for Sunset and Wind. They attempted to bolt! Farmer could hear them snort, and see their eyes bug open. Several times he had to stop the horses, get down from the wagon and rub their manes, faces, noses and talk softly to them.

Now an auto would fly by nearly taking Farmer's hat off, but they didn't seem to pay any mind to it. In fact, when one came up fast from behind and passed them by—Farmer had to hold back on the reins to keep his horses from racing after the disappearing automobile.

A black one that read 'Ford' across the front in large letters came over the crest of a hill, the driver waving as he flew on by towards Plainview. Seeing the Ford triggered thoughts of his friend Benjamin. 'I've been places and seen things that would jus' fry yer ears off with me tellin' it all', he had said. "An' I could never have imagined the likes o' it ifen I wasn't seein' it for myself!" Farmer thought.

Along about mid morning the road crested a hill. From that spot, Farmer looked down in a low area lined with trees. A small river flowed under a log bridge where the road crossed over. Near the bridge on this side of the river were quite a number of buildings—with a large sign, which

Farmer could easily read all the way to where he was—Katie's Stop.

"My o my—We gotta stop!" Farmer laughed.

Farmer felt sort of out of place as he located a place to leave his horses and wagon amid some of the automobiles. He saw numerous cabins—some appeared occupied. He walked slowly by the gasoline pumps to see how the driver was getting gasoline into his auto.

Farmer stepped into Katie's Café. Several patrons were at tables and the talk was noisy. Farmer made his way to the counter, and spoke to the large jolly woman standing behind it.

"Just lookin' ta get a cup o' coffee," Farmer spoke softly.

"Well you just put your fanny at a table and we'll get one right to ya!" she ordered loudly.

Farmer's face flushed with heat, as he turned to a table.

"Hey, ain't you the feller on the wagon?" a man grabbed his arm as he walked by.

"Yes I am!" Farmer replied, looking into a friendly face.

"I passed you by some ways back. You got yerself a good team a horses I reckon, 'cause you made pretty good time."

Farmer smiled and nodded and made his way to a corner table. The young woman who was waiting tables brought his coffee.

The coffee was hot and tasted good. Farmer became immersed in the conversations as he slowly sipped from his cup. He tried to take in every word, for it seemed the talk of the world was going on right here at Katie's. Farm talk, cattle talk, talk of the past war, talk of relatives and friends, talk of churches, the boomin' economy!

Farmer lost track of time until a dusty driver came in smacking his gloves against his leg. "Howdy, howdy," he drawled. "Say, I heard tell in Amarillo that folks heard on a radio that there's a northerner comin' down. There's cold rain, maybe some freezin' rain be blowin' in, probably hit here first of the week!"

This news jolted Farmer into reality that he needed to be on his way. He paid for his coffee and bid everyone goodbye.

On the other side of the bridge about a half-mile he came on the road to Cottonmouth. It wasn't as smooth and wide as the Amarillo road, but still good enough for Farmer to run the team for periods of time—then he would walk them until they rested. The road climbed and dipped over hills and low lands. The land was dotted with brush and cattle for as far as his eyes could see. He was awestruck by the great expanse of Texas!

It must be long 'bout four o'clock judgin' by the position of the sun, Farmer figured when he stopped in front of a huge gate. The beam across the top had T——-R burned in to it in large letters.

CHAPTER 13
A SURPRISE TURN

Farmer had never seen such a large house. There were none to rival it in Holt. He was greeted by a young man who emerged from one of the buildings as the wagon rolled to a halt.

Farmer was directed to the ranch house while the young man informed him he would tend to the horses. As Farmer walked to the house he made a survey of the buildings. All were large and well built. The corral appeared capable of holding a hundred head of cattle with two loading chutes. He saw three black, what he had heard called, trucks parked near a building he figured to be a shop o' sorts.

It came to Farmer's mind as he rang a bell by the massive wooden door, that the ranch was quiet. He had not seen anyone besides the man who took his horses. Farmer rang again!

A middle aged Mexican woman opened the door. "Si?" she questioned.

"My name is Farmer Trevor," he began, removing his hat, "I am come ta visit Mr. Thomas Redkin."

"Senor Redkin is a not here. He and his men working on the range," she pointed past Farmer's shoulder. "They return when sun goes down. You come."

Farmer followed her into a hallway lined with coat and hat pegs and pictures. The hallway opened into a huge living area. The walls were dark wood covered with pictures, trophies, and what Farmer thought must be collected items that had some kinda meaning. Large thick sofas were placed around a stone fireplace, which covered a far wall. Farmer noticed a desk and chair by one of the windows. The room gave him a sense of warmth and friendliness, and he could tell that Redkin was accustomed to having guests.

The woman stopped in the middle of the room and turned to face him. "I am Merrita, Senor Redkin's house-keeper. Come! I take you to your room."

"But, I can sleep outside, or the barn," Farmer protested. He hadn't thought to stay in Redkin's home.

Merrita turned with a frown that told Farmer to refuse Redkin's hospitality would be an insult.

Merrita left Farmer in a guest room. It was bright and sunny, with a soft bed covered with blankets and a colorful quilt. Farmer washed up in a basin atop the dresser. Merrita reappeared with some fresh baked bread and homemade preserves. She had a glass of water, also a second glass of a drink that tasted like cider.

Farmer enjoyed the refreshments, but was too nervous to remain in his room. He went outside, knowing it shouldn't be too long before Redkin and his hired hands came in. He thought to find the young man, looking first in the barn, then on to the stables. He did locate Sunset and Wind who seemed to be at ease with the attention and feed they were given. Several other horses of Redkin's were in stalls, but Farmer made note of how many empty stalls there were, accounting for a lot of men working on the Redkin spread.

As he became more absorbed, he took in how the various buildings were laid out—and their purposes. He discovered a smaller corral with an open roof covering on one side. There were several heifers in this pen of a breed Farmer had not seen before. He watched them for a time until the sound of approaching horses broke into his thoughts.

It was as Merrita said. The sun was dropping into the western hills when Thomas Redkin and his cowboys rode into the stable area. They were loud and boisterous, a mixture of laughs, growls, cowboy remarks and rough talk.

Farmer resisted the urge to run greet Redkin like a little boy and walked instead towards the front porch of the house. It was near dark when Farmer recognized a dusty faced Thomas Redkin walking towards him. Two of his men followed close behind then veered off to disappear around the side of the house.

"Welcome, fella," Redkin smiled as he stepped up on the porch and extended his hand towards Farmer. "Hope you ain't been waitin' long, son, but I have ta tell you, I ain't hiring any more hands right now. Got me a full crew, an' none leavin'."

"I didn't come fer a job, Mr. Redkin. I came ta visit ya!"

"Do I know you?" Redkin eyed him. "Come on in the house."

"I met ya in Holt at a church dinner on the grounds. You was seein' relatives as I recall," Farmer continued as they walked into the large room.

Redkin stopped and eyed Farmer again.

"Hmmm. So why are you here to see me?" Redkin asked, "If you ain't lookin' for work."

"Well..." Farmer hesitated, "mainly 'cause yesterday mornin', the Lord tol' me ta go see Thomas Redkin."

"The Lord told you?" Redkin's eyes narrowed, and he seemed to look through Farmer. "What did the Lord tell you to see me about?" Redkin's voice carried the tone of suspicion.

Farmer's eyes dropped as he felt his face flush!

"Don't rightly—know," Farmer stammered. He felt foolish, and wanted to hide from the ranchers penetrating stare. "He jus' tol' me ta come—an' I did," Farmer went on. "But I..."

Merrita interrupted walking briskly to Redkin.

"Merrita, you must prepare a room for—" he turned back to Farmer, "I don't recall your name, Son."

"Senor Trevor," Merrita remembered his name and introduced him. " I have given him the sun room."

"Very good. Show Mr. Trevor the toilet room, and to his room. Call him when supper is ready. I must clean up now."

Farmer was more than eager to retreat to the sunroom. He sensed Redkin's coolness, and realized he had made a fool of himself. In his heart, he knew that Redkin saw him as an opportunist, wanting a hand out. Farmer dreaded facing the rancher at the table.

It was as an eternity before Merrita knocked on his door. She led him to another good-sized room with a long table surrounded by chairs. The two cowboys Farmer had seen walk around the house were cleaned up and seated at the table. They stood up as Merrita pulled a chair out for Farmer.

The taller cowboy, with ruddy face and neck spoke first, "Howdy, stranger. Name's Red, an' I'm Redkin's foreman."

They shook hands.

"Name's Farmer Trevor from Holt, Texas.

"Me Rocca," the second cowboy, a thin and attractive Mexican grinned. "I keep Senor Redkin's vaqueros in line."

"Welcome, Farmer Trevor from Holt, Texas," Thomas Redkin entered the room. Farmer could tell immediately that Red, Rocca and Merrita respected the elder rancher. Not because he was their boss alone, but a far deeper reason.

"Come on, boys, you must be darn near starved!" After they were seated, Redkin offered grace. The simple, yet heartfelt prayer touched Farmer.

"Dig in and eat," Redkin instructed. Then eyeing Farmer he laughed! "You hesitate Farmer, an' everything will be all eaten!"

Farmer could not believe that. There was meat and potatoes, and biscuits a plenty. Farmer ate until he was miserable.

During supper Farmer listening to the talking, determined that once Thomas Redkin was married. He loved his wife deeply, and they started the ranch together. She caught whooping cough and died young for they hadn't any children. Redkin never remarried, although there were numerous interested women, as Red and Rocca kidded him. Even Merrita got in on the ribbin' as she poured coffee.

Finally, the conversation waned, and Red and Rocca excused themselves to 'hit the sack.' Farmer had learned that the cattle were calving and cowboys had to work long hours and split shifts to watch 24 hours a day. Some of the heifers had difficulty giving birth and needed help.

"Well, Farmer Trevor of Holt, Texas," Redkin turned his attention to Farmer after the other two had left, "thinkin' back on it, an' if I'm rememberin' right, you were the lad who wanted to go west to be a rancher—and your Pa was against it."

"That's right!" Farmer brightened, "an' all that changed with this here official letter from the government."

Farmer produced the letter from the front pocket of his bib overalls.

"Hummm-uh huh-humm," Redkin mumbled thoughtfully as he read—then looking up at Farmer, "so the government wants to homestead some land and had a drawing of applications and you were the ninth pick?"

"Yes Sir!"

"Well, son, what do you want from me?"

"I reckon maybe the Lord—seein' as how He tol' me to come—that maybe ya could teach me some 'bout ranchin' an' cattle an' such . . ." Farmer's voice trailed off as he felt his face get hot, he dropped his eyes. "Ifen you have the time," he added.

Redkin looked at him thoughtfully for some time before he spoke. "Your Pa still against you packin' west?"

"Yes sir. He won't talk ta me or let me come . ." Farmer's voice broke. "He says my place is right there farmin' the land."

"And you're determined to go to Oregon?"

"Yes, sir, with all my heart!"

"You have a family?"

"Yes, sir. Emile an' me have two boys . . . an' she may be with child."

"How are you goin?"

"In our wagon, and I got two strong horses."

"I see," Redkin sat in thought awhile.

Farmer went on to tell him about Benjamin bringing maps he had gathered—and some he had drawn.

"Benjamin had the whole trip figured out," Farmer concluded.

"You understand you have a long, difficult journey ahead of you, Farmer?"

"Yes sir, but I'm determined in my spirit ta go, and the Lord will get us there in one piece. I'd be powerful grateful anything ya can teach me."

Redkin eyed him again, and then laughed a hearty laugh! "That, I can do, son. Merrita!"

"Senor," she answered as she came through the door, and awaited his order.

"First thing, Son is to look like a rancher stead of a farmer. Merrita, find Farmer a pair of jeans, shirt, and cowboy boots. An' he'll need a new hat. You be sure an' gather the things he has now an' burn 'em."

"Senor," she acknowledged and left out.

"And a belt," he called after her.

"Now listen up, son, 'cause we don't have much time," and with that Redkin began to share from his years of experience, while Farmer absorbed like a dry rag touchin' a pond of water.

Sleep came quickly as he hit the bed, and he couldn't remember stirring until Merrita woke him.

"Senor Redkin is ready to ride off for his work today. He wants to see you before he goes. Try these clothes."

Farmer was angry with himself for not rising earlier. He had hoped to join the rancher for breakfast.

Farmer found the clothes, which Merrita had laid out a good fit.

She looked him over carefully when he came out of his room.

"I matched everything to your clothes," she remarked.

"When did ya do that?" Farmer asked with surprise.

"This morning, while you slept," she smiled.

"Well now, Farmer, you look like a rancher sure nuff!" Thomas Redkin rose from his desk to greet Farmer. "Come with me," and he headed through the kitchen to a back door. "Breakfast will be waitin' for you when you come back in the house. I trust you slept well."

"I'm sorry I didn't wake up earlier," Farmer felt guilty.

"No need, there will be plenty of days for gettin' up earlier. This is not one of 'em, son. Now, I best tell you that you are welcome to stay as long as you want, but I hear tell a northerner is bearin' down on us, an' if you're wantin' to get home 'fore it hits, you best leave this mornin'."

Farmer nodded, "I'm beholden to ya for the stay—and these clothes—and yer teachin' last night . . ."

Redkin made no comment, but led Farmer to a large shed. He opened a big door on the front of the building, and then walked in.

"This is what you need for your trip to Oregon," Redkin pointed to a wagon parked in the shadows.

"This was my chuck wagon that we took on many a cattle drive. It's sturdy and can take rough goin'. The cover's good shape and here in the back is built for all your cookin' supplies, even still has some pots and pans."

"But, I can't—" Farmer started to speak.

"Now, I was lookin' over your wagon this mornin'," Redkin continued talking, "and being as how I have some use for it—and being as how we ship cattle only to Amarillo in trucks—and don't do cattle drives—I think we can do an even trade."

"But my wagon is—"

"Deal?" Redkin asked the second time.

"But," Farmer didn't know what to say. This was like a dream-happening so fast.

"Deal?" Redkin spoke again, still holding out his hand. "Son, I haven't all day to get this tied up!"

Farmer grabbed Redkin's hand in a strong grip, "Thank you, sir!"

CHAPTER 14
GETTING READY

The storm caught up with Farmer on the outskirts of Holt. Friday morning, two of Thomas Redkin's men had prepared the chuck wagon for travel. He was on his way by noon and pushed his horses hard—going on much of the night by faint moonlight, stopping only long enough for brief rests and water.

Saturday morning, Farmer could see the black clouds building to the north and advancing closer to him by the hour. Farmer urged Sunset and Wind to as fast a pace as he could. Even though the wagon seemed easy enough for them to pull—by the time they reached Holt, horses and driver were exhausted.

The wind grew stronger and the temperature dropped to a bitter cold. Freezing rain began falling on them as he pulled up to the barn.

Emile and the boys seemed to hesitate, unsure of the wagon until she saw Farmer, then she ran to greet him. She threw her arms around his neck and kissed him and kissed him until he had to gasp for breath!

"Oh Farmer, I missed you so much! I worried! I'm so glad you are home!" she laughed and cried at the same time. "Look at you!" she stepped back to see his new clothes. Farmer's heart was moved as he realized she hadn't even noticed the new wagon. Her eyes were only for him.

The boys on the other hand were already climbing into the chuck wagon, examining every part.

"Where's our wagon, Pa!" Walter asked.

"This is our wagon, our goin' ta Oregon wagon!" Farmer said with a laugh.

"Wahoo!" "Walter whooped—Clifton tried to copy him. Emile shook her head.

"Ya'll get in outa the cold! Quick now! I'll tell all when I come in. Emile, a hot cup of coffee would do me fine!"

Farmer moved the horses into the barn and made sure they were warm with feed and water. He talked to them, how good they'd done and rubbed their necks and faces.

A thin layer of ice was forming over everything. Farmer hurried to wrap and cover the hand pumps so they would not freeze. He closed the chickens in their coop and made sure they had some feed inside. Rushing to the house, he slipped and fell on the newly forming ice. He knew he was more in a rush to tell Emile and their boys all that had happened and what he'd seen, than it was to get out of the cold.

They were iced in the rest of that day and Sunday. They missed going to church, but now had the sense of seeking a new church in a new land. Their hearts were in Oregon. They did use the time to sort through belongings to decide what they had room to take—and what they would sell or give away, and what would stay in the house. There were items that had special meaning to them, but no room in the wagon. Emile was certain they could store those at her parents. Maybe they could even be convinced to bring them along when they traveled to Oregon for a visit.

"When will we leave, dear?" Emile asked.

"Seein' as how the good Lord has given us a route an a wagon, soon as possible. March is near gone, but I'd like us ta be travelin' on before it's over. I think the winter storms are ending, and the quicker we leave here, the quicker we can settle on our lan...ranch."

The sun was out bright Monday morning, and soon melted any remaining ice. For a while, low layers of steam rose from the ground and the roofs of the buildings.

Farmer was doing chores when his brother, Jacob rode up and dismounted off his horse. Their hands locked in a firm clasp, then a hug—patting each other on their backs with their free hands. No word was spoken, but each knew what the other was feeling.

"Mighty fine rig ya got there," Jacob said motioning towards the chuck wagon.

"Ain't it dandy!" Farmer beamed. "It's our goin' ta Oregon wagon. Here, take a look!" and the two walked to the wagon.

Jacob circled the wagon twice, looking it over carefully, thoughtfully. His face grew serious and he grabbed a wheel to shake it.

"Pa sent me with a message Farmer. I didn't much want ta come with it, but I did want ta see you. You know in my mind, I'm right happy for you, but in my heart I'm gonna miss you a powerful lot."

"That's Pa's message?" Farmer was puzzled.

"Naw, dang! That's me talkin', Farmer. What Papa told me to tell you is this, 'He says fer ya ta get over this goin' to Oregon an' ta start workin' the high ground for spring plantin'. It ain't too late to change yer mind and do what's right, but ifen ya ain't a gonna work the land, then get off it now. And don't take nothing that don't belong to you.' That's what he said to tell you, Farmer."

Farmer felt the blow to his heart like a shotgun blast to his chest. He fought back tears.

"Now you know I don't feel that a way 'bout it, Farmer," Jacob went on.

Farmer dropped his head and stood silent for a while.

"Ifen I come ta talk ta him," Farmer swallowed hard.

"Papa's said he'll run you offen his place, 'less you come to tell him yer stayin'," Jacob replied.

"How's Ma?"

"She's been crying a lot, an' her and Papa have loud an' angry words pretty often."

Farmer thought on what had been said, going over each part carefully.

Finally he answered. "Tell Papa, can't change from the course that's set. Me an' Emile an' the boys will be leavin' in a few days. Soon's we have everything in order. Not ta worry, won't take nothin' thet don't belong ta us. We'd be obliged if he would come ta wish us God speed and bid us goodbye."

CHAPTER 15
FAREWELLS

The rest of the week was a flurry of activity in getting ready for departure. Word spread quickly that Farmer and Emile Trevor were leaving for Oregon. Sunday would be their last time in church and a dinner on the grounds was planned in their honor to send them off proper. Then, at dawn on March 31st, they planned to be leaving on their long journey.

Farmer spent time getting the wagon ready. He greased up the axles and packed extra grease so as not to run a dry wheel. He mounted several water containers on the sides to carry them across dry desert stretches. Emily would wait until closer to leaving to stock food, pots and pans and dishes in the racks at the rear of the wagon.

On Wednesday, Farmer and Emile took a wagonload of their things into town. Vivian Holt had cleared space in Emile's old bedroom for keepsake items. She eagerly agreed to bring them when they came to visit. While she, Emile and the boys visited, Farmer neatly stacked their belongings in the bedroom. Some other things were for selling or trading. Margaret Hatchet rummaged through items in the wagon, finally picking out several for trade.

"Whatcha be needin'?" she asked.

"We got enough flour, sugar, an' coffee, but I reckon we could use some canned goods fer our travelin'." Farmer noticed that Mrs. Hatchet placed many more cans of food and fruit than what he thought the trade was worth. When he protested she shushed him, and mumbled he had some right valuable stuff.

When it was time to leave, Margaret's eyes grew watery. She gave him a strong bear hug!

"Farmer, you been a good customer," her voice broke, "an' more'n that, you been like a son to me," she put her hand to her mouth and tried to shake away tears.

"Now you get on to Oregon and you raise cattle like you've a wanted to—an'—an'—ifen I don't see you again, well, one day we'll walk those golden streets . . ." her voice trailed off, then she added with a laugh, "We'll have us chariots there, but no automobiles."

Farmer laughed as he left and walked to the post office. "Thet Margaret don't give up 'bout these automobiles," he mused.

His post office box yielded two letters and a Sears and Roebuck spring catalog.

One letter was from the government affirming the receipt of Farmer's letter, and instructions for when they arrived in Oregon.

The other letter was from Benjamin. He wrote that he had hoped to be there to see them off, but that was not going to be possible. His work kept him busy in the big city. He wrote about his woman friend and time spent at Speak-Easys, drinkin' gin. He said he was making extra money delivering whiskey and some moonshine to these places. Benjamin wrote about the fun he was havin' gambling, drinkin', and dancin', and Farmer's heart grew heavy as he realized his and Benjamin's lives were moving in two directions, not just in where they would live—but how they lived.

On Thursday, several neighbors dropped by to say their farewells, and some purchased a few spare pieces of furniture, extra dishes and cooking utensils that the wagon would not hold.

On Friday, Farmer and Emile were amazed to see the Holts in their Surrey coming down the lane. Susan was riding a horse, running ahead of the wagon. This was the first time they had ever been to the Trevor home.

Walter and Clifton let out a yell and ran to greet them. Farmer and Emile were delighted to see the Holts and invited them inside, as Hirum helped Vivian down from their Surrey.

"Before we go in, I have an announcement," Hirum spoke in his usual gruff voice. "I was thinkin' the other day about your travel, and your ranching, so I decided you needed a riding horse. Here it is," Hirum motioned towards the horse that Susan was proudly mounted on.

Farmer's mouth dropped—Emile gasped!

"Oh Father, thank you so much!"

"A friend brought this horse in from West Texas. It's a Mustang, so it is surefooted on rough or rocky ground. Knows how to cut cattle, I'm told—yet gentle enough for Walter and Clifton to ride," Mr. Holt explained.

"He looks all dusty," Clifton spoke in his tiny voice.

"Yes, he's Dusty, from West Texas," Walter agreed.

"Sounds like they've named him," Susan laughed as she dismounted and hoisted both boys up on the saddle. Everyone laughed with her, and watched as she led the horse around the house. They saw the boys' excitement leap, as they suddenly understood, this horse was for them!

Everyone remained outside until Dusty and its young riders grew tired. When the Holts stepped into the Trevor home they were impressed with its warmth and comfort.

"Thet's Emile's doin's," Farmer gave her the credit.

Emile served coffee and some cake she had baked. The conversation stayed on general things. They all avoided any discussion of leaving for Oregon, until Hirum stood up and announced they must go. He grabbed Farmer's hand and placed in it an envelope.

"Don't open this until you are out of town," he ordered, "and you take good care of my daughter and grandsons, you hear!"

Immediately the women burst into tears and clung to each other.

"It's so far! You all will be so far away!" Vivian kept saying.

Walter and Clifton began to whimper and they ran to their Grandmother Holt and Auntie Susan. The women held on to them tightly as for dear life! Then they hugged Farmer and kissed him goodbye. Sadness he had never known before filled his heart. The look on Emile's face told him she felt it even more.

Hirum picked up each boy and looked at him carefully, he kissed Emile, and with a promise they would come see them in Oregon, the Holt's drove away, Vivian and Susan waving and blowing kisses.

On Saturday, Farmer made his last trip into the town of Holt. He first closed out his post office box.

"You want me to give any mail to your Pa?" Clem asked.

"No, I reckon you best give it ta the Holt family."

"I see you received a letter from my son. How's he a doin'?" Clem went on.

"Seems doin' fine, said he was makin' some extra money. Wrote of a Betty Jean, he's sweet on. I was a hopin' to see Benjamin 'fore we left, but he said he couldn't come right now. I'll miss him; me and Ben, we're best of friends most our lives!" Farmer spoke with emotion.

"I know," Clem answered softly.

"You tell 'em, he knows the way ta Oregon, same as me! Good bye!" Farmer spun around and left out, not havin' the heart to tell Clem of his son's new found lifestyle.

"Take care," he heard Clem call out after him.

Farmer and Emile were glad to be in church on Sunday. Everyone was in good spirits, and Pastor Beckner called them up to the front along with Walter and Clifton to have special prayer for their safe travel. He preached a message on the Promised Land and that they all were pilgrims passing through, seeking a place made by God.

Farmer sadly took note that none of his family was present. He spoke to pastor about it during potluck.

"Your Pa's very angry," Reverend Beckner began.

"He thinks you are throwing away everything he has given you, and you are putting your family in danger. He says this is your place, here, on the farm. You are a farmer."

"Why's it so hard fer some folks ta let go?" Farmer asked.

"'Cause some folks don't do well with change. They are safe with what they know. Remember how some folks opposed Reverend Tunnell when he decided to accept the call of another church?"

"Yes."

"An' maybe they get a little green about somebody bettering themselves," Beckner added. "I think your Pa is afraid to let you go!"

Those thoughts followed Farmer as the time for farewells came. There were some who were cool and did not speak at all. Others were jovial and laughed and wished them well. Some of the women gave gifts and vegetables they had canned from their gardens. There were hugs and tears. One of the lads Farmer had taught last year in Sunday school threw his arms around Farmer's waist and sobbed." Wish't ya weren't goin' way!" Farmer felt that same sadness sweep over him again.

Monday morning as they were eating breakfast, they heard a knock on the back door. Farmer and Emile looked at each other, as Farmer rose to go to the back part of the house. He opened the door to find his mother, Jacob, William and Stella standing on the porch.

"Come in!" he said, "Where's PaPa?"

His mother kissed and held him.

"Pa's workin' the high field. It's dry enough. He don't know we're here." Jacob explained.

"He'd shoot our tails, ifen he knew!" William added, holding his coat closed.

"Pa's been mean an' ugly 'bout the whole matter," Stella snarled.

Emile and the boys were glad to see them. Emile got up to get them something to eat, but they'd already had breakfast. They all went in the living room and were seated, except William.

"I've been a thinkin'," he began. "Where you are a goin', I reckon you'll need a scout."

"Yeah, for huntin' Indians!" Walter acted like he had a rifle and was creeping around the back of the sofa.

"Stop it, Walter!" Emile scolded.

"What kinda scout?" Farmer was almost afraid to ask.

"This kind!" William beamed from ear to ear, pulling a puppy out from under his coat.

Both boys ran to their Uncle to claim their new pet.

"Fellers, this is Scout," William said as he handed the wiggly ball of fur to the children.

"Margaret Hatchet turned me on to this one. It's told his pappy, grand pappy, and great grand pappy was all good hunters. Had to ride a good ways to get it. Hope ya'll are pleased!"

"Ya couldn't a done anything ta please me more, William!" Farmer immediately exclaimed.

"Of course! We need a scout," Emile added. "Can you thank Uncle William, boys."

Both boys happily responded, but didn't look up from Scout, who was bouncing all around them.

The adults watched the boys play with Scout for a while. Emile took mother Trevor and Stella back to the kitchen.

"I want ya ta have the house, Jacob," Farmer began.

"Now what the tarnation would I do with your house?" Jacob appeared uncomfortable.

"I hear ya been courting Dorothy Shipley. Ya two get hitched an', ya already got ya a home!" Farmer could see Jacob's face get red, and William laughed.

"Yer the farmer, Jacob." Farmer grew serious. "Ya have a love fer the land. Ya have a heart fer it. Ya belong here."

Jacob dropped his head.

"You ever comin' back?" William asked.

"I reckon, some day. I'll get me one o' those fast automobiles. Maybe a Ford model like Benjamin Harrison's got. The world's been passin' us by here at Holt. Won't be long 'till everbody's goin' in 'em. I saw all kinds goin' ta see Rancher Redkin. I bet they could go as fer in two hours as it took me two days by wagon!"

With that, Farmer told of his travel, and the sights, and Redkin's Ranch while his brothers sat wide-eyed, hardly believing what they were hearing.

All too soon it was time to say farewell. Farmer felt that same sadness fill his heart again.

They all tried to be grown-up about parting, especially Stella who so wanted to be all growed up. The good-byes were stiff and they made half jokes to each other, trying to tease. But when he looked in his mother's face, seeing how tired and worn she looked, he could no longer hold back. He wrapped his arms around her frail body and cried like a baby. His mother cried also, saying, "Oh Farmer, Oh Farmer!" over and over. Soon they were all holding each other in one big clump, weeping, letting go!

That afternoon, the wagon loaded for the morning, Farmer took a last look around. His gaze wandered over the fields he had worked for many a year. The barn he had built, the house where he and Emile had begun their life together, and where Walter and Clifton was born.

Farmer came to the conclusion. 'Leavin' for a new place is excitin', sayin' farewells is not'.

CHAPTER 16
WESTWARD HO!

It was early morning, March 31, 1925, when Farmer and Emile Trevor placed their sleeping, bundled-in-blankets sons, Walter and Clifton in a crowded chuck wagon and began their journey west to a new life in a new land.

They took a last look at their home, barely visible in the pre-dawn darkness. Farmer could see Emile wipe her face and knew she was crying. He put his arm around her and gave a gentle squeeze. He wanted to say, "I feel it too!" but his action conveyed his thoughts.

He only needed to shake the reins for Sunset and Wind to take off down the familiar lane towards Holt. Scout tried to arouse his young masters by wrestling around in their blankets and licking their faces, but they refused to wake up and kept pushing him off. The pup finally gave up and wiggled into the blankets and grew still.

Dusty, on the other hand was eager to be going anywhere. Even though he was tied to the rear of the wagon, he stayed along side, pulling his rope as far as he could. Farmer found Dusty to be a spirited horse and one he knew would be a big help in Oregon. He also saw how the boys had taken to him, and how good he was with them. He felt gratitude towards Hirum and Vivian for the gift they had given.

"You are quiet, Farmer. Tell me your thoughts. Are you sad?" Emile spoke softly.

"Sorta feelin' both, Emile. I was thinkin' how special it be ta have Dusty, yer folks bein' thoughtful 'bout it an' all."

"And your brothers bringing Scout," she quickly added.

"An' I was also a bit sad 'bout sayin' goodbye ta our home—and I been thinkin' thet any minute I'll see my Pa come riden from behind ta tell us farewell—an', an' thet he loves us."

Emotion welled up and Farmer had to stop. Emile put her arm around his waist and held on tight.

"I was thinkin' 'bout other things too," Farmer went on. "Jacob will be comin' soon ta do the milkin' and feedin'. I reckon Pa will stop in later ta look things over."

"Oh Farmer, what will they do with—our farm? Will we ever come back?" Emile asked.

"I reckon Jacob will live there, and sure there will be a time ta come fer a visit." Farmer replied.

The two rode on in silence, lost in their thoughts. Farmer kept lookin' back—thinkin' he heard a rider, or a wagon, but none came.

The eastern horizon was starting to gray when they passed through Holt. The town was asleep and unaware of their leaving, except for a barking dog back among the houses on a side street.

When the sun broke upon them, Emile opened the envelope that her father had given them to reveal ten new twenty-dollar bills. "The note reads-For your journey and new start," Emile said.

"That's a powerful amount of money!" Farmer exclaimed with a whistle. "Added ta what we already gathered—'twill give us a good boost!"

The sun was well up by the time they arrived at the creek bottom, and so were their boys.

"Let's rest a spell," Farmer helped Emile down from the wagon. The boys were off in a run to explore, and while Emile fixed something to eat, Farmer turned the horses loose to water and graze.

"This is where I met thet Timothy fella from Flag," Farmer remarked as they ate. "Wonder if he an' his misses got their marriage patched up?"

"I pray so," Emile responded to his thoughts.

"I like this place!" Walter broke in. "Is this Oregon?"

"Not yet!" Farmer and Emile answered in unison and laughed.

They retraced Farmers route to the Redkin ranch where they were warmly welcomed upon arriving the next afternoon.

"Well, here you be!" exclaimed Redkin when he entered the large room of his ranch house. "Howdy, Farmer, and you are Mrs. Trevor. And your boys! Look at you two! Tell me your names."

"I'm Walter, he's Clifton, an' we got us a dog called Scout."

"Well, well. How is your journey so far? Is the wagon comfortable enough Ma'am?"

"Oh yes, sir!" Emile was so excited. Farmer could see her face flush, and she spoke so quickly, wanting to tell all at once.

"The wagon is quite comfortable and sturdy. We were able to get more in it than expected. And Walter and Clifton have never seen an automobile before, and we have seen so many, and we are happy to be on our way, and thankful for the wagon. . " Emile's voice trailed off and she dropped her eyes.

Farmer resisted the impulse to grab her and kiss her. He loved her girlish charm.

"Merrita!" Redkin called.

"Senor Redkin?" she answered as she entered the room.
"Do you have our guests settled in a room yet?"

"Si, senor."

"Then I would like for you to show Mrs. Trevor and their boys around the ranch. They will want to see the cattle we have corralled. Mr. Trevor and I have some business to attend to."

Thomas Redkin had a love and interest for his family that Farmer did not quite understand. Were they like a son and daughter and grandchilden he had never known and enjoyed? Or did he feel sorry for them?"

Redkin showed Farmer a personal protectograph he had purchased the first of the year. He explained it was designed to guard the amount line on his personal checks. Then he proceeded to write and stamp a check to Farmer for one hundred dollars.

"I can't accept more from ya, Mr. Redkin. Ya have already done so much!" Farmer protested.

"What have I done?" Redkin queried, eyeing Farmer.

"You practically gave me your wagon."

"That was a trade!"

"Mr. Redkin, we both know thet wasn't a fair trade!"

"Why, Son, was you expectin' more fer your wagon? Well, now, here it 'tis," Redkin's face broke into a wide grin as he handed Farmer the check.

"No—No! I should be a payin' you!" Farmer refused the check.

Thomas Redkin grew serious. "Sit down, son, and you listen to me. I saw your spirit and your heart that day in Holt. I saw how you stood up to yer Pa, but never lost yer respect for him. Now, my wife died when she was young—I loved her dearly an' just never had a hankerin' to re-marry. Never had any babies o' my own, so I have no close kin— but if I did, I think I would like them to be like you and your Emile. An' I would be right proud to have me two grandsons like Walter and Clifton. Now, Farmer, you have many a mile to travel—and you will need a, a grubstake getting started. I'm a meanin' for you to take this check and place it in a bank in Oregon when you get there." Redkin held the check out again for Farmer to take.

"It would make this old man's heart feel good if you will do this."

There were few people that Farmer had given a hug - Benjamin, his brothers and sister, his Ma and Emile's family. Farmer was not the man to hug just anybody, but on this day Farmer graciously accepted the check and gave the rancher a firm hug that said, "Thank you!"

When Emile came back in with Merrita, she found Farmer and Thomas laughing and talkin' cattle and ranchin'.

They stayed at the Redkin Ranch several days through the weekend, attending church with Thomas and his foreman Red. He told Farmer and Emile it was because he wanted to give them as much educating on cattle ranching as he could. But the longer they stayed they sensed it was as much for Redkin as it was for them. It was as if for just a few brief days he had a family of his own. He introduced them with pride to his friends and neighbors.

The ranch hands were glad for the extra days' stay. They lavished attention and teasing on Walter and Clifton.

"Those boys are soakin' all thet up like dry sand," Redkin observed the second day they were there.

There was always an available cowboy to keep the boys occupied. They taught them to better ride and handle Dusty. Red took them out on the range the third day.

"Oh my—I don't know!" Emile said in worried tone when several cowboys asked to take Walter and Clifton with them to herd some cattle. "They are so little—and Farmer is with Mr. Redkin."

"We guard them with our lives, senorita," Rocca assured her, holding his sombrero in his hand.

The ranch hands were also glad for the extra stay to have Emile around. They would fall over themselves to get her attention, and Farmer saw how they were captivated by her looks and her charm. He also noticed something that deepened his love, trust, and respect for his wife. Whenever some of the cowboys would make attempts to flirt—or get a little too bold for her liking, she would draw to Farmer's side and slip her hand inside his arm and get very close to him. She had a way in her words and actions that made it very clear—her heart belonged to Farmer.

In all this, the men appeared to respect them as a family, and acted sad to see them go. Several of the men made that fact clear to Farmer as they shook his hand and wished him safe travel and a good life in a new land. He felt their friendship towards him to be genuine. Merrita too, had enjoyed the company of another woman. She cried and patted Emile's and the boys' faces when she said her good-byes.

"You go back," Redkin directed, "to the road coming outa Plainview and head north. Now east o' Amarillo you'll come to a more traveled road. There's talk o' the government makin' a road clear through from Chicago to the Pacific Ocean in California. This'll be part of that road, and when you turn left on that road you will be goin' west. It'll take you through Amarillo and clear on to New Mexico."

It wasn't until this small band of pilgrims in a chuck wagon turned on this road headed west did it hit Farmer that his dream was coming true. He was really moving his family. He was traveling west! As the reality set in, so did his excitement rise—so much did it overtake him that he stood up in the wagon and shouted, waving his hat in the air, "Westward Ho!"

CHAPTER 17
SOUNDS AND SIGHTS

It was Monday, April 6, 1925 when the Trevors' departed from Redkin Ranch. They did not get an early start, so they had not reached Amarillo when the sun was setting. They camped in a small grove of scrub brush apart from the road, and were on the way again as the sun rose in the east. It was mid-morning when they turned onto the main road headed west into Amarillo, that's when Farmer let loose with his loud "Westward Ho!"

Emile laughed, while Walter and Clifton just stared at him—wondering what did Pa do that for?

As they neared the city, Farmer halted the wagon and retrieved both boys from Dusty's back.

"Aw Pa," Walter objected.

"I ain't never seen so many automobiles on a road at one time. I don't want Dusty ta get skittish an' run off with ya," Farmer explained as he tied Dusty to the wagon.

As they proceeded on they became aware of a rumbling sound. Far away at first, but coming closer, fast.

"What is that?" Emile asked.

"I don't reckon I know, Emile, sounds too loud to be a automobile."

As their eyes scanned the city's skyline, suddenly a large object rose from the north side of the city and headed straight for them. Farmer blinked his eyes.

"What is it?" Emile grabbed Farmer's arm.

"It's a airplane! Look boys! A airplane!" Walter and Clifton stood frozen—eyes wide! Clifton began to cry.

"It's ok! Won't harm us," Farmer calmed them, at the same time trying to settle the horses down.

The roar of the engine grew louder as the plane flew past them—so close they could see the two men seated in the plane—one behind the other. Farmer waved his hat in large movements. Walter and Clifton followed his lead and waved their arms wildly.

One of the men waved back, and both boys jumped up and down in excitement—never taking their eyes off the flying wonder until it disappeared into the sun.

"It had U.S. Mail written on the side," Emile remarked.

"I declare, Emile, I never knew mail was carried in airplanes," Farmer added.

The rest of the way into Amarillo all the boys could talk about was what they had just seen. They put together a makeshift plane in the wagon and played like they were flying the mail airplane, and Scout was their companion.

Nearing the city, the road became hard surface. The horses seemed energized hearing their shoes ring beneath them. As they picked up their pace the wagon seemed to fly the remaining distance into the city.

Downtown Amarillo was alive with sound and sights. Ooga horns blaring, automobiles filled the street, others parked on the side. There were many people walking on the boardwalks—moving in and out of the stores that lined the street. Voices could be heard and at times there were sounds of music.

A young girl walking with her mother upon seeing the wagon, pointed, and asked loudly, "Are they pioneers, mama?"

"They are likely in town from one of the ranches, dear," she replied.

The pace was so hurried Farmer and Emile decided to stop. They saw an open space next to the boardwalk and Farmer pulled the team and wagon alongside and tied the horses to a lamppost.

He attempted to settle the horses down, as they were becoming nervous from all the noise and movement around them.

"Isn't that a sight?"

Farmer turned towards the voice to see a well-dressed man in suit and tie. Thinking he was talking about the wagon he replied, "Yep, it sure 'tis a good wagon ta travel in fer us, mister."

"No, no, not your wagon. In there! Now aren't they some beauties?"

Farmer looked up into a large glass window to see two brand new automobiles inside.

"New company just started this year. These are Chryslers. Selling quicker than we can get them in. They come in four cylinder and six cylinder," the man went on.

"Don't know much 'bout automobiles." mumbled Farmer.

"We call them cars. What you need for your family is that touring car there, plenty of seat room. You all come inside and take a look," he offered his hand to help Emile down.

"My what fine lads you have. Bring them inside too."

Emile climbed off the wagon, eager to see everything. The boys scrambled down with Scout, but Farmer thought it best to place him back in the wagon. Scout started yelping when they disappeared into the building.

"This here Touring Car is the right car for you. Four doors, take a look at all the room in there!" he pointed inside the open door.

"This car is the finest workmanship and materials. Look at the paint! It has a new thermostatic heat control. That means the motor is kept at the same temperature givin' it more power and longer life. All cylinders receive identical charges of gas—for good fuel economy. And Chrysler developed oil and air filters to keep the engine running clean. This car has both filters. Another thing, Chrysler has a theft proof numbering system, and look here on the dash. It has a heat indicator, not showing the water temperature in the radiator, but in the motor. It has hydraulic 4-wheel brakes and pivotal steering. There are no side sway springs; it has Watson stabilators to make the ride smooth for the Misses. There is headlight control with horn button, automatic windshield wipers, and a gasoline gauge on the dash. Total price for this fine Touring Car to take you on your way is only eight hundred ninety-five dollars!" The man waited for their reaction.

Farmer shuffled his feet and looked down.

"Can we buy it Pa?" Walter pulled on Farmers sleeve.

"Yeah, Pa," Clifton chimed in.

"We don't have near thet kinda money, mister."

"Well, I'm pleased to tell you folks that Chrysler has a plan for time payments that we have been authorized to offer our customers. You all from around here?"

"We air from Holt," Farmer answered, "and we air on our way ta Oregon," he added proudly.

"Hmmm." the man studied them, and then went on, "Oregon? Well, heck, can't sell you a car going to Oregon—unless you pay cash price."

"Can't do thet, but it is a mighty fine automobile ya got there," Farmer concluded.

The man looked outside at the wagon thoughtfully, "are you traveling to Oregon in a wagon?" he asked. "Folks stopped doing that some years ago. This is the roaring twenties, for gosh sakes!"

"Yep, thet's how we're a goin'," Farmer said sternly.

"Well, I wish you good luck for a safe journey. There's many a mile ahead that will take you all a long time." The man opened the door for them, and gave a look that appeared one of admiration.

"Luck ain't got nothin' ta do 'bout it. It'll be the Lord getting us ta Oregon," Farmer remarked dryly.

As they proceeded down the street, for the first time, they felt out of place. Farmer searched in vain for another wagon, and was relieved to see one parked by a Blacksmith Shop. Occasionally, they spotted cowboys on horseback, and very few hitching posts.

It was indeed the roaring twenties, and Farmer became aware of Emile's interest in the women's dresses—which most were at the knees, revealing their legs. Then Emile would pull at her floor length dress—then watch women walking on the boardwalk and frown. She attempted to fix her hair, almost unconsciously.

"You look powerful pretty today, Emile," Farmer finally offered, but he felt it was just a feeble attempt to make her feel better, falling far short of its attempted goal.

There was so much to see, it seemed they could barely take it in. Emile spotted a sign in the window of a restaurant that advertised "home cooking" and they decided to use a little of their money and buy lunch. Inside was bright colored cushioned chairs at tables. A man at the counter directed them to an available one, and a young woman promptly brought them glasses of water and menus.

"That box is singing," Clifton pointed out a finished box with knobs that set on a shelf near what appeared to be the cooking area.

"Maybe a phonograph playen' records," Farmer commented, then the music stopped and a voice came on talking about weather and a tornado in the Midwest.

"Must be a radio we heared bout," Farmer guessed. They set spellbound, listening to news about other parts of the United States. Then they announced and played a song, "If You Knew Susie, Like I Know Susie." Farmer caught Emile's smile and knew she was thinking of her sister.

The meal was a treat for the Trevors as it was not often that the family had eaten a meal at the Holt Café. Farmer would stop for coffee sometimes, but seldom the family had ever eaten a meal there.

As they ate their lunch, they heard talk of a dance craze called the Charleston. Two women at a nearby table remarked how lude they thought it was. A phone rang behind the counter, and the man there answered it.

The new song, "Five Foot Two, Eyes of Blue" played on the radio, and Farmer laughed when they spoke of a movie coming to the theatre in Amarillo titled, "Go West" and played by some fella named Keaton. There was news of someone in Germany, about a banned party, and trouble in Panama, and a man in a plane to try and reach the North Pole later in the year. The voice on the radio spoke of Buicks that had valves in head, and everywhere you see the new Chevrolet because it is quality at low cost. They left the restaurant to the sound of the song, "Albany Bound."

"Wrong direction fer us," Farmer laughed and Emile laughed with him.

"I brought something fer ol' Scout," Walter exclaimed as he proudly produced part of his lunch he had wrapped up.

The horses were rested and eager to be on the road. The Trevors in their chuck wagon passed on through the town of Amarillo, to the interest and sometimes, apparent amusement of on-lookers. Farmer felt like his head was spinning from hearing and seeing so many new things.

"I didn't realize we were so behind the times," Emile said. "Holt is so small and isolated. I wonder why my father and mother stay there. Susan told me that styles in women's clothes was changing, but she dare not wear any of the dresses home—now I understand why. The dresses are so short and—and—just awful. I could not be seen in the likes.

"I don't know, Emile, I think ya would be powerful pretty in one of those new dresses. I like ta see yer legs!"

"Oh stop it!" Emile slapped his arm, but she had a smile that stayed with her the rest of the afternoon.

There were numerous cattle pens on the west end of Amarillo, and they passed a place where they saw another airplane swoop down and land. This set the boys off again and they resumed playing airplane.

The Trevors continued west out of the city at a brisk pace for sometime until the horses tired. The sun was dropping, so Farmer found a suitable place to camp. Emile liked the rear of the chuck wagon that folded down to make a table, and all her fixings were right there.

After supper the boys finally fell asleep, leaving their Pa and Ma sitting by the campfire. They were quiet, looking at the stars and the fire—remembering everything that had unfolded during the day.

"You recall thet little girl askin' her ma ifen we was pioneers?"

"Yes", replied Emile.

"Well, I reckon we is, Emile, maybe the last of the pioneers."

"There will always be pioneers," Emile said softly, "as long as there are men like Farmer Trevor".

CHAPTER 18
CATTLE TOWNS

Farmer pushed the team hard the next day. It was midday when they passed through the small town of Wildorado. They found a place to eat a bite, and Farmer replenished the water supply. Grass for the horses was ample along the way so far—and Farmer was grateful for that, but he knew the time would come they would have to carry some feed grain to get across the rough and dry places.

"'Bout fifteen more miles on to Vega," a kindly old man told Farmer. He was seated outside a gasoline station, and Farmer pulled the wagon up and asked him the conditions ahead. "A few miles outa town you'll be on the staked plains."

"Staked Plains?" Farmer questioned.

"Yep. That's 'cause the pioneers staked their trails. Now it's a road. After Vega 'bout eighteen mile is Adrian, then Glenrio on the New Mexico state line, that's 'nother twenty mile.

"What's beyond thet?" Farmer queried.

"Don't know," the old man smiled, "ain't never been there."

It was dark when the Trevor's chuck wagon made its way down the middle of Vega. They had noticed that the automobiles were less frequent. The headlights of one blinded them as it chugged past headed east, probably to Amarillo.

"What did that gentleman in Amarillo say they were called?" asked Emile as the auto moved down the street.

"I'm thinkin' he called 'em cars, Emile."

Vega was quiet. Most of the shops were dark—only a bar or two was lit. Camp was welcome that night on the outskirts of the town. Farmer could hear cattle in nearby pens as he tended the horses. Emile prepared supper, and Farmer watched the boys chasing Scout in the firelight. After the meal was over they slept soundly until morning.

Farmer tried to push the team again this new day, but soon realized the hard travel the previous day had taken its toll, not only on the horses, but on Emile as well. Besides, the road beyond Vega was rough, making their journey much more laborious. Farmer let the boys ride Dusty longer stretches of time. Several times in rough places, Emile got down and walked.

The road begin following next to a railroad track, and in the afternoon Farmer, Walter and Clifton got their first up close sight of a train headed West. Passengers were visible and the boys delighted in waving to get attention. Walter urged Dusty into a run to chase after the quickly passing cars. Someone inside musta said something, because some men and women from the other side joined passengers on their side to peer out the windows, and some waved.

"Oh Farmer! The boys will be hurt!" Emile cried out as she grabbed Farmer.

"They be alright, Emile. The boys' air gettin' good at riden' thet mustang. I reckon they will do a heap o' growin' on this trip—an' we need ta let them".

"Walter is five and Clifton only three. Much too young to be chasin' a train on a horse over rough ground!" Emile retorted.

By now the train was down the track and all that remained was the smoke. The flush faced, laughing boys came trotting back on their horse, bouncing up and down.

"Don't you children do that again!" Emile scolded.

"Why, Ma?" both boys objected. "Dusty is a runnin' horse."

"What if he steps in a ground squirrel hole and throws you—and—and breaks his leg. Would you like that? You ride along this wagon—you boys hear me!"

"Yes 'em," they answered as they swung Dusty along-side.

Farmer turned his head to keep from laughing. When he managed to wipe the grin off his face, he turned to Emile all serious like. She was still fuming.

"I reckon ya saw all these sights, when ya was in school in the city."

Emile's face softened slightly, "That was over five years ago. Everything has changed so much."

They traveled on in silence—only the sound of the wagon and horses.

"Pa," Walter spoke.

"Yes, son."

"The train was sumpon, but the airplane was most excitin'! I'm gonna fly in one some day."

"Me too!" voiced Clifton in agreement.

"If you don't break your necks first," Emile mumbled under her breath.

There was still daylight left when they reached Adrian. The look on Emile's face and both boys—especially Clifton who was in the wagon now, told Farmer they were tired. The horses were dragging and the pace had been slow.

The town was made up of some stores and houses. In all of these cattle towns so far there was a post office as well as several stock pens and corrals. But Adrian had some grain storage sheds by the railroad. Farmer could tell that the ranches herded cattle here to ship to market by railroad.

In town, folks smiled. Some gave a "Howdy." Farmer enquired about any running water.

"None hereabouts," was the reply. "There's some cattle tanks on the ranches. We have cisterns and well water in town. There is a creek in Glenrio though."

On the west end of town, Farmer spotted a grove of trees and decided to camp there for the night. Still he was disappointed that they had not traveled far on this day.

Emile must have sensed his displeasures. She came up to him as he was unhitching Sunset and Wind. She put her hand on his face, turning him towards her. "I can go longer," she said searching his eyes.

Farmer dropped the traces of the horses and took Emile in his arms. His love for her filled his heart and soul to a depth he had not realized before—nor did he understand why it should come upon him so at this particular moment.

"I needs be mindful of ya and our sons, and the horses air tired." Farmer whispered in Emile's ear after he kissed her in a way to convey the love he felt for her.

"Farmer," she pulled back to again look him in the face and search his eyes. "I do think I am with child. I could tell more today."

"I could see it, Emile. You need a good rest fer tonight."

Next morning, the Oregon bound pioneers were indeed rested and anxious to be on their journey. Numerous cars of various kinds passed them on the road. Some traveled east and others were headed west. Few took the time to stop and visit, a point that struck Farmer. It seemed like the automobile quickened everybody's pace so that they didn't want to be sociable.

Long near suppertime, they came upon a car broken down on the side of the road.

"Howdy, neighbor, what's the problem with yer aut—I mean yer car?"

"Don't rightly understand it. This Hudson has been running just fine. There was a loud bang, an' it quit, and here we set!"

Farmer got down while Emile and the boys remained in the wagon.

"My names Farmer Trevor, and this here's my wife Emile and our boys, Walter and Clifton.

"George and Debra Apperson. Glenrio is just beyond that rise. I think they have a garage there.

"A what?" Farmer asked.

"A garage, maybe they can fix it."

"Do you folks have any water? We ran out and it has been so hot," the woman asked, near pleading.

"Oh, of course, you dear people," Emile responded, climbing off the wagon and going to the rear of the chuck wagon to get cups. She dipped water from a barrel mounted on the wagon's side and passed water to everyone.

"I fear the water is not cool," Emile apologized. The couple was grateful and drank their fill.

"It's wet," George responded after he emptied his cup and was ready for another.

"Thank you so much," Debra added. "We were parched."

Farmer looking over the front of the car remarked, "I reckon we can pull ya into Glenrio, ifen it's not thet far."

"I don't know . . .," George questioned.

"I fixed me up a way ta hitch Dusty in front of Sunset and Wind. You know, so's I can get more power." Farmer broke into a grin. The rest laughed when they realized his joke.

The horses strained at their harnesses, and slowly the car began to roll behind the wagon. George sat in their Hudson. He steered the car, while the two women walked on the side of the road and talked. Farmer stopped at the top of the rise. He looked down into a grassy low spot where the town of

Glenrio was nestled. Farmer could see a small creek to one side of the buildings.

The incline of the road to the high spot where Farmer stopped had made for a hard pull and all three horses were drenched in sweat. Farmer was pleased at how hard Dusty had worked out in front. That distance had taken over thirty minutes. Everyone cheered when they reached this point in the road. The rest was downhill into town. While George and Debra climbed into their car, farmer helped Emile and the boys into the wagon. Then he took a moment to talk to each of the horses.

"I'll be keepin' the brakes on so we won't crowd your wagon," George assured them, and down the hill they started, arriving in Glenrio a few minutes later.

The garage was still open, and a young man came out as Farmer stopped the wagon by the gasoline pump.

"Now that's a sight I ain't seen before! A car pulled by a chuck wagon. Yer horses need some gas, sir?" the man teased.

"Nope, their gas grows on the side o' the road, and it's there free from the Good Lord," Farmer replied, his eyes matched his smile.

Farmer untied the Apperson's Hudson, and helped push it inside the garage. While George and Debra spoke with two men, Farmer looked around. There was an array of parts, tires, cans of lubricants, some fenders, and tools of kinds Farmer had never seen. He looked into the open mouth of another car to see the skeleton of a dis-assembled motor. He went outside to Emile and the boys to wait and be sure that the Apperson's were taken care of. Eventually, the couple came out of the garage.

"I would like to give you something for your help," George began.

"Yes, that would have been a dreadful walk," Debra added. "And we were so thankful for the water. I didn't know it could taste so good!"

"Won't take nothing," Farmer answered, "Glad we came along ta help".

"Can we put you up in the Hotel? We'll be staying there. These fellows say they can fix our car tomorrow. Not as much trouble as we feared. Come, let us get you a room at the Hotel."

"Won't take nothing; glad ta help," Farmer answered again but more firmly.

"There must be something we can do!" George persisted.

Suddenly, words came out of Farmer's mouth that surprised even him at hearing himself saying it. "There is something ya all can do—ifen ya promise with yer words."

"Yes, if we can," George hesitated.

"When ya get ta yer home, promise ya'll find ya a good Bible teachin' church an' attend a Sunday Service.

"Well, I guess we could. We've never been church goers."

"I'm askin' yer word—and I see ya ta be a man o' yer word," Farmer stuck his hand out to George.

"By golly, we will, Farmer," George beamed as he shook Farmer's hand. "You can count on it!"

It was a tired but happy family that camped in a grassy glen by a small stream on the edge of Glenrio. Long into the night they heard coarse laughter, cussin', arguin', and once shots rang out. On occasion, the chug and rattle could be heard from a passing car, and its lights flashed on them for an instant as it went by.

"We've seen us some cattle towns," Emile murmured as she snuggled close to Farmer.

"The last—in Texas," Farmer yawned.

CHAPTER 19

TUCUMCARI

W hat day ya reckon it be Emile?" Farmer asked as they ate a hurried breakfast.

"I've been making marks on a small calendar I brought. I think this is Friday, April 10th."

"I walked up the road a piece this morning. I could make out some eatin' places, and saw several cattle pens with a herd of cattle. Thet probably counts fer so many cowboys raisin' a ruckus last night."

"I heard gunshots," Emile mentioned.

"Was there shootin'?" Walter jumped up.

"We think so," his mother continued.

"I could see a railroad station a piece back to the east. An some o' the town is over the line in New Mexico," Farmer changed the subject.

Emile began to laugh.

"What ya laughin' 'bout?" Farmer asked.

"I was just thinking how flat Texas is, and do you remember what the old man at the gasoline station in Wildorado said to us?"

"What?"

"He said that the Texas Panhandle is so flat you can see for two days!" Emile laughed freely and Farmer joined her. Clifton wanted to know, "what they was laughin' for?"

Hard surface road had been left behind at Amarillo. The road from there was mostly graded dirt road. While some stretches had some scattered gravel rock, other parts were little more than a wagon trail made more pronounced by the frequent wheels of the automobiles.

Farmer stopped the wagon on the Texas side of the border and jumped down off the wagon. He walked to where a sign pointed out the state line, and leaving one foot in Texas, he planted the other in New Mexico. "Look, Emile, half in Texas—half in New Mexico."

Emile laughed and clapped her hands and the boys joined her. They scrambled down out of the wagon to join Farmer in the fun.

As they progressed westward, the landscape began to slowly change. The flat land that had been with them for so long, begin to give way to deeper ravines in the earth, and the hills rose higher, and more jagged into the sky. The first evening they camped in a red rock hollow and witnessed a blazing sun drop behind a ragged line of small mountains.

The sun was high overhead on the third day out of Glenrio when they came upon a painted sign stuck in the ground on the side of the road. It read, "4 miles to Tucumcari."

"That's a welcome sign," sighed Emile, and she shifted her weight on the seat.

Farmer looked at her. "Air ya alright?"

"Yes, but I miss our bathing tub and bed."

Farmer thought a minute, then, came up with an idea. "Emile, I reckon this might be a place ta use some of our money and stay in a room with a bath and bed."

"Oh, Farmer! Can we!" Emile perked up.

The road into Tucumcari flattened out, and it was after the noon meal when the Trevors rolled into town.

"The two towns out of Glenrio frightened me," Emile remarked as they rode slowly past businesses and houses—the horse's hooves clacking on a hard surface road. "Why do cowboys need to be so reckless—and—rowdy? And those dreadful men, who were shooting their pistols at—everywhere! And the next town was near as—frightening. Farmer, will we be safe in Oregon?"

"Yes, we will be safe. I don't know why the cowboys were like thet. It was Saturday and they just wanted ta cut loose, I reckon. Oregon will be different—ya'll see!"

They spotted a back-home looking café on the left side of the road with a large open space for the horses and wagon. Farmer was pleased to find a hitching post.

"The last twenty miles was shore nuff dry, and gettin' hot fer the likes o' April. We used up some o' our water and need ta refill here in Tucumcari. I'm a thinkin' ta add another water barrel—or what I can find ta hold more water. We got some desert spaces to pass over, an' it'll be a mite hotter reachin' into summer.

"Whatever you think," Emile agreed.

There were no customers inside the small eating establishment. The lunch patrons had all had their fill and were gone about their business. A young woman dressed in an outfit that hinted of being Indian, warmly greeted them, although she did not appear Indian herself. She seated the Trevors at a sizable table and placed menus before Farmer and Emile. With a wink at the boys, she turned to the counter to fill glasses with some chipped ice and water. Farmer peered over his open menu to see Walter staring after the young waitress—a boyish smile on his face.

"Walter," Farmer said, bringing Walter back from his thoughts. "Air ya hungry as a mountain bear thet's been sleepin' all winter?"

"Yes, sir," the boy's face reddened as he dropped his eyes.

"Are you all travelin' in that wagon," the young woman asked as she placed the water on the table.

"Yes, we are," Emile answered.

"I came from Texas a few years ago with my folks in a covered wagon. I was only seven, but I remember it well."

"We hail from Texas. We come from Holt. Thet's southeast from Amarillo."

"We lived in El Paso."

She wrote down their order, and took it to an older woman in the kitchen area. The food was tasty and filling. Both Farmer and Emile, without saying it, sensed the desire to speak further with their young waitress.

Emile led out, "That was such a delicious meal. We are the Trevors; I'm Emile and this is my husband, Farmer, and our boys, Walter and Clifton.

Farmer stood, and the boys also, saying "Howdo. Won't ya set and visit with us a spell. We haven't had no visitin', 'cept with each other fer three days."

"I don't—know," the young woman was hesitant, then it seemed she melted, and with a genuine smile shook each of their hands. "I'm Lily, and pleased to meet—some Texans."

Farmer pulled up a chair for her, and she sat down, looking at each one of them in turn. "Well," Lily began, "What do you think of our New Mexico?"

"The country is beautiful, and oh, the sunsets!" Emile answered, "But I was fearful for my life in the two towns near Glenrio."

"Oh! You mean Endee? Yes, that is a fierce place. The cowboys come in off the range on Saturdays. There's so many shootings I hear—they just keep graves dug for Sunday burials."

"Oh my!" Emile put her hand to her mouth. "Not every Sunday!'

"I hear—it's so—every Sunday! More bodies in the grave, than in the town. Now San Jon is a tad tamer, but not near as nice as Tucumcari."

"Is thet an Indian name?" Farmer was curious.

"Yes, I hear—it's so. See that mountain peak yonder?" Lily pointed towards a side window. They all looked. "The Comanche's used it for their smoke signals to be seen here in the valley. They named it Tucumcari. Then there's a old tale of two Indian lovers which were killed—but I don't believe that one," Lily laughed.

"Your family came here to Tucumcari?" Emile asked.

"No, they took a homestead between here and Santa Rosa," and Lily's face grew sad. "Father's still there, but my mother—she—had" Lily's voice broke and tears filled her eyes. "She was giving birth, and we lost her and the baby."

"Oh, you poor dear," Emile placed her hand on Lily's arm.

Farmer could see the effect this had on Emile, knowing she thought of giving birth to a baby in a remote land.

"This looks ta be powerful good land fer raisin' cattle," Farmer wanted to change the topic.

"Oh yes! It certainly is, but my father was stubborn to farm—and the land is hard and dry and unyielding."

"Well, we certainly don't have a stubborn farmer here," Emile laughed. "But you aren't living on the farm?"

"I'm still getting my schooling here in town—and work part days to help pay my way."

When asked about a place to stay for the night, Lily recommended a place run by a middle-aged couple.

"They had some nice sizeable cabins built—just for travelers. Well worth paying a little more," Lily told them. Then whispered to Emile, "They have heated water that runs into the bath."

Farmer knew there would be no stopping Emile from going there. When Farmer walked into the office he was somewhat taken back to be greeted by a stout woman of obvious European decent, while her husband was very Mexican. He noted the names Chuvero and Gretchen Lopez, and wondered how in the world did the pair meet. He made up his mind to get to know them better before leaving Tucumcari.

"Ve have a vonderful cabin fer der Hans Farmer, und de Frau vill be happy mit," the woman spoke in a heavy accent upon viewing Farmer's name on the register.

"I get the key, my love," the man rose to take a key from off a hook on the wall. "I'll walk down and open the door."

As Farmer turned to follow the man, the woman took hold of his arm, and then nodding towards her husband said, "Mein Lopez von the var—I make him vork hard to vin mein heart!" Then she laughed merrily, and Farmer went out the door.

Emile and the boys walked into the cabin slowly and peered all around.

"Oh!" she exclaimed with a gasp.

Farmer could tell she was fascinated and pleased.

"Where's our bed?" Walter looked disappointed upon only seeing one bed in the room.

"Yeah!" demanded little Clifton.

"Well, I reckon it's in this other room," Farmer walked to a door to discover a small space with a water closet fixture, a sink and a tub. There was a light bulb hanging from the ceiling with a knob near the bulb. Farmer turned on the light and Emile, curious, tested one faucet on the tub and was thrilled when it produced water. The boys were amazed— they had never spent the night away from their home—apart from times at their grandparents. Still, even the Holts did not have running water in the house yet.

"This is—is—so—so modern!" was all Emile could say.

"An' the boy's bed be in this next room," Farmer called out, and the boys screamed in glee as they charged into where their father was seated—bouncing on the bed.

"I can't wait to bathe," Emile called out from the bathroom. "Do you think the water really does come in hot?" Farmer heard her ask.

"Ifen not, I reckon I'll be buildin' a fire under thet tub," Farmer chuckled.

"Oh Farmer, it is getting warm. Walter, Clifton, you first, come and get your bath." Both boys tore off in a flash, and for the first time in months, they didn't have to be begged or ordered to clean up.

Farmer unloaded some of the things they would need that evening, after he took care of the horses. He had spotted a livery stable not far from the cabins. It was run down, and the owner grateful for any business.

"I reckon since I'm stayin' in a cabin—my horses oughta have their own place," Farmer told the stable owner who had just settled Wind in a stall.

"I'll give them good feed and water, mister, and have some to sell ya for your travel. You're a dyin' breed, you know."

"Whatcha mean?" Farmer questioned.

"Few wagons, anymore—least not to travel far."

"Thet I know," Farmer dropped his eyes. "I aim ta get me one o' those cars first chance I get some money!"

The boys were clean and neatly dressed in their nightclothes when Farmer returned to the cabin. Emile eventually emerged from a long soak in the tub. "I'm all wrinkled," she giggled. "It was heavenly!"

The warm water was heavenly, and Farmer felt he washed miles of dust and grime off his body. They had used a water basin, and a few times had a creek to wash in—but none compared to the feel of this. They all slept peaceful the whole night, and woke the next morning hungry for breakfast. They returned to the small café where they ate the day before. Lily was in school they were told, and the woman who waited on them was not so open to talk.

"Oh Farmer, can we stay one more night?" Emile implored, and Farmer caught a pleading look in his wife's eyes.

"Thet bed was sure soft," Walter added.

"Me too," followed Clifton.

Farmer looked at Emile and then his sons. As eager as he was to be on the road, he realized some rest for his family was in order.

"Well . . . I reckon an extra day won't do no harm."

Emile kissed him happily on his mouth before he could go on.

They shopped in a dry goods store. Emile wanted some course material and heavy thread and needles which puzzled Farmer, but when he questioned why—she smiled and replied, "You'll see. It's a surprise!"

They found some printed postcards with pictures of Tucumcari and determined it time to write folks back home.

Farmer located some suitable water containers, and while Emile retired to their cabin, Farmer took the boys to help him attach the wooden kegs to the wagon. He also purchased some metal ones that was made to hold gasoline—but would hold water. He placed those in the wagon, while the wooden kegs were mounted on the sides. Farmer felt better now, as they had been almost out of water a couple of times, and Farmer knew they would have to carry more to make the desert stretches.

Back at the cabin Emile was writing notes to her folks in Holt and sister Susan who was now returned to Fort Worth. Farmer wrote a few lines to his Ma and Pa to let them know they were well and in New Mexico. He also wrote a card to his friend Benjamin Harrison.

While Emile and the boys purchased some canned goods and food items to restock their supply, Farmer mailed the postcards—and for a moment felt a wave of homesickness, and knew Emile must feel it too.

Returning to the cabin, Farmer stopped in to see the Lopez's. "Ya vant to sleepin' over fer eins more night.—Ist New Mexico gotten its mitts on ya already," Gretchen teased and slapped his arm so hard Farmer near fell over.

"Have ya seen one New Mexico sunset—si, it will be one to remember," Chuvero commented as he stepped through a door from somewhere in the back.

"Only a few," Farmer responded.

"You watch tonight. Senor, it will be most beautiful."

"Well, I reckon ya two have me as curious as a pole cat snoopin' 'round a hen house. How on God's big earth did ya'll meet?"

Chuvero and Gretchen laughed together. It was Gretchen who spoke, "Mein Chuvero—he vas fighting in the var and mit came to my village. Herr saw a fraulein—me—unt vanted a frau—me. I sprecken mit herr Chuvero unt become leibsters. Ve comin' to America."

"What she is saying," Chuvero said, "I was a soldier in the United States Army and saw this beauty in one of the villages. First sight—fell in love. I married Gretchen, and after the war brought her to America—to Tucumcari— home. Started seeing travelers grow in numbers, so took money saved from the war and bought this land, built some cabins—comfortable—like a casa. You happy in your cabin?"

"Very much," Farmer answered.

"Ve have hard road now," Gretchen added excitedly.

"Si, next year the hiway from Chicago to California will pass right here. Si, we will have people from east and west—driving through Tucumcari!" Chuvero proclaimed triumphal.

"Sleppin' in mein cabins," Gretchen finished softly with a satisfied smile.

That evening, as Farmer and Emile stood beside the cabin experiencing a New Mexico sunset; their emotions were full while they held each other tight. Thoughts of home and family lingered. Awareness that the most difficult leg of their journey still lie ahead, uncertain of what they faced, but an unwavering trust and faith in God to spur them on, and a deep love for each other—they were ready to face a new day and be on their way.

"God and Tucumcari have been good to us," Emile murmured.

CHAPTER 20
STORM CLOUDS

T he road west out of Tucumcari soon began to climb becoming narrow and rocky as it wound its way up into the staked plains. Passage with the cars became more difficult, and the horses labored on some of the grades. Farmer counted five times he had to hitch Dusty ahead of Sunset and Wind to help them pull the wagon up a grade.

It took four long days for the pioneers to reach Santa Rosa. It was late on Saturday when they rolled into this old village perched on the edge of the Pecos River. Too tired to even eat, they managed to locate a room to stay in and a place for the horses.

The hotel room was small and crowded, not nearly as nice as the cabin in Tucumcari, but they were too weary to care.

Next morning after cleaning up, and eating breakfast, the family attended a small community church they had spotted on their way into town the evening before.

The people in the church were friendly and glad to have visitors. On one side was a small organ with feet pumps, and a woman played with her whole being—arms and hands flying over the keys, and her feet pumping for all she was worth. The small congregation sang their hearts out, some in English—some in Spanish—some in another language that Farmer had never heard. He took it to be Indian, guessin' from their colorful dress. All three languages blended together on each song, and Farmer couldn't help but feel touched!

"How good it is ta be in church on this fine day," Farmer thought. The order and style of the service was different than what they were used to in their church back home—but Farmer knew the Lord was present in this place in Santa Rosa.

The minister was an older man with a kind and wise way about him. He spoke of the time Jesus Christ calmed the storm, and that storms will come into our lives. But, he added Christ is greater than any storm we will ever face. That part seemed most to be saying something to Farmer.

After the closing hymn, the minister asked Farmer to tell their names and where they were from.

"Ye be the family in the covered wagon!" one woman exclaimed aloud upon hearing—"Holt, Texas".

"I say we need to all pray for your traveling mercies," the minister declared and prayed mostly for the Trevors' protection and safety.

Monday morning early, Farmer, Emile, their children, three horses, and one pup crossed the Pecos River. The sight of the chuck wagon had brought back memories for older ones-to the younger—an odd sight, with its water barrels strapped to the sides. Tools, tubs, and a saw mounted between barrels. A rifle handle could be seen sticking up above the wagon edge where Farmer sat. Pots and pans hung on the back and clanged as the wagon bounced over ruts and rocks.

"What a sight I reckon we be," Farmer laughed.

"We be a pretty sight," Emile laughed back.

The road condition did not improve. Farmer was amazed every time a car passed them—seemingly undaunted by the roughness or steepness of the terrain. They labored all that day, with Emile getting down to walk more often. Even the boys did not want to stay in the wagon and ran ahead with Scout

"Listen for cars," Emile warned them often.

"Emile, I reckon ya can hear one fer miles," Farmer finally said. "Ain't likely one ta sneak up on us!"

Emile flashed him an annoyed glance.

By Wednesday afternoon they had not found a single trace of water, and the sun bore down on them. Passing travelers had become so infrequent that Farmer realized he was wishing for a car to come along, and began to wonder if there was another living soul out here.

As the sun was dying out in a blaze of reds and golds, the brave band of travelers happened on a small creek.

A bridge comprised of two logs with planks across them spanned the creek. Farmer drove the wagon across, and then turned off the road to a level spot downstream near the water.

"I reckon this be a good place ta stay the night," Farmer announced, and they set about putting up camp.

As Farmer tied the horses on ropes so they could eat the scant grass and drink from the creek, he felt a breeze brush his face. Looking to the north, he saw dark thunderclouds growing, and as he kept his eye on them, he began to see flashes of lightning but heard no thunder.

"Thet storm's a long ways from here," Farmer thought, but he spoke not of it to Emile and the boys.

As Emile prepared supper at the rear of the wagon, Farmer noticed her look at the clouds, then at him.

While Emile sat at the campfire and Walter and Clifton made a play airplane in the firelight, Farmer took extra measure to tie down the canvas covering over their beds. He thought to make sure their two hurricane lanterns were full of kerosene just in case they needed them.

"Thet storm seems a slow mover, but even if it rains on us we should be dry and warm," Farmer reassured them as they bedded down for the night.

Suddenly, Farmer was awake. The fire was only glowing embers now, but as Farmer lay in his blankets he could see the lightning flash on the canvas tent. Then he heard the low rumble of distant thunder, and he sensed the restlessness of the horses.

He stayed still in the warmness of the blankets; however, the longer he lay the uneasier he became. After a few minutes, he got up, pulled on his boots, and fumbled in the dark to light the lanterns.

"What is it, Farmer?" Emile sat up.

"We needs ta move from here!"

"Why? What's wrong?"

"Don't reckon I know—jus' know we needs ta move!"

Emile got the boys up and in the wagon, and started piling the blankets in. Farmer went to get the horses.

"Where is Scout?" he heard Emile say and the boys started calling for their dog.

Farmer hitched the team to the wagon, and tied Dusty to the rear. The breeze had picked up and the thunder louder. Farmer and Emile struggled to roll up the canvas tent against the growing wind. They threw pots, pans, and dishes from around the supper campfire into the back and latched down the gate of the wagon.

"We can't find Scout!" Emile cried, as Farmer helped her up into the wagon.

"We can't wait on the pup!" Farmer spoke sharply, "We needs ta leave!"

"No Pa! No Pa!" both boys cried.

"Dang, where is thet dog?" Farmer held up one lantern trying to peer into the darkness.

"Scout!" he heard Clifton say.

"Where?"

"Scout's wrapped up in the blankets," Walter pulled the wiggling pup into his arms.

"Oh, Dear God!" Emile cried.

"Haaw!" Farmer urged the horses up onto the road and away from the bridge. They had moved down the road only a few feet when they heard a loud roar and a crash above the howling wind.

"What was that?" Emile screamed.

"Danged ifen I know," Farmer yelled back.

He climbed down from the wagon, taking one lantern in hand and walked back towards the creek. The sight he saw sent an icy chill down his back and his legs grew weak. The creek bed was full of water filled with limbs and brush rushing by. The water was up to the road, and as Farmer tried to see, suddendly in a lightning flash that lit the road, trees, and creek, he realized the bridge was gone. A sickening feeling moved into the pit of his stomach—a few minutes more—all of them would have been swept to their death!

"Emile, I'm a countin' on ya ta keep the boys in the wagon and the horses calm."

"What is it, Farmer?"

"A wall o' water—I reckon from the storm—crashed down the creek. Took out the bridge an'—an'—everything!"

Emile looked at him with a blank stare into the lantern light. Then she held out her hand towards him and burst into tears.

"Oh, Dear God—Dear God!" she sobbed.

"What's wrong, mommy," the boys huddled close to her.

Farmer took her hand, "The Good Lord done spared us," Farmer brushed tears from his own eyes. "Now we gotta make sure no one else dies in this flood. I'm a tyin' the horses down tight so they don't spook when this storm hits us. Ya keep this lantern ta warn folks comin' from the west. I'll take the other one back ta the creek and pray none come from the east."

The wind blew strong, the lightning lit up everything like momentary daylight. The thunder crashed, and the rain started. Soon it was a downpour, and Farmer was soaked. He checked on Emile and the boys to make sure they stayed inside the cover on the wagon. He calmed the horses—then hurried back to the creek.

"I was wishin' today, Lord, ta see a car, but I sure ain't hankerin' ta see one right now!" Farmer breathed a prayer.

Farmer tried to take refuge under some trees, but the rain found him anyway. He felt chilled to the bone, and at times his body shook from the cold. An hour passed, then another—time seemed to slow to a crawl, and Farmer longed and prayed for daylight.

The water raged by without any let up. Farmer thought he heard some noise mixing with the sound of rushing water. To his horror he spied the narrow twin threads of light coming from a car making its way along the road on the other side of the creek. He started yelling and praying with all the strength he had, frantically waving the lantern. "Dear Lord, I ain't much fer fancy prayin', but I shore need ya ta stop those folks 'fore they perish in the water!" Farmer pleaded, his mind racing.

The car kept coming; Farmer swung the lantern and screamed with all his might. The car kept coming closer to the creek. Farmer's heart froze, he stopped, waiting for the worst, then like an unseen hand held up the car halted on the edge where the bridge use to be.

"Oh, thank God . . ." Farmer drew a breath. He could see people get out of the car.

"Bridge out!" he yelled out. He could hear voices from the other side but couldn't make out what was said.

The car backed up a piece and sat with lights shining down the road to the water. Farmer sensed they were staying put to warn any travelers coming behind them.

Farmer kept his vigil and so did the car, while Emile watched the west from the wagon. Along about dawn the rain stopped and the clouds passed over. By sun-up the creek had receded as quickly as it had risen. A car came from the west. Farmer waved them to stop.

"Bridge washed out in the storm," Farmer hollered. A man by himself got out of his car and surveyed the situation.

"I badly need to get to the other side," the man stated angrily.

"Don't see how!" Farmer said matter o' factly.

The man spun around, cursed under his breath, stepped onto the running board, throwing himself into the seat. He slammed the door twice, backed up, turning back west on the road and sped off.

Farmer put his attention to the other car across the creek, which sat still now. He waded the dwindled creek, climbed the bank and approached the car. Looking in at the windshield, he could see a man and his wife sleeping with a baby in her arms. He knocked on the door, rousing a family from their slumber. Three small children popped up in the rear seat.

"Shore glad ta see ya all well on this beautiful morning," Farmer greeted them all with a smile.

The man jumped out of his car, grabbing Farmer's hand and shook it as if his very life depended on it.

"Mister, we owe you our lives. How can we ever thank you!" the man spoke with deep gratitude.

His wife came around the car from the other side with the baby and kissed Farmer on the cheek.

"You saved our lives, Mister."

"That's the plumb truth!" her husband went on. "We all woulda drowned. I saw your light and slowed down—then saw the water and barely stopped."

"I dare not think of what coulda happened to us had you not been there," the woman turned her head.

"I shore prayed powerful hard thet God wouldn't let ya go in the water."

"I have a fire and coffee, on," Farmer heard Emile say. He turned to see she had waded the creek and was coming up behind him.

"My wife amazes me," Farmer thought.

For the next two hours the grown-ups warmed themselves by the fire and sipped coffee. Emile cooked breakfast, and while the children played around the wagon, Farmer, Emile and their new friends, Bob and Kathleen Buchwald spoke of God's great love and how He had spared them all from a sudden death!

CHAPTER 21
A SCARE

The Trevors and Buchwalds barricaded the road on both sides of the creek before going their separate ways. The Buchwalds were returning to the first town to await the bridge repair. The Trevors continued their journey west.

Farmer could determine by the lay of the land that they were still climbing. The sun shone bright and warm in a clear blue sky, as the horses and wagon made their way slowly and carefully along the roughly graded road. New Mexico had not been a state long enough to have any well developed road system.

The mountains rose taller above the floors of the small valleys the road crossed, while taller and thicker stands of trees became more frequent.

Farmer had been quiet, thinking about the events of the night before, the pictures embedded in his mind. He slowly became aware that although the sun was warm, he was not, and that scratchy feeling in his throat grew more noticeable and troublesome by the hour. Farmer asked Emile to wrap a blanket around him, but even that didn't help. He felt chilled to the bone.

Long before sunset, Farmer could go no farther. He located a good camping spot in a grove of trees a short distance from the road. It was all he could do to unhitch the horses and get them settled for the night.

Emile was working on setting up the tent canvas, and Farmer helped her finish that. As soon as the blankets were spread out Farmer lay down and covered up. He could not stop shaking, and his throat felt on fire. Emile felt his forehead and pulled another blanket over him. She was saying something to Farmer, but it did not make it into his head. His mind seemed stuck on building a campfire, and he played it over and over. Finally, he called out to Emile that he would ready a fire. Farmer remembered seeing her face as she came under the canvas and reassured him she had already started one.

Then Farmer slept, for how long he didn't know—maybe a minute. He was awakened by Walter asking him if he and Clifton could ride Dusty around. Emile's voice followed, telling him not to disturb his Pa.

Farmer refused supper. He felt as though he was freezing and sometimes shaking so hard that it made his insides hurt. Then his mind got stuck on waterin' the horses, after that how he could stay warm in the night air. Farmer spent a fitful night, all the while thinkin' he would feel better by daybreak.

When the sun finally rose Farmer was so sick he couldn't get up. He refused breakfast, but drank some water. He ended heaving that up behind the wagon.

"Reckon I'll be some better in a bit," Farmer told Emile as she helped him back into his blankets.

"Oh Farmer!" he heard her say. "You are burning up with fever!"

Farmer tried to lie still, but the shaking would become almost violent at times as it over took him. He tried to fight it, but seemed no match for what was inflaming him!

His mind wandered into a dense fog. He couldn't open his eyes. To swallow was nearly impossible and painful. Some sounds were so loud they hurt his ears and head, other sounds he could barely make out.

Outside the canvas tent Farmer heard one of the children ask, "What's wrong with Pa?" He never heard what Emile said.

How much later, Farmer did not know, for he had lost understanding what time it was, but he remembered opening his eyes to see Emile near him. She had felt his face and placed a wet, cool cloth across his forehead. When he looked at her she began to cry, "I don't know what to do; I don't know what to do!"

Then he had restless, horrible dreams. Once he didn't know if it was a dream—or really happening, but he opened his eyes to see Emile's face filled with fear.

"Farmer, you've got to fight! For me! For the boys! For our unborn baby! We need you! Don't leave us alone out here! Farmer! Listen to me! Don't leave us! Get well!"

Farmer fought, but he felt so weak that his effort made no difference—then he remembered nothing—nothing, until he awoke. It was dark and Farmer wasn't sure if he was dead—or alive!

"Emile?" he coughed in a raspy voice. He heard a gasp.

"Yes! Farmer?"

"I'm so hungry, I reckon I could near eat one o' the horses," Farmer remarked as he sat up.

In an instant, Emile's arms were around him—she was crying and laughing all at once. Her hands went to his face and she kissed his cheeks, chin, his mouth and his nose as she sobbed, "Oh Farmer! I thought I was going to loose you! You were so sick, outa your head, burning hot as fire with fever. Scared me and the boys near to death. We prayed and prayed for you. Oh thank God you are better!" Then she got up and slipped on her coat, and disappeared into the dark.

"Emile, what in thunder air ya doin'?" Farmer wanted to know.

"I'm building up the campfire. You're going to get the biggest, best breakfast any man—my man ever got," she called back.

CHAPTER 22

RECOVERY

In the dark hours before dawn, Farmer learned from Emile he had been delirious for three days. They sat around a roaring campfire, and true to her word, Emile had fixed a whopping big breakfast! Farmer was so hungry he hadn't given much thought to what he was eating.

"Emile, where in thunder did we get eggs?" Farmer blurted out.

"Folks coming by were very kind, most of them," Emile explained. "Oh Farmer, I don't know where to start, telling you three days of all that happened in just one breakfast. You don't know how I wanted to have someone take you to a doctor. One family told me the nearest doctor was in Romeroville. You remember we passed through the morning before the storm?"

"Yes."

"They were afraid to get out of their car or get too close—thought you might have the plague. That frightened me even more. They promised to send help back, but wasn't too long and they were returning. Couldn't get through because of the bridge being down an' all . . ." Emile snuggled close, putting her arm around Farmer's waist.

"I'm so thankful to God you are better," she went on. "The third day I was nearly loosing my mind not knowing what to do. Another family said they were from Pecos, said that town is near Santa Fe and there was a doctor there, and one in Santa Fe. Said Pecos was near fifty miles. They had some cough medicine and some liniment they thought might keep your fever down."

Then Emile spoke sadly, "They wouldn't get out of their car either. Didn't want to catch your sickness, so they sat the medicine and the liniment on the ground and drove off. They never came back, so maybe the bridge has been repaired . . ." Emile's voice trailed off as she thought.

"Word must have gotten around that the bridge was out. Not many cars—almost no travelers the last two days."

Farmer felt an ache in his heart for what he had put Emile and the boys through. He remembered that another was on the way, and came to the realization with greater resolve that he must protect Emile from anything that would harm her and the baby. He felt such a love for her and held her tight for the longest.

He got up to pile more wood on the fire against Emile's protest, and upon completion of such a simple task, could tell he would do no travel this day.

"Well, woman," Farmer kidded, "thet was a mighty heap o' informin' which you done—but I still haven't any idea where we come by those eggs!"

"Oh!" Emile laughed. "This old man and woman came down the road. They had fresh eggs and gave us some. I'd near forgot that man was the only one who would look in on you. He climbed under the canvas, prayed for you, said the eggs would fix you up."

Emile smiled sweetly, her eyes glistening in the firelight. "I wasn't quite sure if he meant before or after you recovered," she added jokingly.

Walter and Clifton were excited upon waking, to find their Pa up and better. Nothing would do until he saw the play fort they had built off in the trees. Farmer, later in the day gathered enough strength to have a round of Indian war with his sons. They fought imaginary braves surrounding the fort as though their lives depended on it. Emile loaded their stick rifles so the battle waged on until they all lay on the ground panting for breath!

That afternoon Farmer found himself growing restless and irritable. "I can tell you are ready to move on," Emile remarked without looking up from the supper meal she was preparing.

Farmer knew immediately her remark was in response to the way he kept snapping at her.

"Just upset with myself fer costin' us so much time," Farmer mumbled. He walked away, following a deer trail through the trees to the other side where he could look across the plain to mountains which rose in layers, north and west of them.

Walter joined him–then Clifton came running up a moment later. They stood in silence, drinking in the sight of a land, rugged, unsettled, expansive, even the boys seemed to sense the sacredness of what Farmer felt. The irritability gave way to peace that came from knowing they were in God's Hands doing what He wanted them to do. He had spared them from a watery death, and from the fever. The scene said so much—without words. It was felt!

"I think God lives here," Walter spoke with emotion Farmer had never seen in him before. Farmer scooped both of them up in his arms.

"Yes, God lives here!" Farmer answered.

"Our cows here?" Clifton wanted to know.

"No, son, we have a long way ahead o' us."

That night after supper around the campfire, the family did a heap of serious talking. They spoke of home—the one they had left, of missing papas and grandmas, aunts and uncles, memories on this trip already fixed in their minds. Of the home they were headed towards. Of dreams for the future, of dreams coming true.

CHAPTER 23

A REASON TO BE IN SANTA FE

The road veered again to the northwest making its way across level plains until again Farmer and his family found themselves in mountains. Stands of juniper and pinons were denser where the road wound around sides of steep grades, cresting over a pass to drop into a flat area, then to climb into another mountain.

The road in some stretches was in fair shape and passable. Farmer and Emile were thankful when faster and more comfortable travel was afforded by good road. However, longer portions of the route were rutted and rough, a condition left from the long winter months. Some places in the mountains were narrow, twisting, carved out along the sides of cliffs, full of sharp curves. Emile usually opted to dismount the wagon and walk, until she would tire out and have to ride again. They didn't let Walter and Clifton ride Dusty in these rough places for fear that the horse would bolt off the road down the steep side, possibly in search of grass and water, which also was in shorter supply. The ground had become dry and rocky and the recent rain had failed to revive much grass.

One thing Farmer had been thankful for was that the climb into the mountains had not been such that the horses could not pull the wagon up them. Few times he hitched Dusty up in front of Sunset and Wind, thinking the team probably could have made it without the extra help.

"Get up here an' earn yer keep," he whispered once in Dusty's ear as he hooked him to the wagon.

The pioneers passed through tiny towns of Bernol, Rowe and Pecos, camping alongside the headwaters of the Pecos River. They were told in Pecos that there were Indian Villages nearby, but they never saw them. They did see an increased number of Indians. Some in beaded dress, others in buckskin. Farmer felt less a spectacle, as there were more horses and wagons still used in this area.

They did take a little time to look at the site of a Civil War battle when they rolled through Glorieta. Signs had been mounted in various locations telling all about the battle. Leaving there they traveled on to Santa Fe, which proved to be larger than Tucumcari.

"I reckon you'd be glad to find one o' those cabins here, Emile," Farmer remarked casually. He had eyed her turning and looking with fascination at the many shops and stores with wares of blankets, jewelry, dresses, hats of such an assortment to attract any shopper, and Farmer knew Emile could hardly wait to go looking. But she didn't respond.

"Now Emile, my dear. I know we got us a little money, but we can't be spendin' it all in Santa Fe," Farmer went on just as casual.

"Silly," Emile popped him on the leg with her hand.

Walter and Clifton had been captured in fascination themselves, peering over the side of the wagon. They crawled over behind their Ma and Pa and Walter pulled on Farmer's sleeve, wanting to know if the Indians might attack their wagon?

"Reckon those days are gone, boys," Farmer replied with amusement.

"What ifen they sneak up on us in the dark?" Walter voiced concern.

"Yeah," Clifton echoed.

"Well, from the looks an' the attention we get from folks lookin' at our chuck wagon, they might figure we's such strange ones not ta bother with us," Farmer smiled at passerby's on the boardwalks.

The Trevors lodged at a guest inn with adobe rooms near a place that could care for the horses. After three days of travel, a night's stay was welcome, even though the facility was not up to the standard set by the cabins in Tucumcari.

The adobe walls were painted. Decor of Indian and Spanish origin gave the room interest and several other guests shared the bath, so Farmer and Emile had to wait for the room to empty or for water to heat. The beds on the other hand were comfortable.

Farmer was up early and out of the room while Emile and the boys still slept. He went to get some information about the road to Albuquerque, as the road map Benjamin had given him was lacking details about those blank spaces. It had also occurred to him in the night that he had lost track of time, and he was unsure of what day it was.

The sun was coming up splashing into light on the mountains and the faces of the buildings. Farmer saw someone at the desk in the lobby, so he detoured inside.

"We been lost up in travel an' outa touch, an' I reckon I haven't a notion as ta what day this is," Farmer announced as he strode into the open room.

His sudden entrance startled the pale skinned man behind the counter. The man eyed Farmer with a scowl.

"Not sure what year it is . . ."the man replied.

Farmer was uncertain if the man was serious, or funnin' him.

"Sounds as ifen yer day ain't too bright, my friend," Farmer responded.

"Not when I have some fool come in before sun-up wondering what day it is. Sounds like a goose, sticking its head up in the morning wondering where it's at."

Farmer felt the back of his neck get hot and anger began to smolder inside him.

"Let's try this again," Farmer tried to control his temper. "I'm a guest here at this establishment, an' where I hail from, we don't treat our guests with them kinda stabbin' words. Now somethin's done got ya agitated this mornin'— an' it ain't the likes o' me."

After a moment the man broke his gaze. "You're right, I was with some friends last night, someone had booze; I drank too much; head pounds," he uttered in short gasps. Then looking up at Farmer he asked, "You ever get drunk?"

"Never had me any interest," Farmer responded.

"It feels—good. I hate it! Got its hooks in me! Won't let go!"

"Drink somethin' else," Farmer offered as advice.

"But I like the way—it makes me feel!" The man shot back.

"Can't be all thet wonderful I reckon from what yer a tellin' me."

"How would you know? You never been—drunk. Get drunk—an' you might be the same."

Farmer looked on this man thoughtfully, searching his mind for words, feeling God's love moving his heart.

"My name's Farmer," his face broke into a warm smile, as he extended his hand.

"Peter," came a muttered reply, but he didn't offer his hand.

"Sounds like ya got a big ol' empty place in yer heart an' life you's tryin' ta fill. I can tell ya booze won't fill it—but I reckon I can tell ya what can."

"What?" Peter looked up.

"It's the fella who walked up to a fisherman who was also named Peter, an' also had him a big empty place in his heart. This fella tol' Peter—drop everything and come with me. He filled Peter's empty place with Hisself."

"What fellow are you speaking of?" Peter questioned suspiciously.

"Jesus Christ, the Son of God," Farmer breathed the name reverently, staring into nervous eyes surrounded by a freckle filled face topped with bright red hair. Peter's expression right then was one of someone hit firmly in the face with a board.

"I opened my heart ta Jesus Christ an' believed He would fill my empty place—an' He did, so's I don't need no liquor," Farmer went on.

Peter dropped his eyes, shaking his head in a resolute—no. With eyes on papers he shuffled through, he remarked sourly, "The answer to your question Mr. Farmer, it is Thursday, April 30, 1925."

CHAPTER 24

STEEP GRADE

Farmer found out that same morning—from another source since Peter had closed the conversation—that the road took a southwest turn through Indian Territory. There was connecting road, but the blank spaces on the map denoted where there was wagon trail left over from bygone years, or some of it old stage routes.

After some time for Emile, and the rest of them following her in one store upon another, for looking, they took their leave of Santa Fe. In a small gift shop tucked in a corner building the boys had spotted some metal toy airplanes. They begged and pleaded for them, as Farmer had never seen them carry on so before. Now they were zooming their toy planes in swoops and dives, trying to duplicate the sound of airplanes with their voices. They played in the small area they occupied in the wagon located directly behind the seat at the front where Farmer and Emile sat.

The road continued winding its way over passes and across small valleys. The stretches of trail were deeply rutted and so rough that Farmer thought it might shake the wagon to pieces. He could see the toll the jarring was taking on Emile, but she bravely held on. He decided to have her ride Dusty over some of the worst of the trail, which seemed some better for her.

Making their way back and forth around sharp curves over a trail strewn with small rocks, in a particular rough place, as Emile held on to the seat of the wagon, bouncing up and down, she chattered with an impish grin, "Not—not—too sure—if—all the—kickin'—kickin'—in—my—stomach—is—the wagon—or—the baby."

Off in the distance mountains grew taller, as the road climbed higher. The third day out of Santa Fe they began climbing up into the tallest of the mountains, which they could see. The juniper and pinon transformed into taller and thicker stands of pine and fir trees. Grass at this level grew abundantly.

The pace became slower, and Farmer found he needed to stop more often to let the horses rest. At one such time he studied the map of New Mexico for the hundredth time.

"I reckon us ta be right about here," Farmer showed Emile where he pointed on the map. "Albuquerque I figure ta be on the other side o' this mountain we is climbin'."

"Do we go over the top? It looks so high," Emile questioned looking up and shading her eyes from the sun.

"Must be some way through—I reckon to come on a pass soon," Farmer studied the skyline.

Yet the roads way grew steeper and the journey more laborious. Few cars came up from behind them driving up the mountain, but several came flying down the grade—honking their horns on the sharp curves—kicking up dust and rocks as they whizzed past.

"Top's near!" One driver shouted as his car rattled by on the downgrade. This news encouraged them all, but they appeared no closer to the top as they labored up the grade. They made camp as the shadow of the mountain fell on them the third night. Farmer fell asleep determined to beat that mountain the next day, and by daybreak he was up, campfire built, and coffee brewing.

"Let's get movin'," Farmer called out to a sleeping Emile, Walter, Clifton and Scout. "Let's make the top 'fore it gets too blazin' hot!"

Emile emerged from under the canvas tent in her night-gown. She yawned and stretched her arms over her head, revealing the shape of her figure, and a tummy beginning to show. Farmer watched her and heard her familiar, "Good morning, Farmer."

Now Farmer knew she would never agree, nor understand, but right then at that moment as she warmed herself at the fire, hair all over her head and in her face, in her nightclothes, she was the most beautiful woman in the world—his world. She would laugh and jokingly say, "I'm the only woman here," Farmer thought to himself.

Emile caught his look, smiled, turned red, and retreated into the tent to get dressed.

After a hurried breakfast, Farmer hitched up the team and placed Dusty up front.

"Pa, how 'bout I take Scout and see ifen there's Injuns ahead?' Walter mimicked from a book on pioneers going west that Emile had read to him.

Farmer ordered them all in the wagon, and urged the team out onto the road again.

The wagon moved up the grade, winding, curving its way even higher up the mountain. Then the incline upward, which had been difficult for miles, worsened. The wagon rolled slower, maintained for a few hundred yards, then slower to a crawl.

"Hahh—Hahh!" Farmer shouted flapping the reins across the horses' backs. "Pull Wind! Pull Sunset! Go Dusty—Go!" Farmer urged the horses on while they strained against the harnesses. Out of the corner of his eye he saw worry on Emile's face. She held on tightly! Another fifty feet, "Whoa!" Farmer pulled the team to a stop and quickly yanked the long brake handle down tight.

"Emile, I need for ya ta take the reins. Boys, ya get out and walk ahead of Dusty, maybe he'll try followen' ya. Take Scout. I'm gonna try an' push an' turn the wheel."

"Oh, Farmer, we can't do this long, and I can't see the top of the pass. What will we do?" Emile cried out.

"Start the team, Emile, and pull the brake off. Ifen the team stops, pull the brake on pronto, else we'll loose the wagon and everthing."

"I don't know if I can," Emile was crying.

"Yes, ya can! Ya gotta help me, Emile! Ya can do it! Set yer teeth tight an' do it!"

Farmer heard Emile shout to the horses and felt the brake release. Up ahead Walter and Clifton in boyish voices called, "Come on, Dusty, pull thet ol' wagon. Sunset! Wind!"

Farmer pushed with all his might against the rear of the wagon. Slowly it began to roll and move, inch by inch up the steep grade. Farmer darted back and forth from pushing to helping roll the rear wheel by pulling on the wagon spokes with hands, sometimes hopping on a spoke with one foot to apply his weight.

The road curved sharply and leveled for a short distance where the wagon picked up speed—then up another sharp incline. The wagon lost the gained momentum and again the horses struggled under the load. From where Farmer pushed on the wheel he could see Emile was having trouble with the horses. They kept pulling to the side, wanting to go over the edge of the road. He ran to the front of the wagon and pulled the brake!

"Whoa, Emile—Whoa!" Farmer shouted as he climbed up into the wagon seat to take the reins.

"Let me go up with the boys," Emile said as she climbed down.

Farmer waited for her to reach the boys and give the horses a rest, before he urged them on again.

"Haahh! Haahhh!" Farmer shouted, flipping the reins. The team dug in pulling with all the strength they could gather, and the wagon inched forward, little by little up the incline. All three horses strained against their harness, the traces were taut as the wheels kept slowly turning.

The horses came into a patch of loose dirt and small rocks. Sunset's hoof kicked out from under him and he went down. Wind reared and with a shriek Sunset wrestled to get back up. Emile was up the road screaming!

In a flash, Farmer had the brake tight and was on the ground. He held Wind still so Sunset could get his footing. Their eyes were wild and both covered with white froth. He patted their faces and talked to them until they calmed down.

"Farmer, whatever can we do?" Emile and the boys were by him.

"Don't reckon I know," Farmer removed his hat and wiped his face on his sleeve. "The horses jus' can't make this steep a grade!" He exclaimed and spit.

Farmer paced back and forth thinkin'. He could unload the wagon to see if that helped—but how to get their belongin's over the top! Maybe make several trips. But he didn't think their belongin's was all that heavy.

Into his racing mind, the chugging of an automobile down below pushed its way into his worried thoughts. He felt some relief just to know there was someone else on this mountain. Soon the car came into view on the curves below, making its way up the graded road. Farmer recognized the car as a Model T, but unlike any other he had seen. This one appeared to have a small wagon on the back. Within a few minutes, it emerged through some trees coming into the curve below them and braked to a fast stop behind the wagon.

The side door opened and a tall man in western garb stepped out. His skin was brown and tough as leather, no doubt from long days in the burning sun. He wore cowboy boots and hat, and under vest, Farmer could see the butt of a side gun in its holster. His hat brim shaded the warm smile that formed as he eyed the stalled band and their wagon.

"Appears ya got yerselves stuck," the man spoke with a low gravelly voice. He walked up alongside Farmer and touched his hat brim to acknowledge Emile.

"Our horses jus' can't pull this grade," Farmer answered.

"Well, son, this here is Tijeras Pass, an' both sides er 'bout the hardest climb in all New Mexico. Yer gonna near wear out yer brake goin' down the other side in the canyon. When road crews re-worked this road, they didn't make it fer wagons."

"I reckon not!" Farmer agreed. "Our horse jus' fell down, an' they air dead tired. I'm at a loss as ta gettin' ta the top."

"Oh, we'll get there fer sure. My name is Flint Parker. Own a ranch along the Rio Grande."

Farmer introduced himself, Emile and their sons. He told Flint about the horses, and Scout, and how they came to have the chuck wagon from Thomas Redkin. Parker told Farmer he knew Redkin from some cattle deals some year's prior.

"Yer goin' to Oregon in a wagon!" Flint Parker exclaimed in surprise when Farmer told him of their destination. "Y'all believe in doing yer trip the hard way," he added with a low laugh. After walking around the wagon, as if calculating a plan, he asked, "Ya got some strong rope?"

Farmer produced a length of rope, and after inspecting and pulling it, Parker grunted, "Will do."

"Now ya un-hitch yer lead horse and tie the rope solid to yer wagon tongue," Flint instructed. "I'm gonna pull yer wagon over the top with my pickup."

Farmer unhooked Dusty while Flint moved his rig carefully past the wagon and horses. They attached the rope to the rear axle of the Model T and the other end tied firmly to the wagon tongue between Sunset and Wind. Then Farmer tied Dusty to the rear of the wagon and joined Emile and the boys who were already in the wagon.

"'Tis one o' those times the good Lord sends an answer ta prayer fer I have time ta pray it," Farmer smiled at Emile.

"How do you know I wasn't praying it?" Emile replied, looking straight ahead—then when she looked at Farmer her eyes sparkled.

Flint put the pickup in gear and Farmer released the brake on the wagon. They started moving ahead and about then the rear wheels of the pickup started bouncing up and down—throwing rocks on the horses and dust up in a cloud. Farmer's heart sunk!

Flint Parker was out of his rig—thinking. "Let's unload from yer wagon to the pickup. Need some weight on the back tires."

While they moved the heaviest things from the wagon to the pickup bed, Parker told how he traveled to Amarillo to buy something new Ford had manufactured just for farmers and ranchers. They say it can pull a plow!

"Like havin' a wagon bed on yer car—first one out—no one else makes one yet!" Flint Parker talked about his Model T pickup. "Now we will see how tough it is—let's try again."

This time the rear wheels dug down, took hold, and began moving up the road. Soon the horses were nearly running to keep pace with the Model T. A mile or two more and they crested the pass where the sky shone clear blue through a cut in the trees. As they rolled to a stop, the valley below spread deep, rising to a high plain beyond.

"Well folks, told ya we'd make the pass," Flint drawled, pleased with himself, and proud of his pickup's performance.

"This be the Sandia Mountains, an' before ya is Tyeras Canyon," Parker spread his hand in a grand motion. "Road drops fast. Y'all be hearin' car horns honkin' 'cause some curves and places be so narrow, only one can pass at a time. This road drops right into the main part of Albuquerque."

"Mr. Parker, God surely sent you!" Emile blurted out.

"Don't know 'bout that ma'am, but do know rightly I'd been to my ranch days ago, ifen I didn't get tied up on the other side o' Romeroville while they fixed a bridge washed out."

"We was ther an' saw it!" Farmer exclaimed, and proceeded to tell Flint how God had spared their lives.

"Anyhow, we air beholden to ya, Flint. We was stuck shore nuff an' couldn't a made the top without yer help." Farmer clasped Flint's hand in a firm shake that expressed Farmer's gratitude without any further words to be spoken.

Flint Parker bid them, "so long," leaving the Oregon travelers with his best wishes for a safe journey. With that he again tipped his hat to Emile, nodded to Walter and Clifton, caught Farmer's eye for an instant, climbed into his pickup and rumbled off into the canyon.

"Got me two things I have ta say," Farmer remarked thoughtfully as the wagon began rolling again.

"What's that?" Emile looked up at him.

"I'm powerful thankful ta the Lord fer delayin' Mr. Parker so's he could pull us over thet steep grade . . ."

"And what else?" Emile asked.

"We jus' gotta heve us one o' those Model T Ford pickups when we get ta Oregon."

They both laughed and broke into singing an old hymn they learned in church- "What a fellowship, what a joy devine, leaning on the Everlasting arms..."

CHAPTER 25

RIVER CAMP

Albuquerque afforded no available services for horses that Farmer could locate. It seemed the automobile market had well replaced horse and wagon in this city. Farmer and Emile felt a spectacle again in their chuck wagon, so sought refuge on a grassy bank of the Rio Grande River. They decided to remain in camp the remainder of the day to relax and let the horses graze and rest.

"Albuquerque was certainly a busy place," Emile reflected on their ride down the wide dirt road named Central Avenue. "Do you know I didn't see any other wagons—not one?" Emile continued, voicing the thoughts that Farmer also had.

"I reckon times have passed us by, and we have a bit o' catchin' up ta do," Farmer remarked as he tethered the horses.

"Was our life so bad, Farmer?"

Farmer stopped to look over at Emile. He knew her thoughts had drifted home—to what used to be.

"No Emile, not so bad."

Later as Farmer stretched the canvas tent and staked it down, Emile walked by smiling coyly. "Lets go swimming," she invited. "The boys are already at the water's edge."

Farmer found a suitable spot to swim and the four of them laughed and splashed water at each other, and played into the afternoon. Scout yapped from the shore until he could stand no further excitement and jumped into the water paddling his way to the boys.

A hundred feet down river several Mexican women with their children stepped through a line of bushes down to the water's edge. They had apparently come to wash clothes and let their children splash in the water on a warm day. They appeared amused at the gringo family's antics in their Rio Grande, and Farmer noticed they kept looking and pointing at the wagon, speaking words in their language that Farmer could not understand.

That afternoon, after the Trevors had dried themselves and built a campfire, the Mexican women and their children approached the campsite. The boys had busied themselves building a soldier's fort, but when they spied the Mexicans they ran quick into camp. Emile was at the back of the wagon starting supper. Farmer had just dropped an armload of wood gathered from a grove of scrub trees.

"Senor," one woman called out.

"Ma'am," Farmer acknowledged them and tipped his hat.

"Habla Spanish?" she asked.

"Don't reckon I know Spanish, Ma'am."

The women appeared embarrassed and shy.

"English," she shook her head and holding two fingers close together trying to say she didn't know very much English.

She pointed to the wagon. "Rancher? You work?" she asked. Her companions shook their heads yes.

Farmer stood confused. "Not sure what yer a wantin'," he shrugged his shoulders.

The women spoke among themselves for a moment with animated gestures, then, one disappeared through the bushes. The others graciously dismissed themselves and returned to where they had hung clothes.

Farmer and Emile dismissed the meeting until the woman who had left emerged again through the bushes accompanied by a younger woman. When the other women down the river saw them, they hurried to the Trevor's campsite. The young Mexican woman walked to Farmer with an embarrassed smile and glance as she held out her hand.

"I am Angelina Running Bird," she introduced herself with a soft voice.

"Oh, you are an Indian woman," Emile spoke as she joined them coming from the back of the wagon.

"I am Laguna Indian. I moved to Albuquerque to attend special university. My friend came to me because I can speak English. These women believe you must be from a ranch," Angelina motioned to the other women who all nodded in agreement, even though they had little idea of what she spoke.

"A ranch—we are going ta a ranch," Farmer questioned, puzzled.

"Oh, you mean the wagon," Emile laughed. "They think we are from a ranch because we are in a chuck wagon."

"Si, they want to know if there is work on the ranch. For them or their men," Angelina relayed the women's question.

Farmer and Emile told how they were pioneers headed to prove a homestead in Oregon, and they traveled in a wagon. When Angelina translated the tale, the women's eyes got big—then they laughed, speaking quickly at once.

"Stop, Stop!" Angelina pleaded. "I can only listen to one—at a time!"

Farmer and Emile invited the women to join them around the campfire for some afternoon coffee Emile had brewing over the fire. The children eagerly joined Walter and Clifton in play as they proudly displayed the fort they worked to build. Farmer marveled that the children seemed unaware of differences—cultural or languages. All they knew was that they had found new friends to play with.

The women were full of questions, mostly to Emile. She answered with charm, Angelina interpreted and they would laugh and chatter. They asked about Texas, the people there, travel in a wagon and sights seen along the way.

'They don't seem to have any problem getting' along,' mused Farmer. 'Reckon it's men who's always goin' ta war, but this shore is a woman's place.' Farmer sipped his coffee and listened to his wife and the women.

The older woman eyed Emile, but said little. Her only expression was to smile as the others laughed. By and by she arose from the rock where she sat and stepped to Emile. She cupped Emile's face in her hands and studied her face and eyes for some time. The rest sat silent.

"Nino?" she asked Emile, then rubbed Emile's tummy.

"Nino" she said beaming.

"Ma Ma says you are having a baby," Angelina translated.

"Oh! Yes, I am!" Emile exclaimed joyfully.

Three of the women threw up their hands. Running Bird covered her mouth. This news set them all to talking at once as they surrounded Emile.

'Good Gosh!' thought Farmer. He got up to check on the horses and the children, and leave the women to their visiting.

That night as he lay looking out at a million stars sparkling across the sky, his heart was full of happiness and pride. Pride in his God, his wife and boys, of the child on the way, the life that had been given him. More than that he felt an ever-greater awareness of God's filling and over-flowing love.

CHAPTER 26
DESERT

Of the women who had visited their campsite the day before, whether they be Indian or Mexican, or both, Farmer could not tell. Nor did it make any difference to him. He had found them to be a cheerful and humble people, who seemed to carry a quiet strength about them. They made the most of simple things and enjoyed life. He did know that he, Emile and their sons were grateful for their company.

These women through the lips of Angelina Running Bird had given him three important pieces of information.

"Don't take water from Grande River. Rain, in high country, fills the water with much dirt and other things not good for drinking," Angelina translated their words. "Take much water, you must travel many days through dry desert before you reach Gallop."

"Malpais," the elder woman spoke in a growl.

"Badlands!" Angelina matched the woman's tone of voice. "New Mexico Badlands."

That meant before the Trevor family continued on their journey they rolled the chuck wagon on Central Avenue once again in search of drinkable water. They thought also to bolster up their food supply. At a friendly Trading Post they found both.

The clerk upon seeing their wagon gave some advice.

"We are given word in Albuquerque that the new East-West hi-way may come right down this street aimin' at California. In makin' plans they have graded a road straight through Central Avenue, 'cross the Rio Grande, and straight West up the bluff. I was told it to be seven or eight miles to the top. Maybe too much for your team, but if you follow the old road a short distance along the river—well, that's the old wagon road that will get you up to the high plain."

"How 'bout feed fer the horses, and water?" Farmer inquired.

"Feed is sparse. Very few stopping places—Grants is the biggest. Little water. You folks are coming along a good time of the year. Still not blazin' hot, but hot enough. Watch for coyotes and mountain lions," the fellow warned. His last statement caught Walter's attention.

"Any wild Injuns?" Walter burst out.

"I think they are all tame by now," the clerk laughed and tousled Walter's hair.

It was fifteen minutes after nine that morning, but took the chuck wagon pioneers until the sun was straight overhead to crest the bluff.

A mile from the Trading Post, Central Avenue crossed the Rio Grande. The constructed bridge over the water was long, wide, and sturdy. Numerous cars were on the road—that Tuesday morning in May, and the lumbering wagon soon lined up cars behind it, unable to pass for oncoming traffic. Some cars to the rear began to honk their horns. Farmer urged the horses to hurry, but they were no match for the swifter moving automobiles. Some in the cars smiled, others gave disgruntled looks, as they worked their way around the wagon. Dust flew when the cars hit the road again at the end of the bridge, and soon they could be seen moving up the side of the bluff.

Farmer found the old wagon road just as the clerk had said. The road wound back and forth making an easier grade, but it also added more distance. Farmer and Emile walked alongside Sunset and Wind for some distance, and the boys rode Dusty. The sun grew hotter as it rose in the sky, and the horses were tired. Farmer put Emile and the boys in the wagon, and then he hitched Dusty up front. As the horses trudged up the grade, Farmer could see cars moving steady up and down the new road to the south of them. Oddly, there had been no one else using the old wagon road all morning.

"Well, I shore am glad ta get here!" Farmer declared as they rode out onto the plateaus.

"Not near as glad as our horses," Emile wiped her face.

Farmer halted the wagon to let the team rest. Emile got down to walk around. The boys followed to run and play with Scout.

Farmer stood up on the wagon seat to gaze into the distance. He saw desert with clumps of scrub brush and patches of cactus. Small mounds of gravelly sand were scattered amongst the brush and cactus. The desert seemed to slowly rise to meet Mesas off in the distance.

"What do you see?" Emile was looking up at him.

"A might empty land as fer as I can see. Horses won't be findin' much ta eat out here," Farmer remarked dryly.

They all drank water, and Farmer gave some to the horses, and they were on their way again, soon joining up with the new road.

One could tell that the people of Albuquerque had worked on this road—hopeful to attract the attention of the commission who was deciding which roads and trails to connect to make a hi-way from Chicago to the Pacific Ocean. There had been talk in Amarillo, Tucumcari, and Santa Fe and certainly signs of preparation were seen in Albuquerque.

The new road was wide enough for two cars to pass. It looked to have been recently graded. In some low places, small gravel was spread, and the horses were more easily able to pull the wagon at a faster gait. In fact, they did so well Farmer left Dusty up in front of Sunset and Wind.

The sun was ready to touch the distant horizon, when Farmer rolled the wagon to a stop in front of a small aging Trading Post.

"This must be the crossing of Rio Puerco," Farmer remarked as he studied the map. Ahead they saw an iron bridge—spanning a wide wash.

"Oh," remembered Emile, "I believe this is where Angelina told me the Laguna Indian Reservation begins—her home."

Near the old Trading Post there was a building going up. It looked like it might be a gasoline stop. Behind that two cars were parked and families were busy setting up tents and making camp before it got dark.

Farmer and Emile followed their example, selecting a site along the bank of the stream, which had dwindled to a thin ribbon of water. Camp was erected in a hurry, and Walter and Clifton fell asleep as they tried to eat some supper. The headlights of passing cars illuminated the outline of the iron bridge, and the lighted windows of the Trading Post blinked out. Desert chill settled in, and out somewhere in the distance, yapping howls of coyotes pierced the night stillness.

Emile placed extra blankets on the boys, and also over her and Farmer. She snuggled up as close to Farmer as she could to get warm. They both shivered until their bodies warmed the blankets tucked around them.

"I've never been out in the desert before," Emile whispered in his ear.

"Well, I ain't never been anywhere—'cept Abilene," Farmer snickered.

CHAPTER 27
BADLANDS

It was near noon the next day when the chuck wagon made its way into Correo.

"Oh look! A little post office!" Emile pointed, delighted. I must post some letters that I started. She crawled back into the wagon and dug through belongings to find her writing materials. While Farmer located water for the horses—and to replenish what they had used out of Albuquerque, Emile hurriedly finished several letters to family and some friends. She had also written one to Farmer's family.

"I wanted to give these a happy ending to a worrisome beginning," Emile spoke somewhat jokingly—and seriously.

"How ya mean?" Farmer asked.

"Because I started writing when you were so sick," she leaned close and kissed him. Then bounded off the wagon to go inside the small concrete building.

"Stamps for first class—two cents apiece," the postal clerk informed them. "Didn't expect to see folks in a wagon today—unless they was Lagunas," he went on.

"Well, we never expected ta find us no post office out here," Farmer spoke in his Texas drawl. Everyone laughed.

"The government built a post office here in the middle of the Laguna Indian Reservation. First postmaster lived in a small room in the rear. Slept here—did his cookin' here. First mail come off the railroad not far from Corres," the mail clerk explained. "Handful of businesses built up later. Where you traveling to—California?"

"Oregon, to raise us some cows," Walter answered proudly.

"Yep, Oregon," Clifton echoed.

"Oregon! My, I declare," the clerk peered at the youngsters over his glasses.

"Any idea 'bout the roads?" Farmer queried.

"Not up there, but you have badlands as you get closer to Grants and razor sharp lava rock, hard and cutting. An' folks travelin' through two weeks ago told me of spottin' some cougars. You best watch your horses. Cougars will bring a horse down right in front of you!"

"Dear God!" Emile gasped as she took hold of Farmer's arm.

"Feed is sparse. Some grass beyond the town of Old Laguna, but I don't believe you will get that far today. You can buy some grain at our General Store."

Emile licked the stamps, placed them on the envelopes, and handed them to the clerk.

They made some purchases at the suggested store. They were hungry and the odor of home cooking from a small café drew them to the other side of the road to eat lunch. They were tempted to spend the night in one of the small cabins, but wanting to make the most of the remaining daylight, they moved on down the road.

A short distance out of Corres, the road crossed over the railroad, turning west again to follow near the steel track. That afternoon the boys spotted black billows of smoke from a train approaching from the east-behind them. It was the first train they had seen in days, and Walter and Clifton were thrilled when the engineer waved and blew the whistle several times as the train and its line of cars rumbled by.

The rest of the afternoon they felt left alone. No more trains, not even a passing automobile. A suitable campsite was not to be found. The ground was hard and covered with small rock. Fuel for a campfire was lacking and what Farmer managed to gather did not burn well—generating more smoke than flame. Supper was cold—the night air dipped to freezing.

"Can't recall bein' so glad ta see the sun come up," Farmer grumbled as he climbed out of the blankets.

"I'm so cold I dare not move," he heard Emile say.

They were traveling again by daybreak.

"We're hungry," both boys cried.

Emile opened a can of beans and they ate as the wagon bumped and jolted along.

"Beans cold," Clifton complained.

Farmer felt anger well up inside him. Not so much at Clifton, but he felt helpless to do anything about the condition they were in that morning.

"Sure would do fer some hot bacon an' eggs," Walter remarked.

"Be thankful ya have somethin' ta eat!" Farmer snapped.

Both boys' eyes dropped instantly as they cleaned their plates in silence.

"Boys," Emile finally spoke, "there was no good wood for a campfire to cook with and keep us warm. It won't be like this forever." She smiled at Farmer, and he made up his mind to store wood on the wagon and not get caught like this again.

As the day wore on, it appeared that the long plain seemed a long continual ascent. Some stretches of the road were in fairly good condition and there were no steep grades, so the horses pulled the wagon with little effort. They appeared to make good time, yet the town of Old Laguna never wanted to appear.

And just knowing there was no available wood to build a fire and cook a delicious meal, made their hungry stomachs more demanding. After awhile, it seemed to consume Farmer's thoughts. He daydreamed about slabs of fried ham with biscuits and white gravy. He could taste potatoes sizzling in a pan, and as the sun grew hot, his mouth watered for some cold tea.

Finally, he spoke out! "Dang, Emile, I've been some hungry before, but this is plumb crazy. All I can think 'bout is eatin' an' been longing fer one of these cafes ta appear!"

"I know! Me too!" Emile murmured.

At that time the boys who were riding on Dusty came back to the wagon. Pulling Dusty in and turning alongside, Walter spoke excitedly.

"Saw us a rabbit, Pa! We could shoot one fer supper!"

Emile giggled, and they both knew the boys had the same thoughts they did.

That afternoon the road passed close to pueblo ruins up on the mesa that rose above the plain. Miles further, the road became winding and the hills and mesas cast shadows across the valley floor.

"I reckon we have ta be near on top of Ol' Laguna," Farmer muttered to himself as he studied the map. "Shows ta be by a San Jose river."

And sure enough, suddenly the road dipped down into the river bottom. They crossed a wooden bridge that felt like it swayed when they reached the middle. Old Laguna was on the far side of the bridge.

"The river is nearly dry," Emile called out, looking over the side from the wagon.

Old Laguna consisted of a few houses, a church and a Trading Post, but offered no place to eat or spend the night.

However, the weary travelers found firewood in the trees, which grew near the water, and some patches of grass blew in a gentle breeze. A small stream of water still flowed in the San Jose, affording a comfortable campsite.

Emile cooked a hot supper that evening, and thanksgiving offered for the meal to God was truly heartfelt. They made their beds near the fire, and Farmer got up numerous times in the night piling more firewood warding off the stinging cold.

The next day the Trevors came upon a rather active village named Cubero. The first thing to greet them was a sizable and old cemetery. The scant homes were built near a stream that gave life to a grove of tall cottonwoods. A mile or so beyond was a newer portion of the village, signs that read Villa de Cubero. Cars were parked in front of the trading post. They enjoyed an early lunch at the café, and were anxious to continue on their journey.

Outside the café, Farmer helped Emile to the wagon seat and then walked next door to a newly built gasoline station. Behind the station were two cabins, some areas unfinished, denoting these too, were new.

"Needin' a room to stay the night?" a man emerged in the door of the station. "Your misses looks tired and ready for a rest."

Farmer looked back at Emile who sat waiting for him.

"How fer is this Grants town?" Farmer asked the attendant.

"Going by wagon, you'll not make Grants tonight. You have the Badlands to pass through."

Farmer weighed a night in the cabin, bath, and rest— against time. It seemed they had lost precious days already. They still had a full afternoon ahead, putting them that much closer to Grants.

"Reckon we'll be goin' on today," Farmer decided. As he looked to the northwest his eye caught what looked like clouds. Storm coming, he wondered.

The man followed Farmers gaze.

"Naw, that's the snowcap on Mount Taylor. Pioneers looked for that land mark, as it meant the continental divide was near, and Arizona after that."

Farmer thanked the man and as he headed the team back out onto the road, he pointed out Mount Taylor in the distance. This was their first glimpse of high mountains, and soon the landscape they moved through changed. The road followed the south side of an apparent long valley while the rock and sagebrush covered hills rose higher above the valley floor.

That afternoon as they followed the road along the base of the hills, they saw the black line of smoke from the engine of a train on the track running along the opposite side of the valley. They faintly heard the whistle blow.

The valley dropped and the road joined the base of a rocky mesa. A car coming from the west stopped as it came upon the wagon pioneers.

"Howdy there, travelers," the driver spoke loudly above his car's engine, "are you faring well."

"Yes, farin' well, can ya tell me how far ta Grants?" Farmer asked.

The man looked at the dashboard for a moment.

"I would say, about fourteen miles. Left there no more than an hour ago. Course, the lava rock slows you up. You're coming to it. See that high pass between the hills back there?" the man pointed. "The road goes down into a big valley, all full of lava flow. Road narrow an' rocky. You'll have to be careful for your horses and watch for cars and places to pass."

He told them he was from California on his way to Santa Fe. He had plans to make a movie there he said, and thought Farmer and Emile—'On the Oregon Trail' in their chuck wagon had merit for a movie idea. With a, "Good Luck," his shiny, dust covered Packard bolted away from the Trevors.

"I wander what one of those moving pictures is like, Farmer," Emile spoke thoughtfully. "Remember, we passed by a movie house in Amarillo."

"Ye hear what thet man said, you all? Grants, is an hour away. We can make thet town I reckon fer sundown!"

Someone had named the valley that the Trevors descended into, "The Badlands" for a reason. The growing shadows from the surrounding hills made the black rock appear as flowing rivers coursing along the valley floor—in places filling it up from side to side. The rock was hard as flint with razor sharp, jagged, protruding edges.

It was impossible to build a road through or on top of the lava flow, so the route went along the edge. Sometimes, the black rock pushed close to the sides of steep hills. Farmer urged the horses faster in a race against the approaching dusk.

"Where in thunder is thet town!" Farmer exclaimed in disbelief. As far as he could see was a black river of rock with an occasional juniper bush.

"Maybe it be down in a hollow—hidden from us seein' it. Come on Sunset, come on Wind!" Farmer slapped the reins against the horses' backs several times pushing them to a run. The wagon shook and bounced roughly.

"Yeh, Pa!" shouted Walter. Both boys stood up holding onto the sides of the wagon.

"Oh, Farmer!" was all Emile managed to say.

Farmer held the horses to a run. He just knew Grants would be around the next curve. Grants, where there would be warmth and rest for Emile and the boys. A place for a hot meal, a safe place.

That curve yielded no Grants, but Farmer thought he could see the telltale lights of a town past a outcropping that lie ahead. He discovered that the outcropping was not the entrance to Grants. Not even to a town, but the narrowing of the road between split rivers of lava. Dangerous jagged pieces of rock stuck out on both sides.

Both horses sensed the danger, and Sunset pulled away from his reins. Farmer could not control them, and Sunset rammed Wind against the rocks on her side before Farmer could pull the team in to a halt. Wind shrieked in pain, and Farmer was off the wagon. Both horses were snorting and wild eyed. Farmer led them down to where the road widened again. Farmer could hear Emile crying.

"That was some ride!" Walter said in awe.

"Hush that talk!" Emile ordered sharply.

"Wind, ya cut yer leg," Farmer spoke softly as he stroked Wind's twitching neck. Blood ran from a gash in her front leg. Farmer examined her hind leg also, which had some scratches.

"Emile, need the balm, and some cloth. Wind has a cut on her leg," Farmer called out.

Emile joined him in a moment. She shoved the balm and a torn strip of cloth roughly in his hand.

"Farmer Trevor, I'm so, so angry with you! I—I could slap you! Have you lost your senses? Are you crazy? You could have killed us all! Why are you in such a all-fired hurry to get to Oregon? We got all summer!" Emile's eyes blazed.

"But—" Farmer started to explain.

"Don't say another word. We ain't moving from this spot, you hear!" Emile spun and marched to the rear of the chuck wagon, noisily dropping the back gate down. She sobbed away her anger as she unpacked cooking utensils.

There was no Grants in sight. The hour had passed, the sun went down, and the Trevors camped in the blackness of the Badlands.

CHAPTER 28

GOD'S PROTECTION AND PROVISION

Grants was exactly where the man said it was. One hour away. That was true for his Packard, but it meant five hours for a chuck wagon. Nevertheless, it was a welcome sight, after passing beyond the lava flow, to see the small community settled along the foothills on the north side of the valley.

Dusty was now alongside of Sunset, and his mustang spirit showed. He pushed and bit at the other horse fighting the confinement. Wind trailed along behind the wagon with a slight limp.

Farmer and Emile were tired from a restless night camped on the side of the road, but not because of the biting cold alone. Farmer put the last of the wood they had in the wagon on the fire sometime after midnight. Mostly, the restless sleep came from not making up with each other. It was over a cold breakfast the next morning that their hearts melted. They held each other tight and both cried. Forgiveness was given and love restored, even though nothing was said.

Emile looked weary and Farmer knew she needed to rest, so he determined to find a cabin.

The road smoothed out as they neared Grants and joined up with the railroad. Rolling slowly through the middle of town, they passed a nicely painted sign, which pointed out—Peace Treaty Signed Here Between Kit Carson and Chief Manuelits.

"I remember studyin' Kit Carson in school," Farmer commented.

"Was he a Injun fighter?" Walter wanted to know.

"Looks like he made peace with 'em at Grants, son," Farmer smiled as he glanced back at his boys in the wagon.

They found a cabin and couldn't wait to get baths! After that they ate lunch, talking and laughing with other patrons. They found Grants to be a quiet, friendly place.

While Farmer got Wind's leg looked after, Emile took Clifton to shop in some of the stores. Walter remained by Farmer, and followed his Pa's every move. After a hearty supper they all collapsed in bed, not moving until the sunlight shining in the window ended their sleep.

The valley out of Grants opened wide and the road seemed to make a slow steady climb. On the second day out of Grants, Farmer wondered if the horses might be sick the way they labored and breathed. When they came upon a sign at the side of the road, Continental Divide Elevation—7,275 feet above sea level. Farmer became conscious that he, too, was having difficulty breathing, and then knew how the horses felt.

"Down hill from here," Farmer laughed, and sure enough the plain started a long decent down the westward side to dump into the New Mexico desert.

The road lay in a straight line across the face of the desert floor. The ground was mostly barren rock, with patches of sand and gravel. Bushes were scant and no higher than a couple of feet. Farmer could see no sign of life except for small birds, or a hawk. And of course, the cars with their passengers helped break the monotony of hours of slow, plodding travel. When the road would reach a rise in the floor, it continued on in its monotonous path across another valley.

The first morning in the desert the temperature jumped as soon as the sun came up. By ten o'clock Farmer could see waves of heat rising off the ground.

"Stop the horses a few minutes," Emile suddenly commanded. She climbed over the seat crawling back into the wagon. Soon she climbed back onto the seat with three pieces of fabric.

"What is thet?" Farmer asked, puzzled.

"My surprise!" she announced proudly, holding up what resembled three hats.

"Dang, Emile, the boys an' me gets hats!"

"They're not for you, Mr. Farmer," Emile teased as she climbed down from the wagon. "Remember me buying this material in Tucumcari? I made hats' for Sunset, Wind and Dusty." She put the horses' ears through the holes and adjusted the hats.

"All finished," Emile said with a satisfied smile as she took her place beside him on the wagon seat.

"I swear, Emile!" exclaimed Farmer. He kissed her passionately knocking her bonnet back off her head. She blushed as she re-tied her bonnet. Then she winked at him.

The minutes turned slowly into hours, the hours into days. The sun burned with miserable heat; the nights were bone chilling.

"Will this desert never end!" Emile cried out in exasperation.

"Is Oregon much longer?" Clifton would ask more frequently than Farmer wanted to hear.

In the hottest afternoon on the third day in the desert, when the wagon topped a rise in the road, Farmer could look down the road marking a line across a long hollow valley. Farmer made out a car stopped on the road several miles away. He could see movement of a figure of a man walking around the car. Emile straightened up as she saw it too.

It took almost an hour to reach the car, and as the wagon neared, a man stepped out of the car to wave them to stop.

Farmer had to chuckle.

"Mister, are we glad to see you!" The man ran to the wagon.

"Oh, thank God! We thought you'd never reach us!" a woman cried out, stepping down from the passenger side of the car.

"Sorry ma'am, I reckon our wagon is a mite slow," Farmer replied.

"We've been stranded since this morning. A radiator hose burst and we have no water," the man explained.

His wife reached the wagon. Her actions revealed fear, and her voice was high pitched. "My mother in the rear seat! I'm afraid she is having a heat stroke. She needs help!"

"Oh dear God!" Emile gasped, grabbing a wash towel and dipper from the side of the wagon; she opened one of the water containers.

"The water is hot!" Emile cried.

"That's no matter! Please hurry!"

The two women disappeared into the rear of the automobile. Farmer drew a cup of water for the man, who gulped it down.

"Slow down, fella, you'll make yerself sick," Farmer warned.

"Never knew water could taste so good!" the man panted.

Soon Emile was back to the wagon for another dipper of water. She looked grave.

"She gonna be alright?" Farmer asked

"Don't know yet." Emile climbed back into the car.

The man paced back and forth beside the car, while Farmer watered the horses. He got the boys to help.

"Is somebody dyin'?" Walter whispered, and Clifton began to whimper.

"I don't reckon so," Farmer answered, "But we can shore pray they isn't."

By and by Emile and the woman climbed out of the car helping an elderly woman out.

"Farmer, we need to set her on something in the shade of the wagon so she can get some air," Emile shouted.

Farmer quickly unpacked a keg, and the woman plopped down on it.

"This dreadful desert! This horrible desert!" the old woman gasped for breath. "No breeze! No shade! Anywhere! Torturous heat! No water! Boiling sun!"

"Now, now," the man and woman tried to calm the old lady. "These good folks are here to help us. God has heard our prayers, Mom!"

"Thank you!" the younger woman looked at Emile and Farmer with tears in her eyes.

Farmer gave everyone more water to drink.

"The car was running fine, when all a sudden steam came pouring out from the motor," the man explained. "Well, I seen that a hose had a hole in it an' the water was lost. I had a spare hose an' tools to change it—which I did that task right quick but to what good without water. I kicked myself many a time today for not having spare water to fill the radiator. Cars coming by didn't have spare water either. One family gave us a little, but we drank that, an' in this heat—didn't last long. Then mom got down, an'—well, we were most scared! I admit I'm not much of a praying man, but I thought we could die in this God—well—er forsaken land. I, we did some serious prayin'. I looked up and couldn't believe my eyes! A covered wagon coming down the road! Thank God for you, sir!"

Emile had all the while kept wet rags on the old woman's face and neck in an attempt to cool her temperature.

Farmer filled the radiator and the man started the car.

"I reckon ya'll be on yer way," Farmer remarked warmly, whipping sweat from his face.

"No, we must return to Gallop. Find a doctor. Come Mom, let us help you back in the car. We must take you to a doctor."

The old woman grumbled a complaint, but complied. Emile helped her to the car.

Turning to Farmer, the man reached in his pocket, " I want to give you something for your help."

"No need," Farmer shook his head.

"I insist!" the man was firm.

"The Good Book tells me ta give a cup o' cool water in His name. Jus' sorry mine was warm—but it was water. Don't reckon we'll take anything but yer thanks."

The man studied Farmer a moment, then spoke, "You most certainly have our gratitude and thanks."

Turning to Clifton, who stood near, the man whispered in the lad's ear and placed something in his hand. Clifton grinned and shoved his hands deep into his pockets.

The woman hugged Emile, and tearfully smiled at Farmer. She held both boys before climbing in their car. Then they backed the car around, and threw dirt and rock from the tires in a quick start.

The Trevors' resumed their slow steady pace down the road. Their gaze followed the dust from the car across the long flat desert floor in front of them. At one point the sunlight glinted off the cars window. Shortly after, the car went over a rise and out of sight. It was then Clifton tugged at Farmer's sleeve.

"What, son!" Farmer looked back to see Clifton holding up his hand.

"That man tol' me to give this to my Pa." Clifton opened his hand to reveal a folded one hundred dollar bill.

"That man tol' me to hold it tight in my pocket and not give it to ya 'til I couldn't see the car no more. Is it money, Pa?" Clifton asked.

Farmer felt a lump in his throat and tender emotion swept over his heart. He looked at Emile who had been watching his face. He knew she felt and understood as he did.

"Hadn't tol' ya, Emile, but we used all our own money at Grants. I've been prayin' we not heve ta dip into the cash yer Pa gave us, an'—an' just looky here what the Lord has done—without our askin' those fine folks."

""What we gonna do with it, Pa?" Walter asked as he climbed up to view the bill.

"Well, I reckon it means we's gonna get us a cabin an' eat a whoppin' meal in Gallop," Farmer laughed as he stood up to go to whoopin' and waving his hat in the hot air.

Emile clapped her hands and shouted, "Thank the Lord!"

CHAPTER 29

GALLOP

Farmer rose quietly at daybreak. He had some talking to do with the Lord. He stood a piece from the camp and studied the desert. For the first time he saw more than just a bone-dry harsh land. God created this place just as He had other places that seemed more lovely to look at.

The desert held a quiet calm. Just the expanse of what lay before him was breathtaking. And off in the distance, was row upon row of purple mountains, majestic, with their tips of gold given by the rising sun.

As he beheld this scene, he felt very small before the Mighty Creator. He wondered how God could tend to so many different things. Bein' so busy—yet He spared the lives o' that family yesterday. 'How easily they could have perished in that deadly heat,' Farmer thought, an' You sent us along with some water to help.'

"An' thinkin' on water, Dear Lord," Farmer prayed aloud. "We's almost out an' I haven't any idée how far to Gallop, so help it last—or maybe send one o' them racin' cars with some."

Emile's touch startled him. She had gotten up and walked quietly to his side. Arm in arm they silently watched the light of the rising sun fill the desert floor.

"Farmer," Emile began speaking. "We were so intent with that dear family yesterday—we don't even know their names."

"Uh huh," Farmer agreed.

"I shudder to think of what—they could have died out here!"

They both stood thoughtfully in silence looking out into the desert.

"Farmer?"

"Yes."

"We are almost out of water ourselves, using so much yesterday."

"I know."

"Will we make it? I mean, will it last?"

"I'm hopin' and prayin' so. I reckon we will heve ta make it last as long as we can," Farmer held Emile close.

And to make their remaining water supply last, they drank only when thirst drove them beyond the point of holding out. Dusty and Sunset had to be watered, but they held back on Wind.

The desert sun was relentless, and by afternoon the Trevors' water was gone. Farmer had stopped taking any to save precious drops for Emile and the boys. He began to see water where there was no water, and moments of panic would seize him. He knew they too could die in this cruel desert.

No cars passed by all afternoon. Finally, one came from the west. Farmer waved them down, and the travelers gave them a Mason jar of water.

"You'll make it now. See that draw in the mountains— right there. That's Gallop," the driver told them.

"Oh, thank God!" murmured Emile.

The Trevors's were so weary when they arrived in the settlement; all they wanted to do was find a place to sleep. They saw more Indians in Gallop than any other town they passed through. They saw no cabins or hotels, but passed by saloon after saloon. Drunken men staggered along boardwalks. Some were passed out lying against walls of the buildings.

"How dreadful!" Emile turned her head. "Get out of sight boys!" She ordered as she shoved them down in the wagon.

"Ain't even night yet," Farmer commented.

They located some cabins farther into town run by an old Hopi Indian. Farmer unhitched the wagon next to their cabin and led the horses to a stable. On his return to the cabin, he found Emile and both boys sound asleep. Only Scout greeted him.

"Reckon we's just too tired to eat," he thought and laid down next to Emile.

'Now why is thet woman taken a bath in the middle o' the night,' he thought.

When he opened an eye he realized the sun was up, and Emile was bathing.

He looked in on her and smiled.

"Good morning," she said sweetly. "If you'll get some things from the wagon, I'll make coffee and breakfast on the little stove this cabin has."

Farmer heard Emile as he dressed and pulled on his boots.

"It felt terrible—us going to bed all dusty and dirty—from the desert. I just couldn't keep my eyes open. The boys fell asleep before—I could—even undress them. I don't—remember you coming to bed. Oh, Farmer, this bath is wonderful—I'm in cool water!"

Farmer was shocked when he went to the wagon. The back deck was down, some pans were on the ground and the food supply was gone. Looking in the wagon, Farmer could see someone had dug through their things, and his axe was gone from the side.

As he stood there—dazed, anger replaced shock.

"Emile!" Farmer stormed back into the cabin. "We've been robbed!"

Farmer went back out to the wagon. He was thankful he'd had the habit of carrying his rifle and shotgun indoors, but upon examination, the ammunition was gone along with their food store and the axe.

Soon Emile was in the wagon trying to determine what was missing.

"My jewelry and one of my dresses is gone," Emile announced dryly—then she broke down in tears.

"Oh dear, they took some of my undergarments! Why would any person—do—that?"

Farmer felt rage. He wanted justice! He wanted revenge! He wanted to strike back—he wanted to defeat—but who? He was ready to report the robbery to the Gallop sheriff when he saw a young Indian woman walking towards them. Farmer turned and she hurried to the wagon. She carried a bundle wrapped in a blanket. She wore a plain dress, but her feet were clad in moccasins. She had a silver and turquoise bracelet, her jet-black hair was braided on both sides of her head. She was thin of frame, and her blue eyes darted from Farmer to Emile to the wagon to the open door of their cabin.

She placed the blanket on the ground and opened it. Farmer recognized their stolen things.

"Are these yours?" the woman spoke in broken English.

"Oh yes!" Emile exclaimed. "Where did you find them?"

"My—husband," she went on. "He comes to the saloon. The drink—makes him do bad things. We hungry—he bring this."

The Indian woman holds her hand toward the blanket. Farmer noticed a tiny baby strapped to her back.

"I ask him—you steal? We fight! He said he took from a wagon. When he sleep in the dark, I walk in the dark to bring—to return. Please, don't tell—the—law. My husband will—be jail. Please!"

Farmer looked into her pleading eyes.

"Oh you poor thing!" Emile cried out from the wagon.

Farmer felt compassion for this family.

"Do ya have anything ta eat," he questioned the woman.

"No," she replied.

"Well, Emile, I reckon we should give our food ta this Indian and her baby."

"Oh, yes!" Emile agreed.

"You leave the clothes and jewelry here. Where is the ammunition?"

"No understand," she questioned.

"Bullets! Where are they?"

She shook her head—no.

"I don't see my axe!"

Again she shook her head no.

Emile climbed down to collect her dress, undergarments, and jewelry.

"Ya can take food an' go, God love ya. We' won't be turnin' yer man over ta the law," Farmer told the woman.

She nodded, bundled up the canned goods, and hurried away, her baby bouncing up and down on her back as she ran.

Farmer felt warm and happy inside, that they had been able to help this Indian family. He was thankful for the return of Emile's things, especially the jewelry. Those had been given to Emile over the years—some handed down from her grandparents. He regretted the loss of the axe, but would purchase another.

Once Farmer and the boys were cleaned up and dressed, they sought out a nearby café. They were famished! As they ate, they went over the events of the morning. The Indian that stole from their wagon in the night, to make up for money thrown away on illegal drink and his squaw walking in the dark desert to return what was taken.

"An' you gave them y'alls food!" a woman at a nearby table broke into their conversation.

"Reckon we did," Farmer answered.

"Couldn't help hearin' and can't take no more," she spoke gruffly.

"You had yer hat pulled plumb over yer eyes, aw mos. You didn't see it comin' neither. That's their game—some of 'em. Men can't leave the whiskey alone—ever penny they get goes to drinkin'. They steal from travelers like you, and their women bring it back. All they care about is the food—an' know y'all feel sorry for them an' they get that anyway, 'cause you give it to them. What else they want just doesn't come back with the squaw. They get food, and y'all don't call the law. That's their game, an' you fell fer it!"

She shook her head and turned back to her plate.

Farmer was stunned and Emile devastated. He felt anger boil inside again. Not only had he been stolen from once—but twice.

It was in Gallop that Farmer made up his mind that Indians were no good lying thieves.

CHAPTER 30
HASHKNIFE OUTFIT

I t was on Sunday, May 17, 1925 that the smooth, wind worn, red rock of Arizona greeted the Texas travelers.

There was a somber mood among the Trevors, not the excitement they felt at the Texas-New Mexico Border—none of the silliness of one foot in one state-the other foot planted in the other state.

Instead, Farmer and Emile felt gratitude towards God for keeping them safe—alive!

As the wagon slowly rolled towards the Arizona border, Farmer's mind recalled what New Mexico had afforded them. They could have perished in the flashflood, the parched desert, burning by day, freezing at night. And the towns they journeyed through. Some left pleasant memories—some less so. They learned a bitter lesson in Gallop that not only bruised their pride, but also was costly.

Stolen food had to be restocked on the wagon, not to mention a new axe and replacement of the rifle and shotgun shells that had also disappeared in the night. That and staying two days in a cabin used up much of the money given by the family in the desert. Farmer knew they would have to soon dip into the cash from the Holts.

Emile had remembered that money in Gallop and was near panic. "Oh, Farmer, did that Indian steal our money too?"

"No, thank the Good Lord! I keep that an' the check from Mr. Redkin in my money belt," Farmer informed her.

So it was when they stopped on the Arizona line, they offered a prayer mingled with the anticipation they were closer to Oregon—yet apprehension as they remembered the difficulties they had encountered in New Mexico.

"We sure been gone long time," Walter spoke, looking up into his Ma and Pa's faces. "Thought we should been in Oregon by now."

"I'm tired a bumpin' in this dang wagon," Clifton complained.

Emile showed surprise at Clifton, and then looked at Farmer.

"Well, wonder where that came from! Would you like to walk?"

Clifton dropped his eyes, "No ma'am!"

Farmer and Emile knew they would have to keep the boys occupied as the trip wore on. Wind was healed enough to take her place again alongside Sunset. Dusty was more than pleased to take on the lighter load of Walter and Clifton. Scout was growing and able to run at the horses' hooves for a mile or two at a time.

The road here was well graded. It followed at a distance the railroad, and over the border into Arizona, the road dropped into a river valley walled on each side by deep red rock. The first trading community lay next to a high, red wall on the right side of the valley. The river lined with brush and scrub trees coursed its way down the middle.

"Welcome to Lupton," a deep gravely voice came from under a wide brimmed cowboy hat. "Where ya hail from?"

an old man with rugged appearance looked up at them with keen steady gaze.

Farmer 'whoaed' the team at a gasoline pump where the enquirer stood.

"Holt, Texas," Farmer announced with a smile.

"Dang! Dust my britches! Fellow Texans! I hailed from Dennison way. Drove cattle on the Chisolm Trail. How long ya been gettin' here, an' where ya headed?" the old man spoke with that familiar Texas drawl and a warm humor that made Farmer and Emile feel they had known him forever.

He listened with interest as they told of leaving Holt the last day of March, and the tough travel through the Badlands and desert.

"Not to pour sand on ya, but the Navajo here—'bouts say this, 'New Mexico desert is bad, Arizona desert, badder. New Mexico desert hot, Arizona desert hotter'."

With those words hanging over them Farmer and Emile left Lupton discouraged, but it began to dawn on them the saying maybe was not true. The road was well defined and the grade out of the valley onto the high plain gradual.

The road and railroad followed the Puerco River. Ample water still flowed in the riverbed, which eliminated concern for grass and water.

There were numerous settlements as well, which broke up endless miles of empty desert. The pioneers in their chuck wagon rolled through Allantown, Houck, Querino, Chets, Navapache, Chambers and Navajo. Farmer observed some of these to be railroad station stops. Others were trading posts, with some more settled, boasting a café or a few houses owned by railroad workers. Gasoline stations with repair garages had sprung up in several locations.

A few miles east of Adaman, Farmer halted the wagon at a crossroads. A post with a sign on top read, "National Old Trails Road." Directly under that sign a board nailed to the post pointing back the way they had come, painted in faded white—Gallop 78 miles, one pointing north read, "Fort Defiance." South read Fort Apache.

When Farmer read, Fort Apache, Walter jumped up. "Ma tol' me a story 'bout Apaches," he said with excitement.

"An' the sign west says—Holbrook 24 miles," Farmer finished.

Near the crossroads was a rock Stage Station, abandoned with the advent of the automobile. A hundred feet to the west stood a railroad station, adjacent to the track and near the bank of the Puerco River.

Farmer had the plan to go as far as they could with the rest of the daylight, but another two miles brought them to the southern entrance to the newly formed Petrified Forest National Park. They decided to follow some other travelers down the side road and into a flat desert floor strewn with logs and chips of wood turned to stone.

Farmer and Emile chased the boys, and they all examined pieces of petrified wood, while the horses rested. Scout scared up a rabbit and took out after it with both Walter and Clifton running behind, screaming and shouting. Farmer felt joy and love swell in his heart as he watched them.

"I hope Oregon will be good for them," Emile spoke wistfully.

"Reckon it'll be good fer all o' us," Farmer put his arm around her shoulder and pulled her close.

"I love you, Farmer," Emile spoke softly, "and I trust you. For them, for me, for the child I carry. I think I felt it move today and fear it will be as restless as it's father."

Farmer kissed her lovingly.

"Emile, my restlessness is past. Reckon I'll be right content when we reach our place in Oregon."

Emile looked deep into his eyes.

"Farmer, you know I would follow you to the end of the world, but I long to settle down and raise our children."

"An' I powerful love ya fer thet, Emile."

Pulling back onto the National Old Trails Road, Farmer remarked dryly, "Right some educational, eh boys? Thet was a sight ta look at, but ya can look at rock logs fer jus' so long."

He paused.

"Sure would make powerful sorry campfire wood. "

Emile laughed.

They camped that night on the edge of Adamana, and were on their way by sun up. Farmer wanted to reach Holbrook before nightfall.

The sun rose hot! At one of the frequent stops to water the horses, Emile fitted the hats over their ears. The road passed through what was known as the "Painted Desert."

"This place has a beauty all its own," Emile observed. "It is as if God brushed colors onto the rocks—and look there how the sun and shadow brings them out so richly. I've never seen anything like this."

"Me neither—course, I only been ta Abilene," Farmer turned his head away to stifle a laugh.

"You silly man," Emile giggled and hit his arm.

A few miles from Holbrook, a train passed nearby headed east. They could see passengers in the windows as the cars moved swiftly along.

Suddenly, a large herd of cattle came up out of the river bottom surrounded by eleven cowboys on horseback. Within a minute the chuck wagon was in a sea of moving— bellowing hooves and horns.

Walter and Clifton were on Dusty and didn't have time to get into the wagon. Farmer could see Walter's bewilderment as he tried to maneuver the mustang into the cattle.

"Oh, Farmer, help them!" Emile cried.

Farmer stood up and waved Walter back away from the herd.

"Oh, hang on, Clifton," Emile yelled out.

Then the cattle cutting instincts of the mustang took over, and he worked the cattle to keep them together, same as the cowboys.

"They'll be hurt!" Emile was near panic.

"Emile! Settle down! Walter is good on a horse. He can take care o' hisself."

"He's a little boy an' Clifton is three!" Emile retorted, "and all these huge cows around us!"

The cattle moved ahead of the wagon and appeared to adjust pace to stay with the wagon. The cowboy, who Farmer figured to be a trail boss, pulled his horse in until he rode along Farmer's side of the wagon.

"Howdy folks, ya got some young cowboys over there."

The cowboy smiled broadly from under his hat. He had a red bandana tied around his neck, leather vest over a faded shirt, and chaps over Levi's. The faint jingle of the spurs on his boots could be heard in time to the movement of his horse. The cowboy and horse were covered with dust. All Farmer could see of the cowboy's face were his eyes and teeth.

"Cattle are used to a chuck wagon behind. They feel right at home," the cowboy mused. "Y'all from these parts?" he asked. "Thought you belonged to one of the spreads."

"Naw, we hail from Texas—goin' ta Oregon ta start our own cattle ranch."

"Do tell," the cowboy's eyes narrowed as he studied them hard.

"These yer cattle?" Farmer motioned to the herd moving slowly down the road in front of them.

"Nope! We're the Hashknife Outfit."

"Oh dear!" gasped Emile. "They're rustlers!"

The cowboy heard her and laughed.

"No ma'am. These cattle belong to the Hashknife Ranch—all legal. The biggest spread in Arizona."

The chuck wagon trailed behind the herd, until the cowboys directed them into railroad pens for shipment. Walter had difficulty turning Dusty back to the wagon, but finally responded to his young master's commands.

The trail boss told Farmer to go to the Brunswick Hotel. "That's where the Hashknife Outfit operates in Holbrook," he laughed then his face grew serious. "I want y'all to meet the boss."

Farmer located the hotel and tied the horses alongside the building. The cowboy joined them at the wagon directly.

"Been drivin' these cattle for days and the hands are itchin' to drink, an', er" he glanced at Emile, "find them some female companionship, but sure nuff, there will be hell raisin' in Holbrook tonight! Come with me—the boss wants to talk at ya."

He led Farmer into the hotel lobby and approached a man seated in one of the parlor chairs. He was well dressed, but his features were that of a man who knew life on the open range.

He stood to his feet.

"This is my boss, Jack Winter," the cowboy said.

Winter greeted Farmer warmly and firmly.

"Have a seat. I'm told yer from Texas—on yer way to Oregon—in a wagon. I need a man like you, mister, and could use another chuck wagon."

Jack Winter, long time right hand man to the General, owner of the Hashknife, immediately ordered the hotel staff to situate Emile and the boys in the Brunswick's finest room. Then over the next two hours he tried to convince Farmer he belonged with the Hashknife Outfit.

CHAPTER 31

TOUGH DECISIONS

T he room at the Brunswick was the most luxurious they had ever stayed in, and the beds soft and plush, but Farmer spent a fitful night.

Mr. Winter had offered him a job with salary beyond imagination. The Hashknife Ranch would buy the chuck wagon, and had a sizable, comfortable home on the ranch for Farmer and Emile to move into. When Farmer didn't commit, Mr. Winter offered use of one of the cars to drive into Holbrook when they would need supplies—or just go to town.

Farmer wasn't sure what to do.

"Darn, man, what else can I offer you?" Jack Winter exclaimed in exasperation. By now he was standing directly in front of Farmer.

"I reckon I gotta talk ta Emile 'bout it all."

"You do that. You talk good to your misses tonight. You tell her that the Hashknife Outfit will make sure she has doctorin'—her and the baby."

"What!" Farmer was surprised.

"Sure, you all are expecting another child. It shows. You tell her she'll have doctorin'," Winter smiled triumphantly. He figured he'd nailed the deal down with that final offer.

When Farmer told Emile the Hashknife proposition, he could tell there was something inside his wife that wanted to cry out "YES" to it all.

The night seemed endless as Farmer wrestled back and forth between Arizona and Oregon. He rehearsed a mixture of conversation, feelings, and thoughts over in his mind. He cried out to God, but it seemed his prayers were lost into the darkness of the night.

When morning finally arrived, Farmer was exhausted.

"Oh, Farmer, whatever shall we do?" Emile asked before he was even out of bed.

"Don't know!" he snapped sharply. "I'm a thinkin' on it!"

Farmer dressed and walked out on a balcony off their room to drink in the morning air. Arizona had its beauty—that he could not, nor would he, deny.

Emile joined him while the boys played with their airplanes in the room. She slipped her hand under his arm like she always did when she wanted to get close to him.

Farmer spoke first.

"It's like God ain't sayin' what we should do. Seems as He's meanin', ya can go or stay. It's fine by me, an' ya have my blessin's, but the outcome will be different. An' Emile, thet's what worries me—I reckon I have no idea o' what those outcomes would be."

He felt his throat tighten.

"I did me some powerful thinkin' in the night. I determined I needs think 'bout ya, an' the boys, an, the baby. Here we'd have money comin' in, a home, a doctor—in Oregon we just got a piece o ground. Nothin' else!"

They stood in silence for a while.

"Farmer, I told you I will go wherever you go, and that I trust you—with our lives. From the time you were a little boy you had a dream, a dream of going west and starting your own ranch. When we met in school, I dreamed that dream with you. I dream it with you now. If you take this offer, you'll be working for the Hashknife Outfit, and that's all it will ever be—working for them. Money can be made in Oregon, a house built, a doctor found—Farmer, don't loose sight of our dream!"

Later, Farmer and his family joined Jack Winter at breakfast.

"Good mornin', Trevors! Breakfast is ready and soon as you eat, we'll finish this up, and you can put a long journey to rest," Winter spoke brightly.

Farmer and Emile evaded discussion of the proposal and made general conversation over breakfast.

When they were finished eating Farmer broached the subject. "Mr. Winter, may I ask ya a question?"

Winter nodded.

"When ya was growin', did ya dream o' workin' on a cattle ranch?"

Winter pondered a minute before he answered.

"No," he hesitated and became grave, "I wanted to be a preacher."

Farmer felt shock rip through him.

"What happened?" he asked.

"A long story I don't care to discuss, seeing as how I just met you folks yesterday. Anyhow, the Almighty wouldn't want me now."

"I reckon thet ain't so, Mr. Winter. I'm thinkin' ya lost sight o' yer dream and somewhere took a wrong turn—just as I'd be a doin' ifen I accepted yer job with the Hashknife Outfit. Now mind ya, Mr. Winter, I reckon ya gave 'bout the most generous offer I ever had made ta me in my whole life. An' it is most temptin', but it's not the dream I've had since I's born. So's, I reckon we'll thank ya fer yer kindness, and be headin' on ta our ranch in Oregon."

"And you, Mr. Jack Winter, need to follow the dream and call that God placed on you!" Emile spoke up boldly.

CHAPTER 32
TWO GUNS

May sun was hot and strong on the Arizona desert. Farmer was thankful that the high plain was level and the road in fair shape. Ever since they left Holbrook it appeared the land was a slow but steady incline. They were surrounded on all sides by low mountains that unfolded in layer behind layer from the level plain of desert. The rich red rock seemed faded in the intense brightness of light and heat.

Farmer noticed that Emile grew more restless and sensed she became uncomfortable more quickly, although she was not one to complain. Therefore, he was almost as relieved as Emile to see the buildings of Joseph City in the distance.

"Oh Farmer, I do hope they have some ice water to cool us down," Emile said hopefully.

"Ol' Scout is plumb tuckered out," observed Walter, looking at the dog sprawled out on the blanket covering the wagon floor. The heat had long before driven both boys off of Dusty and into the shade of the wagon canopy.

On arriving in Joseph City, Emile had to dismount from the wagon and walk. The back of her dress revealed the large dark spot soaked with her sweat. Yet, she walked with grace and determination. Farmer tied the reins on the wagon seat, and jumped down to lead the horses. Together, hand in hand, they walked into Joseph City, going directly to an establishment that displayed "Ice" as part of its overhead sign.

They walked into a general store, much like Margaret Hatchet's back in Holt; with the exception this one had two tables and chairs. The elderly couple who ran the store offered sandwiches and cold sodas.

"Ye look hot and tired," the woman remarked to Emile.

"Indeed I am! I could drink a gallon of tea," Emile replied, wiping her face and pushing back her hair.

It was too hot to eat, but they drank plenty of ice tea and sodas. The old couple seemed friendly enough. They told how they moved there in 1890, buying the business from a Mormon.

"Joseph City was settled near the railroad by Mormons migrating out of Utah. Named it after their leader, they did."

"Are ya folks, Mormon?" Farmer asked.

"Lands no!" the woman said.

"They sure have tried to make us one of them," the man laughed."

"Hadn't been for travelers, we'd never stuck it out. Mormons won't do business, 'cept with their own kind."

"How do ya know we ain't—them kind?" Farmer teased with a straight face.

"Heck! You can see em comin' a mile. Might just as well carry a sign. You ain't one, I can tell," the old man laughed.

"Hush now!" his wife scolded.

Before they left, Farmer inquired about the road going into Utah. The old man was uncertain, but went out of the store a few minutes to reappear with another man that he seemed to know well.

"Lem here drives to Flagstaff often on his business. He can tell you about the road into Utah."

"Never driven far on that road, but I can tell you this much," the man called Lem began.

"You're headin' into some desolate country—all the way to the Colorado River crossing, and there's only two places to cross. I seen your wagon out there—the easiest route—and it's not easy—is to Marble Canyon. Mind you, the Mormons made several different trails in there, and you can get confused. Now you reach that road a mile or two this side of Flagstaff, watch careful—not well marked!"

Farmer and Emile thanked Lem for the information. While Emile selected several items in the store that had captured her interest, Farmer gave the horses a second round of water.

Emile wanted to send post cards home that she found in the General Store. They had pictures of the Arizona desert dotted with sangura cactus and yucca plants. One card she purchased had a scene from Flagstaff.

"Mail east goes out on the mornin' train when it comes through Joseph city. Just leave it with me," the storeowner told Emile.

On the way out of town, Lem caught up with them.

"Your sons reminded me of my lad," Lem panted, "so I wanted them—to have—this!" He thrust a metal toy automobile towards Walter and Clifton.

"Golly Gee!" Walter breathed.

"What do you boys have to say?" Emile reminded them of their manners.

"Thank you, sir," the boys responded in unison as they eagerly accepted Lem's gift.

"We take thet kindly, Lem." Farmer shook Lem's hand. "Yer son all growed now?"

Lem looked sad and was silent as though his thoughts were remembering. Then his memories became words.

"Thirty mile beyond Winslow you'll see Two Guns. Thought to have gained the name 'cause of two outlaws who got in a shoot out in an empty building. Shot one of the fellas dead and they buried him right there. Fact is, if ya look, 'tis a unmarked grave on the edge o' town. That be his. Thet town was built on violence and murder. 'Fore it was a town, a whole wagon train was massacred by a band o' warpath braves. When the Army came up—ever last man, woman and child was dead. Buried the remains in a mass grave back side o' Two Guns."

"Oh!" Emile covered her mouth.

"Some short years later some Apaches stole some Navaho women. Navaho men chased the Apache raiders into a cave hidden in the rocks a short walk from town. The Apaches slaughtered the women, and when the Navaho realized their women were dead—they built a fire at the cave entrance and filled the cave with smoke and bullets 'till ever last Apache was dead.

"Dear God!" Emile gasped.

"Sorry, lady," Lem apologized, "but I was such a fool to live in a place of fightin', killin', taken—death—as Two Guns!" By now Lem's face was wet with tears.

Farmer and Emile stared at him speechless.

Lem lowered his voice, "One day some wild drinkin' cowboys and freighters got in a gun fight. My wife—an' my boy—tried to get—outa. . ." Lem covered his eyes with his hand. After a pause he continued.

"I buried them here in Joseph City, and I've never gone back to Two Guns! I drive around it, and when you folks get there, you ride straight through. Don't you stop for nothin'. Death is there!"

CHAPTER 33

MOUNTAIN LION

The Trevors spent that night camped alongside the Little Colorado River somewhere between Joseph City and Winslow, Arizona. They camped one more night, and arrived in Winslow the following day, wind blown and tired. Since it was the Lord's Day, Farmer sought out a hotel where his family could clean up and find rest.

The second day out of Winslow the chuck wagon jolted and bumped along what was marked as Hell Street in the dreaded Two Guns.

Farmer felt Emile shudder as they remembered Lem's brutal description of Two Gun's violent past—yet they found the town peaceful. Some of the saloons had been taken over by more respectable businesses. A whorehouse was boarded up. Men, women and children walked the board ways without fear, and cars filled the streets instead of gunslingers. Travelers driving into town seemed unaware of the death that once blackmarked the area.

As the wagon rolled past the main section of town the Trevors came upon a building with the word "Mountain Lions" painted in large black letters. Through the bars

217

protecting a large front open window, one of the large brown cats could be seen pacing back and forth. It seemed symbolic of the violent, wild nature of this western town. Yes, caged for now, but if turned loose—would strike again!

Emile shuddered again, and Farmer hastened the team through town without stopping as Lem had implored them to do.

The road markers read "Beale Wagon Road" and rose up to a high point. It took them three hours to reach the top of that long slope. They stopped there to take in a breathtaking view.

"Look, there!" Farmer stood up from the wagon seat. It was the first time they had seen snow capped mountains of such majesty. The sun was setting in front of them turning the snow on the peaks a golden splendor.

"Can we camp here, Farmer?" Emile asked. "The mountains are so beautiful!"

"Is that Oregon?" Walter pointed.

"No, son," Farmer laughed, "but I reckon our home will be ever bit as pretty as those there mountains."

Next day the desert yielded to stands of juniper, then lush pine trees. Each hour of the slow steady pace of horses and wagon, the majestic snow covered mountains drew closer and grew taller. The stands of pine rose denser, covering the landscape with a beautiful green coat.

Farmer had never been to a place that quickened his heart more than these Arizona Mountains. He wondered if Oregon looked like this.

Emile must have read his thoughts.

"My husband, if Oregon compares to what we are seeing right now, we will surely live in a most beautiful place!"

That night they camped by a small fast tumbling stream in the forest. Feed was plentiful for the horses, campfire wood ready to be picked up, and Emile cooked a bountiful supper over a roaring fire.

Next morning Emile was not well. While she lay still under the canvas tent, Farmer rode Dusty up the road to see if he would come to Flagstaff. He laid his head on Dusty's neck and gave him free rein. He began urging 'run'—talking in Dusty's ear. He could feel the horse stretch out underneath him in long powerful strides. His hooves thundered on the packed road, as the trees slipped by.

Suddenly, horse and rider broke into an open area, and Farmer pulled Dusty in. The horse was gasping for air, and Farmer felt he was laboring to breathe along with his horse. He spied a road sign, which indicated this was not Flagstaff, but Winona, elevation 8,127 feet. Farmer then understood the heaviness on his chest.

On the north line of pine was the large log building, Winona Trading Post. Situated among the trees, Farmer spotted numerous houses, businesses and many cabins. He spun Dusty around and headed back to the wagon at a gallop.

"Ma throwed up," Walter announced upon Farmer's return.

Farmer quickly broke camp and helped a pale and weak Emile into the wagon. Before reaching Winona she leaned over the side and heaved again. Farmer gave her some water and told the boys to set still and be quiet. He pushed the horses and soon the chuck wagon emerged into the Winona clearing.

Farmer secured a comfortable cabin nestled by a grove of trees. He got Emile and their sons settled, then he tended the horses. Finding a doctor was the next task. Farmer inquired at the Trading Post and the other business establishments. He was told the nearest doctor was in Flagstaff, fourteen miles away.

Farmer determined to ride Dusty to Flagstaff, but first would fix Emile and the boys some hot soup on the small stove in their cabin. Emile ate only a few spoonfuls of the soup, and asked for more water. She didn't feel like she had a temperature, but her face had none of its usual color.

Farmer was saddling up Dusty when a tall, thin man approached him. He was well dressed in a casual way that gave the impression his clothes were expensive.

"Are you the party in this wagon?" he asked.

"Yes," Farmer turned towards him.

"I'm Dr. Lloyd Tennison from Pasadena, California. I'm vacationing with my family on our way East. When I stopped for gasoline I heard talk that your wife is ill. I came to see if I could be of assistance."

"Yes, Doctor, my Emile fell ill this mornin'. I would be right grateful if ya could see ta her. Needs tell ya she is with child."

"Let me get my bag," the doctor walked away to re-appear a few minutes later with a small brown leather satchel.

Farmer escorted the doctor into the cabin. He sent Walter and Clifton outside to play. Doctor Tennison asked Emile some questions then checked her with a stethoscope, first Emile's heart, and then he listened for the baby. He pressed on her stomach, thought a moment, and then spoke.

"First, your baby has a strong heartbeat."

Emile attempted to smile.

"I don't believe you are trying to miscarry, but your stomach is rather nervous. I think you ate something that didn't agree with you, or ate too much. Good rest should put you back in the saddle-er- wagon."

They all laughed.

"But, Mrs., you don't leave this cabin until you feel up to it." Doctor Tennison made the order clear.

Emile slept the rest of the afternoon and through the night.

"Farmer, I'm eager and ready to be on the road," she declared the next morning, "and I feel wonderful and rested."

As they left Winona, Farmer remembered the words Dr. Tennison spoke to him in private.

"Heat and cold and bouncing in your wagon are hurting your Mrs. She is tough, of fine pioneer stock, but there is a limit to how much she can take. You must slow down and take frequent breaks."

By afternoon they knew they must be close to Flagstaff. Dust was constant from frequent cars passing in both directions. They had not found any road turning off to the north. When a gasoline station appeared after a curve in the road, Farmer halted the team next to the pump. A young man stepped out of the building. His face held a mischievous look. He laughed as he motioned towards Sunset and Wind.

"Want me to fill their tanks? Looks like two horse-power," then seeing Dusty, "Nope, three!"

Farmer wasn't in the mood for jokes. The Texan in him thought he'd had enough comments about his team and wagon.

"Lookin' fer the road thet's headin' north to Utah. Ain't seen one, so's it must be ahead o' us?"

The attendant's face went straight when he saw the Trevors' were not amused.

"You missed it."

"Missed it!"

"Yep, nearly a mile back."

"We saw no road goin' north."

"Don't go north. Remember the log house on your right? Just before a bridge over a creek down below. A long bridge."

"Yes," Farmer nodded his head.

"By the log house, the trail goes to your left, coming from the direction you were. Anyway, the trail goes south, down into the creek bottom, then turns north—under the bridge. Follows the creek for a piece. That's the road you're lookin' for."

The Trevors backtracked and found the road they had missed. Clear water bubbled over rocks in the creek bottom, moving ever upward into higher elevation than even Flagstaff. Snowcapped peaks loomed above them, and pine and fir trees were tall and the forest dense. The noise of the water sounded like wind blowing in the trees. Once the Trevors tasted the crystal cold water, they seemed unable to satisfy their thirst.

Over the tops of the trees Farmer could see dark storm clouds hanging onto the high peaks. In the shadows now from the setting sun, Farmer watched for a campsite, close enough to get water, but high enough to be safe if the creek should flood.

Farmer, Walter, Clifton and Scout gathered plenty of wood to last the night. Already, the chill of the night air went through their coats. Campfire built, the horses tied in a patch of grass nearby, all of them were eager to close in around the fire's warmth.

After supper they talked and laughed. They sang songs that Walter and Clifton could join in. Hymns came to mind and they sang from their hearts to a loving God beyond a million twinkling stars overhead. They felt a peace in that place different from any other they had ever experienced.

Emile tucked their sleepy boys under a pile of blankets inside the canvas tent. She helped them "Thank God for Grandmas and Grandpas, Aunts and Uncles, and please protect us while we sleep."

Farmer had finished piling more wood on the campfire when Emile re-joined him. She had traveled well that day and appeared strong. She had a way of putting her hand inside his arm and snuggling up close next to him. This always sent a thrill through his whole being and melted his heart.

"I wish this evening could go on forever," Emile murmured. "It is so beautiful out here."

They spoke of the future, their dreams, their children—Walter and Clifton—the one to come. They talked of the adventures of the trip, of their love for each other. A soft falling snow drove them into the shelter of the tent and under the blankets.

Something startled Farmer out of a sound sleep. He looked out from the tent. The campfire flickered with a low flame trying desperately to stay alive. The snow had stopped.

Farmer listened! Nothing. . No! The horses were moving around. He heard a muffled neigh.

The still night air was split apart by a shriek that sounded like a woman in terrible agony.

Emile screamed and sat straight up—reaching to find Farmer.

"What was—" Farmer placed his fingers on her lips.

Walter struggled to get up, and Clifton began crying.

"Keep them quiet!" Farmer instructed Emile. He pulled his boots on, grabbed the rifle, and struggled to light a lantern. He could hear the horses straining at the ropes and pawing the ground.

The piercing shriek, again—even closer!

Farmer heard Emile scream out in fear from inside the tent. Both boys were crying loudly.

Farmer reached the horses. Their eyes were wide with fright, hot breaths blowing rapidly in the cold air. They were pulling against the ropes and pounding the ground. Dusty reared up pawing the air. Farmer stepped a few paces in the direction the horses were looking, placed the lantern on the ground, stepped back and raised his rifle into ready position—straining to look into the dark woods.

He caught the flash of two red eyes.

"Crack!" He fired at the eyes.

Emile screamed again!

"Crack!" Another shot.

"Crack, crack." Farmer fired twice more towards a sound he heard. He scooped up the lantern holding it high and walking to where he had seen the eyes. His rifle ready—but he found nothing. He moved deeper into the trees in the direction he fired last. In the light layer of snow he could see giant cat tracks.

He left the lantern near the horses, while he went back to build up the fire. Emile joined him soon by the campfire.

"I have never heard such a sound! Farmer, what was it?"

"Well, I reckon that mountain lion escaped from Two Guns an' followed us all the way up here," Farmer remarked in a slow Texas drawl.

"Farmer Trevor! This is certainly no time to make fun! I've never been so scared in all my life!"

"Wasn't meanin' no harm. Just a checkin' to see if Scout was doing his job o' warnin' us. Ya know, Emile, that dang dog didn't bark once."

Emile stared at him, then burst out laughing!

CHAPTER 34
HENRY WILD EAGLE

The road, which degenerated into no more than wagon ruts descended down the north slopes leaving the snowcapped mountains behind. The forest thinned until it gave way to desert again. The map of Arizona from Benjamin revealed they would be on the Navaho Indian Reservation, but little else. The marked roads on the map were now sketchy, showing sections with no road at all; however, an old timer in Winona had insisted the road went all the way through to Salt Lake City.

Farmer remembered Doctor Tennison's orders and tried to go slower and take more breaks.

"Farmer Trevor, this young'n will be born in a chuck wagon if you don't move us along!" Emile blurted out in exasperation.

Farmer was feeling frustration as well. Settlements were few and small, and it had been three days since any car passed them. Sometimes the wagon trail went off into the desert in several directions, and Farmer didn't know which one to take. Time was lost in back tracking, the desert heat was cruel and the water supply was approaching the critical level.

"Is there a town soon?" Emile asked hopefully.

"The map shore don't show none," Farmer snapped looking at the now well-worn map.

"It's been four days since the last one," she said nervously, her eyes searching the horizon ahead.

"I reckon we best be careful o' our water. There sure ain't none out here," Farmer remarked uneasily.

That afternoon a dust storm came up quickly. Farmer covered the front of the wagon. After he covered the horses' heads to protect their eyes and noses, he joined Emile and the boys. They huddled inside the wagon until the storm passed.

Next day yielded no settlement or any sign of water. That night amongst coyote yaps and howls, Farmer quietly asked God for help and protection for his family.

As the chuck wagon lurched ahead the next morning to begin another day's journey, Emile spoke, seemingly on the verge of tears.

"I've lost count of the days. I don't know which day it is, or month, or where on earth we are!"

"I don't rightly know myself, Emile. Just know the nearest place to cross the Colorado River is this here Marble Canyon. We gotta find that!"

Five hours more and the road forked. There were no signs.

Farmer breathed a prayer and felt he should go left. Yet as he studied the two roads, the one left hardly seemed used and appeared to disappear into the rock and sand. The road to the right was well worn and led towards a pass in the distant hills. Farmer chose that road, upon which they plodded along the rest of the day and most of the next.

Walter and Clifton were ahead of them when they pointed back down the road.

"We see dust a comin'!" Walter yelled.

Farmer was relieved to see a car approaching from the rear. It caught up to them in about fifteen minutes, pulled alongside the wagon and stopped—choking dirt filled the air, and then cleared.

"You all look lost or something," the driver laughed. He and his companions peered through dust-covered goggles. Teeth showed white on dirty faces.

"We're headed towards Marble Canyon," Farmer motioned ahead.

"Marble Canyon!" The driver laughed again joined by the rest of the occupants in his car.

"You are lost, pardner. This road turns northeast up ahead. You remember the road divided miles ago?"

"Yes," Farmer answered.

"Shoulda taken the other road."

Farmer felt the hot flush of embarrassment and anger as he turned the wagon around. They had lost a whole day's travel. Emile tried to heal his wounded pride with, "I picked this road too, Farmer."

As the sun dropped below the western horizon, the Trevors set up camp in the shelter of some large boulders. Farmer and the boys gathered dead branches from desert bushes and built a campfire while Emile busied herself with fixing supper.

"How's our water supply, Farmer—Oh!"

Farmer was startled by Emile's cry and looked up to see an Indian man's face outlined in the fire's glow. Farmer jumped to his feet and reached for his rifle.

"We don't want no fight with ya!" Farmer stammered.

The Indian's keen eyes surveyed the campsite in one sweep.

"If I came to kill, I would already be done," the man spoke in good English that hinted of an education. He looked eagerly at the meal Emile was ready to set over the fire.

"I am Henry Wild Eagle. I have been walking with my family crossing this desert. We have no food or water. . ."

Farmer gripped his rifle tighter, remembering what had happened in Gallop. He slowly cocked the hammer back.

"Oh, where are they?" Emile asked looking into the darkness. "Do have them come!"

Farmer wanted this Indian gone. He was just there to take anything he got his hands on.

"I don't –" before Farmer could finish Henry Wild Eagle motioned.

Farmer raised his rifle. What if braves surrounded the wagon! He recalled the massacre of the pioneers at Two Guns. He heard the crunch of footsteps and a slender Indian woman and two children stepped into the light. Emile was already pouring some water.

The Wild Eagles tried to be reserved, but thirst drove them past that. Henry had to slow the children down, so they would not make themselves sick.

"Oh you poor dears!" Emile exclaimed, pouring more water from the dipper she held.

"Emile, we don't have much left ourselves!" Farmer objected to her generosity.

"This is my wife, Hettie. These are our children, Curtis and Omney."

"I am Farmer Trevor—wife, Emile, an' our boys –" Farmer stopped and smiled to see both of his sons had tucked toy pistols in their pockets, "Walter and Clifton."

"And one more in here!" Emile patted her tummy.

Henry motioned and the Wild Eagles disappeared into the blackness of the desert night.

"What the tarnation they be doin'?" Farmer took off his hat and ran his fingers through his hair.

Soon the Indians returned with armloads of sticks for the campfire. After two more loads they proceeded to clear rocks away from the campground. Emile hurried to finish supper, and Hettie tried to help.

Curtis and Omney looked to be eight or nine. They sat quietly gazing into the fire and watched Walter and Clifton with curiosity and humor. They played with Scout when he came near to them.

At supper the Wild Eagles did not appear as savages, but ate with dignity and manners. Their hunger quickly drove dignity and manners from their intentions and they devoured their food.

"We—thank you," Henry spoke softly. "We will go now."

"Wait!" Farmer's curiosity about this family had replaced any fear of them.

"Where we come from, ifen ya eat at our table, we expect ya ta spend the night in our home. I reckon this is our home fer tonight, and I'm a bidden ya ta stay with us and share our fire."

Henry studied Farmer with an intense gaze for a moment, and then nodded his head.

Emile invited Hettie to the back end of the wagon where she hung a lantern and they cleaned up dishes.

"Are ya Navaho?" Farmer asked Henry.

"Crow," Wild Eagle answered proudly.

"Where do the Crow live?" Farmer ventured.

"Montana."

"Dang, ya walked all the way from Montana! Or air ya headed there?"

"We left the Crow Reservation many days ago. There remained no freedom for my people. I saw a picture once of an eagle with its leg tied to a stick upon which it perched. Henry Wild Eagle was becoming that Eagle. Word has told us of mountain valleys in California. We are going there!"

Farmer reflected on what Henry had said before he spoke.

"I too felt my feet were tied ta my Pa's farm. I reckon I'd dreamed of findin' my place—an' freedom fer as long as I can recollect. Seems strange—ya runnin'from the reservation in Montana to start fresh in California—an' me runnin' from my farm in Texas ta raise cattle in Oregon."

The two men sat in silence for a long time. The only movement was the times Farmer stoked the campfire with more branches.

Henry was the next to say something.

"You talk to your God about the food we ate?"

"I thanked Him for it."

"I went to a mission school for three seasons."

"Ya learn bout Jesus Christ?"

"Did not understand the Man. He seemed to be strong, but when His enemies came—He did not fight them. They killed Him, and all His friends ran away."

Farmer thought for some time and breathed a prayer for words and wisdom from God.

"Henry, let me tell ya a story," Farmer began. "There was once a powerful landowner. He had an only Son who He loved more powerful 'an anything. His place had mountains an' trees—clear, fast runnin' streams, flowers, birds an' animals. Now this landowner had lots o' workers, but one day an evil worker talked some o' the others ta try an' take over an' make him the new landowner. There was a big battle an' the evil workers got throwed out. By and by, the landowner had a boy and girl come live there. He loved them powerful too, and He took good care o them. One day the evil worker slipped in an' talked the boy an' girl into sidin' with him. Now, there was a law thet ifen they sided with the evil worker they'd get throwed out too. But the law also said the boy an' girl could be bought back—ifen someone special paid fer them with their life. Let me ask ya a serious question, Henry. Ifen ya had ta give a life to buy back that boy an' girl—which would be the harder life ta give—yers or Curtis?"

Henry seemed to struggle with the question for a long time.

"Curtis Wild Eagle!" he grunted.

"Thet's what God did, Henry. I an' Emile, was thet boy an' girl. You an' Hettie—ya was that boy an' girl. God sent His Son, Jesus Christ, to die and buy us back. Thet's why He didn't fight. He loves ya an' gives ya real freedom."

Henry jerked like a lightning bolt had struck him!

"Can ya read?"

"Yes."

"Ya own a Bible?"

"No. It is a white man's book about a white man's God."

"Where'd ya get that notion, Henry Wild Eagle? Why, I reckon Jesus was more Indian than white where He lived."

Farmer dug out a Bible from the wagon and handed it to Henry.

"Promise me ya all will read this," Farmer requested.

Henry tried to turn down the Bible.

"It's a gift ta ya! Promise on yer word ya'll a read it!" Farmer insisted.

Henry nodded and took the book.

In bed, suspicions begin to fill Farmer's thoughts. He had visions of the Wild Eagles cutting their throats—stealing the horses—stealing food and wagon—leaving them stranded in the desert—or dead!

His suspicions exploded into fear that gripped his heart like an iron vice. He got up, rifle in hand, and slipped into the rocks out of sight, but able to see. Every so often he would build up the fire.

He vowed to keep guard all night, but finally sleep overtook him. He was startled awake by the sun and realized there was a portion of the night he could not account for.

He stumbled out of the rocks—expecting the worse—but found Emile and the boys sleeping peaceful. The Wild Eagles were gone—touching nothing of the Trevors' except maybe their lives.

CHAPTER 35
THE COLORADO RIVER

That morning Farmer and Emile scanned the desert floor for any sign of the Wild Eagles. Emile felt compassion for them.

"Walking such a distance in a harsh land!" she chided Farmer when he shared the suspicions he had the night before.

"Shame on you, Farmer Trevor! It's not fair to judge a whole race because of the deeds of a few." Farmer knew she was right.

Later in the morning, while the horses rested, Walter and Clifton came up to their Ma and Pa. Walter wouldn't look up and seemed to be searching for a way to say something. He walked away, but in a few minutes came back.

"What ya want, son?" Farmer finally asked.

Walter stammered—then rattled off the words as fast as he could speak.

"Gave my airplane to Curtis an' Omney!"

Farmer wanted to burst out laughing, but he held a straight face. He saw Emile turn her head.

"Got my airplane." Clifton added cheerfully.

"Why'd ya do thet?" Farmer queried.

"They had no toys," Walter spoke sadly, "'sides, I seen ya give their Pa yer Bible."

"Oh!" Emile pulled Walter into her arms, and Farmer felt a surge of pride in his children. He realized this trip was building qualities in them that would shape their lives later.

"Reckon I'm right proud ya did that, Walter."

"Shoulda given my airplane," Clifton mumbled.

"An' just what toys would you boys have?" Emile laughed as she pulled Clifton next to Walter and squeezed them tight.

It took the rest of the day to return to the fork in the road.

"Shoulda listened ta the Lord 'stead tryin' ta figure it out myself," Farmer thought. This miscalculation cost them two days.

"But ifen we'd gone the other road, would never seen the Wild Eagles. Reckon God had it all figured out after all," he reasoned.

Next morning when Farmer gave some water to the horses he realized how critically low their supply was. He determined to drink only a few sips and prayed they come to the Colorado River soon.

The wagon slowly creaked along. As the day burned on, the hours felt like days. The sun bore into them with its blistering heat. Farmer felt his lips parch, and Emile refused water and passed it to Walter and Clifton. The heat became unbearable by mid-afternoon. Farmer stopped and put the horses in the shade of the wagon. He insisted Emile drink some of the last of the water. Watching her he saw signs that she was weakening.

The temperature dropped as the sun did, and the thirsty pioneers made the best of the remaining light. But when darkness fell and camp was made there still was no sign of the river. He could hear the restlessness of the horses and knew they could not continue long without water.

Farmer awoke in the middle of the night feeling the heavy weight of responsibility for Emile, the boys, the unborn baby, the horses and Scout. An icy grip of panic swept over him. He tried to shake it off, but it clung to him as in a life or death hold! Only, as he recalled every time on the trip when God had provided and protected them, was that icy grip broken and Farmer slept.

The sun was straight overhead that day when Farmer thought they could go no farther. His mouth, dry as the desert sand, now burned, and he knew Emile and the boys suffered as well. Sand caked on their clothes soaked in places from sweat.

Farmer pulled the reins, but the horses threw their heads and broke into a trot. He pulled back, but they fought him and leaped ahead into a run.

"Oh Farmer, what are they doing?" Emile cried out as she held to the wagon seat.

The trail went through a cut in the rocks and when the wagon rattled out the other side, the Colorado River shown in the bright sun below them.

"The River, Emile! The River! They smelled the water!" Farmer shouted and they all sent up a cheer!

There was no slowing the horses until the road reached the water. He had to fight Sunset and Wind back to keep them from drinking too much too fast. Dusty strained against his rope at the rear of the wagon. Emile already had gathered cloth to strain the muddy water into containers. They resisted gulping down the cool water and took sips, until they cooled off.

Farmer took Walter, Clifton and Scout to locate a suitable campsite. Finding one, he moved the wagon and set up camp. Chores completed, he pulled the boys into the river and splashed water on them. Scout bounded in after them. He left them at the rivers edge, laughing and popping the water with their hands while he went for Emile.

She shook her head, holding up her hands and backing up. Farmer grabbed her up in his arms and carried her to the water. She kicked, protested and struggled against Farmer's strong grip. By the time he sat her down in the river, she was laughing so hard she couldn't stand up.

"You're dreadful!" she sputtered, throwing water at him.

The Trevors played and swam the rest of the afternoon in the Colorado River.

CHAPTER 36
A SHADOW OF DEATH

The straining cloth turned dark red from the sandstone silt in the river water. Emile poured water through the cloth several times to clear the water as much as possible. However, they were relieved just to be able to refill all their water containers.

A flat ferry barge with boarded up sides was the means of fording the river. A cable spanning the water kept the barge from drifting down into the mouth of Marble Canyon.

Farmer had to stand with a nervous Sunset and Wind on the barge to hold them steady. Dusty tied to the rear of the wagon planted his mustang hooves steadfast to the barge floor and never moved.

The town of Marble Canyon consisted of three sun bleached and sand worn buildings, the larger of which was a poorly stocked General Store. Farmer purchased a few needed items, and Emile brought her calendar book up to date. She was shocked to discover it was the fifth of June. It had taken eight days to come from Flagstaff.

"I lost track of time out in the desert," she admitted while Farmer assisted her up into the wagon.

The road out of the Colorado River basin climbed back up onto the high Arizona plain. The desert floor rose into the Kalbob Mountains. The road here was carved out of the sides of the mountain, jagged and steep in places, but the days were not as hot, which the travelers thanked God for.

Passing cars were very sparse. They went two days without seeing any living soul, and four days before they came to the small settlement of Jacob Lake, high in the mountain range. There was food and running water so Farmer figured this would strengthen all of them.

Now the road descended down the other side of the range and out onto the desert floor again. Farmer grew aware that Emile had become more and more frail. She never mentioned it or complained—she just held tight to the wagon seat, but she walked less.

This awareness made him more conscious of rocks and ruts, for it seemed the jolting of the wagon was more severe. He tried to slow the pace down and steer the team over the smoothest parts of the road, if there were any.

Days drug on in the brutal Arizona sun. Farmer became alarmed one morning when he awoke to find Emile not in bed. He found her out in the desert brush, vomiting.

"We hafta find us a doctor in the next town, Emile," he told her.

"I'm alright now," she insisted.

They did not travel until that afternoon, and the next day they pulled into Fredonia.

"We ain't got no doctor here," they were told upon inquiring. "Closest one is in Hurricane or St. George."

"Which ya reckon is closer?" Farmer asked.

"Hurricane be closer. An' you have a choice of how you're getting there. On the west end of town the road separates. South goes through the Injun reservation. North goes through Zion Park."

"Which route ya reckon is quicker?"

"North across the park is less miles—prettier too."

"Not interested in pretty—just gettin' my wife ta a doctor," Farmer spoke with irritation.

Next day Emile was too weak to set on the wagon seat. Farmer made a thick cushion of blankets on the wagon floor so Emile could lie down. He kept Walter, Clifton and Scout away from her and riding Dusty as long a duration as the boys would stay in the saddle or run alongside the wagon with Scout.

"Look, Emile, Utah!" Farmer pointed out a small sign that marked the state line. Emile struggled up to peer over the wagon side—then collapsed.

That night, something pulled Farmer out of his deep sleep to slow wakefulness. He could feel Emile's body shaking.

"Emile? Emile, air ya—alright?"

He heard her sob.

"Emile, what is it?"

She turned towards him.

"Oh Farmer, I am so afraid I'm going to lose our baby!"

"Now why would ya be thinkin' thet?"

"I'm hurting—like when you have labor pains—and I've been bleeding some."

Farmer gathered her in his arms and held her. Emile's body shook as she cried quietly. Farmer tried to console and comfort her, but the words seemed empty and unable to convey any meaning. Just holding her close and gently patting her back and face spoke what his words could not.

When sleep came back, Farmer tucked the blanket around her. He got up and walked out on the desert. The night was mild. Stars were brilliant across the dark sky. He could barely make out the ragged rock formations to his right.

For the first time in his married life, a sickening sense of fear lay hold of his heart and enclosed it in ice. What if it was her time, or the baby's time? In the hush of the desert night, under silent stars, Farmer wrestled with—was Emile and the baby God's to take or Farmer's to keep? In his heart, he knew he must surrender them to a loving and merciful Heavenly Father—but everything in him cried out to hold on! He finally fell to his knees in the gravel, crying out, "Lord, don't rightly know how I'd make it without Emile—but she's yer daughter. An' the baby is yers as well. Ifen ya've decided ta take them ta where ya air—." Farmer couldn't find the words, but his heart surrendered.

Travel was slow the next two days and there was no relief from the cruel sun. Farmer kept a cool wet cloth on Emile's face and neck. She drank water, but had not eaten for some time.

"Didn't reckon my cookin' was thet bad!" he tried to joke, but Emile was expressionless.

Zion National Park displayed a majestic kind of beauty. It lifted one's thoughts towards God. Farmer was vaguely aware of what he was seeing. His thoughts were fixed on Emile. She seemed to be slipping away, and Farmer felt helpless to know what to do. The road went on and on winding through canyons. Would they never get to Hurricane? Would they be too late? Waves of panic washed over him. He pleaded to God to spare Emile and the child. He began to regret ever making this fool trip. His Pa was right! He was a chaser of dreams. What a horrible price to pay—the life of your wife and baby over a dream.

It was midmorning on Wednesday, June 17, 1925, when the chuck wagon came out onto the flat plain, upon which the community of Hurricane sat.

Off to the left of the road, glimpses of the Virgin River far down in a gorge, could be seen. Reaching the town, Farmer immediately set out to locate a doctor. Two women directed him to a house on the next block.

A distinguished, serious faced man came to the door, and Farmer described Emile's condition.

"Is your family Mormon? This is a Mormon settlement, and I only serve our own kind."

"I'm a God fearin' Christian," Farmer retorted.

He turned to the wagon to fetch his rifle. He would not tolerate such nonsense.

"There is a mid-wife who is very good with expecting mothers," the doctor hastened to add. "She will help you. Come! She is near. I will take you."

The doctor led them down streets of Hurricane past houses to a nicely painted two-story home. A small white fence surrounded the property.

"Emile, we got ya some help," Farmer rubbed her shoulder and lightly patted her face. She did not respond.

"Oh Emile, don't leave me," he cried aloud in desperation.

A robust woman greeted the doctor at her door with a warm smile. They were out of Farmer's hearing.

"Oh dear! O dear!" she ran through the gate in her fence and came to the wagon—stretching to reach in to feel of Emile's face. She turned and motioned to the doctor to come.

"Hurry! Hurry! Help us get her inside!"

"Ruth, these people are not Mormon."

"Don't be ridiculous, Jacob. Hurry, or I'll tell the authorities you have ten wives hidden, and I know where they are. Come on, help her up."

The doctor did not comment, but he complied with the mid- wife's order. Farmer could see his neck turn scarlet and his jaw set. He left as soon as Emile was in the house.

"You keep those lads occupied—you take them in the backyard—go on now while I tend your wife," she shoved them out the back door.

Farmer paced back and forth, while the boys made up games and played. He prayed with all his might knowing full well that Emile's life—or the baby's, or both hung in the balance. After what seemed ages, the woman came out. She motioned him inside and sat him at a small table in the kitchen.

"Your misses is trying to miscarry her baby. I gave her something to settle that down. She has given out more liquids than she is taken in. The sun and heat got her down—and the bouncing of your wagon. But all that to say—I think they will both get past this. The baby kicked hard, and your wife is a fighter."

Emotion welled up filling Farmer's heart. He tried to contain himself. His lip quivered and tears filled his eyes, spilling down his cheeks.

"Thank ya!" he managed to say.

The mid-wife studied his face carefully for some time.

When she spoke, her pushy edge had softened.

"What are your names?"

"Farmer and Emile Trevor. Walter and Clifton air in yer backyard. Sounds as ifen they got their dog Scout outa the wagon."

"I'm Ruth Riggs. Where you folks from, and where you traveling to?"

"Hail from Texas, and we air goin' ta prove our homestead in Oregon."

"In a wagon . . .," Ruth spoke thoughtfully.

"Yes'm, in a wagon," Farmer echoed.

Farmer thought not to spend money on a cabin that night, so he and the boys made camp in a small tree lined draw. He was amazed it still ran a small stream. The summer sun should have dried it up by now. There was abundant grass here for the horses, and plenty of firewood. The Riggs' house was an easy walk from the campsite.

Next morning the three of them ate breakfast and bathed. Farmer could hardly wait to see Emile.

"Look at you!" Riggs greeted them at the door. "All fancied up. Emile is much better this morning. Had some appetite too, she did!"

As long as he had known her, Emile had different kinds of smiles, but there was one reserved for Farmer alone. That's the one he saw when he walked into the room! Walter and Clifton ran to her side and crawled up on the bed to sit by her. Farmer was so pleased to see her better.

"Emile Trevor, ya plumb had the liver scared outa me!" he blurted out.

Ruth Riggs gave them time alone before she entered the room.

"Now doesn't she look pretty this mornin'? Got some color in her face again. I could hear your little baby's heart beating strong. Should arrive in November if I figured right. And Farmer, don't get any notion of going anywhere—least for a week or two. Emile has got to rest and regain her strength.

CHAPTER 37

HURRICANE

Hurricane was a strange community with a strange name that produced some interesting characters. Each day Farmer nosed around, the more questions popped into his head. The questions peaked his curiosity, until his thoughts were in a whirl wondering about it all. He determined to learn about this place and it's people, seeing as he had spare time while Emile and the baby were on the mend.

Ruth Riggs seemed a good one to start with. The opportunity came on the third day. Emile had fallen asleep, and Ruth offered Farmer a cup of coffee in the kitchen.

Farmer was the kind of man that gave thought to how he would ease into a conversation—like putting a foot into a cold stream, then the other foot. But when actual time came to talk—Farmer usually just spoke what came to mind—like holding your nose and plunging in the water.

"Ruth, got me a heap a questions jus' achin' ta be asked —'bout this place—the people—ya'll," Farmer began.

Mrs. Riggs stared at him a moment and blinked in surprise. Then a smile spread across her face.

"Well get to askin', Farmer!"

"Air ya—one of—a Mormon?"

"Ha!" she laughed. "Little you know. Would I be given ya coffee if I was?"

"Don't know," Farmer replied.

"They won't touch it. Sinful to drink coffee they say. My late husband was a doctor and a Mormon. I was called one because of him—but never really believed—not in my heart. He taught me everything I know about doctorin' and medicine. When he passed away, folks said I lost all my rights if I didn't marry another Mormon."

Ruth smiled thoughtfully, "They came knockin' at my door. They said I should marry and have babies. Well, I decided to help other women give birth and didn't love any of those men—not to marry. They argued love would come, and I ran them all off. Then they tried to run me off, but I'm a stubborn, headstrong woman that refused to budge. That's when the church called Doctor Jacob G. Edwin to be Hurricane's doctor. Ha! And they don't know what to do with me!"

Then she got a sly smile on her face.

"I know too many of their secrets." She whispered.

"Air they thet wicked?" Farmer asked.

"No, of course not! Most of them are good, hardworking honest folks. They care for their families—and their own. Some Elders will be coming around to talk to you about becoming a Mormon."

Farmer thought on that for a while as he sipped his coffee. Finally, he spoke.

"Reckon I don't understand why ya have ta be anything but a Christian."

"Oh, they have an argument for that!"

"Nothin' ta argue. Either ya have the Lord Jesus in yer heart or ya don't. Ya don't argue people into a church, ya tell them about what the son o' God did on the cross fer them."

Farmer studied Ruth's face. She was lost in thought. Her features softened.

"My grandmother told me about that when I was a little girl," she spoke tenderly. "I had forgotten . . ."

"I ain't no prophet, Ruth, an' not always the smartest man, but peers ta me ya had some hard blows in yer life, and Jesus would like ta come in an' make it better."

"I—don't know how!" she searched Farmer's eyes.

"Plumb simple—ya just ask Him. Thet's what I did."

Ruth seemed to pull back. Farmer held out his hand to take hers. She slowly took his hand.

"Ruth, I ain't a preacher, and I don't know fancy words fer prayin'—but will ya pray with yer heart as I pray? Please?"

She nodded her head.

"Our Father, I'm a prayen fer Ruth Riggs. She's had some deep hurts, and I reckon she wants ta heal her heart and soul. We both air sinners, needin' yer mercy. I pray ya help her ta see yer Son on thet awful cross—a dyin' fer her. Help my new friend believe in what ya did there, an' help her ta open up her heart an' ask ya in. An' Lord, I thank ya fer Mrs. Riggs helpin' Emile and the baby. Amen."

Farmer felt Ruth's grip tighten on his hand. When he opened his eyes and looked up, tears were streaming down her cheeks.

"Darn!" she exclaimed in amazement. "Darn!" she exclaimed again shaking her head, laughing and crying at the same time. "Something happened! Farmer, I believe, and I believe He did come—into my heart!"

Now Farmer was the one that was amazed. Ruth's excitement and joy kept overflowing. She was so happy she went in and woke Emile to tell her about it. Then she went out in her backyard, and Farmer saw her through the window, draw Walter and Clifton to her breast and hug them.

"Dang, Lord, ya did a powerful heap o' changin' in Ruth," Farmer said as he watched the transformation take place. He had never seen God's Spirit do a saving work in someone before his very eyes. He had observed change in others in Holt, but it was later—after they had accepted Christ. This was different—and thrilling. He saw it happen. His thoughts drifted to Benjamin. How he longed for his friend to experience what Ruth just had.

The next morning, Farmer made a call on Doctor Edwin. The Doctor was polite, but cool. He did not invite Farmer into his house.

"How is your wife—and the child?" Doctor Edwin asked.

"Doin' right proud. Reckon they will be ready fer travel soon."

"I am glad to hear that. Now, how may I help you, Mr. . er . .?"

"Farmer Trevor's my name. Got a question in my head thet's really been eaten at me an' I reckon I jus' needs ta ask."

"What is it?"

"If ya was the only Doctor in this town, would ya have helped my Emile?"

"I told ya, I only treat those who are Mormon. I would have sent you to Provo."

"Then I reckon we both be in need of forgiveness."

"How is that, Mr. Trevor?"

"Ya fer being willin' to send my wife ta her death—an' me fer being willin' to send ya to yers. I was headed ta get my rifle."

Farmer felt his eyes narrow in a hard gaze and calm resolve took over.

"Reckon ya never been married, Doctor Jacob."

"It's Doctor Edwin—and yes, I am married."

"Oh, I ferget—ten times, an' ya wouldn't stand up fer yer wives?"

"Wife! Not to take a life."

"Well, thet's how we're different!"

"I really don't have time to discuss this with an ignorant farmer," the doctor's words cut like one of his scalpels. He retreated inside behind a slammed door.

Farmer had the strong urge to kick the door down and drag Jacob Edwin out into the street and beat those words back into his mouth. He was still fuming when he reached Ruth Riggs' house. Emile knew something was troubling him, but he never told her or Ruth of the conversation with Dr. Edwin.

"We sure got a powerful heap o' God doin' some savin' o' yer soul Ruth, with my first question—but thet was jus' my first," Farmer teased.

"Humm, don't know if I can stand up to a second," Ruth remarked, straight faced. "Better hurry an' ask it while I still have enough daylight to answer."

"Reckon it's two questions. Fer the life o' me, I can't figure out the name Hurricane. Ain't those in the ocean or some place?"

"Named after the Hurricane Cliffs," Ruth answered.

"Well, thet don't make no sense either."

"Ha!" Ruth laughed. "It doesn't."

"An' fer the life o' me, I can't figure where the water comes from. I see fruit orchards, crops, and the stream where I'm campin'—shoulda been dry a month ago. The Virgin River is hundreds o' feet down in a deep gorge."

"Now, that's an easy one, Farmer. A Mormon Elder got the idea years ago to go up the Virgin River to where it's higher than this plateau, where Hurricane is situated. He got workers. They built a canal—tunneled through mountains— built flumes—brought part of the Virgin River into Hurricane. Finished around the turn of the century. We've had canal riders who go horseback the length of the canal to clear rocks and such that fall in and block the water. They ride day or night keeping it open. It is the life of this town."

When Emile was strong enough to join Farmer and the boys at the camp, he took them in the wagon to see the fields and orchards. They were able to see the canal from a Vantage Point. Some afternoons they spent hours looking in the town's shops. They found plenty of folks who were kind and friendly.

"You can look around, but don't you dare leave 'till Emile is well," Ruth warned when Emile left the house to join her husband who was eager to have her back, "or I'll hunt you down and bring you back like bandits!"

One morning, the sky seemed especially blue and Farmer announced, "This be such a beautiful day, let's go have a picnic lunch in Zion Park."

"Oh yes!" Emile squealed and prepared a lunch. Emile had been too sick to see any of the Park, and Farmer realized how much he had missed. He had seen it, but it didn't register in his memory.

They walked slowly hand in hand back into deep caves where water fell from ledges above into emerald pools. Lush hanging gardens bloomed in the canyons. There was majesty in the massive cliff towers, and the Great White Throne that demanded each traveler bow in reverence to the Mighty Creator.

The boys stayed ahead of them, exploring every side trail. They seemed oblivious to the magnificent scene rising in glorious golds, yellows and reds before them. They were content to throw rocks in the pools. Once the boys came running back to them breathless, "Pa, Ma, we saw a deer! It just stood there lookin' at us!"

Three times, two Mormon Elders came to visit the Trevors at their campsite in the draw. Their purpose was to invite the Trevors to become Mormon. Some of their persuading was strong. However, there was something in Farmer's heart that told him to leave their teaching alone. These men were polite, but strictly business, not so loving and kind as Farmer recalled church folks back home.

The third invitation included an offer of some land and help with a house.

"We do take care for our own," one of the men emphasized.

"An' I reckon only yer own," Farmer retorted. "Des thet mean I can have me ten wives?"

Emile snickered.

The Elders stood up to leave. Anger and disgust showed in their faces.

"You'll be leaving Hurricane as soon as your wife is able?" the one asked gruffly.

Farmer took what he said as telling and not asking.

"Certainly aim ta," Farmer drawled.

CHAPTER 38
GREAT SALT FLATS

G ood-byes with Ruth Gibbs were tearful. The two women clung to each other, which deeply moved Farmer. Ruth held both boys and then patted Emile's tummy. When she turned to Farmer, he bolstered himself to retain some semblance of manliness. She held him tightly.

"Thank you, Farmer," she whispered, and Farmer knew exactly what she was thanking him for.

It was on the street through town that his emotions overflowed and Farmer could no longer hold back the tears. They burned his face. He turned his head so that Emile or the boys could not see him.

"It is the Fourth of July—Independence Day," Emile announced, pointing to the flags and banners. "I feel much better and stronger now," she spoke brightly. Her face glowed in the early morning sun.

Farmer found the wagon trail Ruth told him about that cut through a canyon and connected to the main road that came from Los Angeles to Salt Lake City. This shortcut that bypassed St. George would save miles and time.

The California road was well traveled, plus it was summer and America was learning to vacation in their automobiles. Farmer was more aware of the spectacle they must be in a chuck wagon, as drivers and passengers stared or pointed from their passing cars. Hurricane still held a few horse drawn wagons, but they saw none now.

Farmer commented on it one night around the campfire.

"The Mormons call themselves latter day saints—I reckon we air latter day wagon pioneers. Emile, America is growin' big and fast! People air on the move. Ya know, I see em buildin' better roads—a bridge across the Colorado, faster cars—gasoline stations and towns springin' up ta take care o' them. An' we're—you—me—our children air gonna see it, be a part o' it, by golly!"

Emile held his arm with both her hands. Looking up into his face she spoke lovingly, "Farmer, I just want you to be happy. To find where you—we—are to be."

Farmer felt a deep love for her fill his heart. He put his arm around her and held her close.

"Emile, when ya was ailin' so bad—and I was sore afraid, ya might go on home, I found out thet my dreams—they was all empty if ya wasn't gonna be there."

The road to Salt Lake City was scattered with many settlements. They were able to find water and feed for the horses. The landscape afforded a unique natural beauty as well as ample campsites. Some nights they camped near other travelers.

Farmer used those occasions to gather information as to the best route—across the Great Salt Flat or up into Idaho. He found no traveler who had actually crossed the Salt Valley—but all agreed it was by far the shorter way.

Farmer discussed this with Emile, and voiced his concerns that the Salt Flat might prove too much for her.

"I believe I can make it, my dear husband. Besides it cannot be worse than the deserts we have ridden across!"

"Well, God has the final say so," Farmer concluded the matter for them.

Having so many travelers on the road made the time pass more quickly. Sixteen days after leaving Hurricane, the latter day pioneers rolled into Salt Lake City.

"Emile, we needs ta decide which way ta go," Farmer mentioned when they settled in the cabin they had taken for the night. "I'm a thinkin' ta go north inta Idaho and then west would be easier fer ya—an maybe safer," he went on.

Emile gave a half laugh. "When have we sought to find a safe or easier direction on our travel, Farmer? What is the Lord telling you?"

"Not sure He's been tellin' me which way. Like He ain't sayin'."

"Two weeks was wasted in Hurricane while I lay in bed getting well. We must take the shorter-quicker way. We must cross the salt desert!"

"Yer restin' time wasn't a waste," Farmer protested. "I don't want ya an' the baby ta get down again—I worry 'bout thet!"

Emile drew close to Farmer looking deep into his eyes. She smiled sweetly.

"I trust you, my love, to take care of us."

Her words made his responsibility for them even heavier, but in that instant he knew he would give his life to protect them if need be. The next morning they struck out into the white sea.

By noon their eyes burned and watered from the brightness of the sun reflecting off the salt. He stopped the wagon.

"I'm a thinkin'," he talked while he began setting up the tent canvas. "Look at this road—straight and smooth ta those distant mountains which I reckon ta be Nevada. The horses can pull easy, we can cross this flat pretty quick like, but not in the blindin' sun. We can hang a lantern, like the lights on the cars. We'll sleep in the day ta pertect our eyes, and anyways the nights air cooler! The lantern lets us see the road."

And that is how they crossed the Great Salt Flat.

CHAPTER 39
STUTZ BEARCAT

As the sun rose on the fifth day in the Salt Flat, Farmer halted the team. Emile and the boys had fallen asleep. He tied the horses against the shade side of the wagon and gave them some water.

"We've made good," he spoke to them as he rubbed their necks and their faces. "Why ya was near as fast like a automobile—an' not near as noisy!"

He set up the tent and staked it down for the day. The dark ribbon of mountains that stood in contrast to the white salt loomed larger, and Farmer figured to reach the Nevada line before the next dawn. He also noticed an object moving fast in his direction. If it were a car it would be the first in two days.

The closer it approached it changed from a dark speck to a yellow object. Yes, it was a car, and within a few more minutes the roar of its engine could be heard.

Emile poked her head up in the wagon and looked around.

"Air ya dressed fer company?" Farmer drawled.

She sat straight up.

"Heavens!" she declared and retreated back under the canvas cover of the wagon.

By now Walter and Clifton were climbing up on the wagon seat for a better view.

In a few minutes a long yellow car came sliding to a halt along side the wagon. This model was open, except for a windshield. A man in long coat and cap peered at Farmer and the boys through dark goggles. Farmer walked to the car, following on his heels was two curious boys and their dog.

"Fancy this! Seeing you bloaks here abouts. Yes! Yes! You are actors in a western moving picture show! I was so hoping to meet some actors—how absolutely stunning!"

"Nope, reckon we air the real McCoy's—headin' ta Oregon ta start us a cattle ranch."

"Oh!" the man replied. "Do tell, cowboy. Hmmm, Oregon, hmmm."

"I sure like yer automobile!" Walter yelled out to be heard above the engine. "I've never been in one."

"What! You have never ridden in a bloody car. Climb in—come—all of you—come—don't dally!" The man opened the small passenger door, and they piled in on the one seat. The car took off, picking up speed.

"Won the car in a San Francisco card game," the Englishman yelled to be heard. "It's a Stutz Bearcat. I got the speed meter to 75 on the flat. Hang on tight!"

The car leaped ahead in a burst of power. The ground alongside the car became a blur. The road before them came and vanished under the car so fast, Farmer felt lightheaded.

Walter was having the time of his life, but Clifton looked as white as the salt.

Slowing the Stutz down, the driver left the road and sped out across the salt deposits. He spun the car in circles back and forth, around and around in wild hilarious abandonment.

Emile was standing beside the wagon when the British man returned his passengers. Farmer feared his legs would collapse when he stepped out of the car.

"Returning your men, madam, with nary a scratch."

He smiled and tipped his hat. In minutes the Stutz Bearcat was a yellow dot in the eastern sun.

"Did that ride make you ill? You look pale," Emile inquired, studying his face.

"I'll tell ya what made me ill," Farmer answered shaking his head as he pointed to the disappearing car. "He will travel the distance ta Salt Lake City in two hours thet took us four days."

"Pa, we'd be in Oregon already if we had us one of those Bearcats."

"I was scared, Pa!" Clifton revealed.

"Me too!" Farmer laughed, dusting his hat off against his leg.

Chapter 40
ALMOST HEAVEN

Nevada was endless sage-covered rolling hills and long valleys. The days seemed endless, and Farmer felt himself like Walter, 'wish he had one o those Bearcats.'

They had been gone so long Holt Texas seemed a lifetime away. Emile chattered and laughed, and Farmer was thankful how she helped pass the long days. He just wanted to hurry and get to their land, but Emile seemed to be happy wherever they were.

They connected with the Applegate Trail coming out of Idaho. This was a southern route off of the Oregon Trail blazed by the Applegate Family. It had been well traveled by pioneers migrating into Oregon for over two decades— now it again had a wagon on it.

The Trail followed the Humboldt River to Winnemucca, then turned in a northwestern direction across Black Rock Desert. Pioneers on the Applegate Trail considered this a very treacherous part of the journey. Passage of time and the coming of the auto age had not changed this unforgiving piece of ground.

They saw many days and miles of rock and sagebrush. So much that Farmer began to wonder if this was the kind of land the government was giving away and if the trees the letter referred to were the scrubby little juniper he saw stuck among the rock and sage here and there.

They were out of water two days when they came to a place marked on the map as Surprise Valley. A fast running stream flowed under a log bridge. Before they drank, they stood together and "Thanked God!" Farmer was reminded of when God brought forth water from a rock..

Farmer had worn the pages thin and torn most of the maps Benjamin had given them. He did not know what he would have done without them. No map marked some of the route across the Colorado River in Arizona and Utah. Benjamin had the good fortune to find a man who had traveled through there, so Benjamin marked the route the man told him about on the map. Much of the old Applegate Trail was not on the map either, but Benjamin found the route in a history book, so he penciled that out also on the map.

The old trail touched the southern tip of Goose Lake then turned almost due west climbing in elevation to a long, wide valley filled with rich farmland.

Excitement was stirring in their hearts when they pulled off the trail a short distance into a small town called Tulelake. They knew that the Oregon State line was but a stones-throw away. They purchased some food stock they were short out of and were eagerly on to Oregon.

When they reached the border they got off the wagon and jumped with both feet over into the state that was to be home for the Trevors. The next few minutes was a mixture of laughing, crying, shouting, praying, dancing, hugging and kissing until they were spent and fell to the ground.

"Oh look!" Emile pointed south to a majestic snow-capped peak.

"And look!" Farmer nodded to another one with only the tip seen above the range of mountains.

"Thet mountain down there is Mount Shasta, and thet smaller one up there is—where it be? Oh, Mount McLoughlin."

"Do you think we will be able to see them from our place?" Emile asked.

"Reckon we can. . ."

The Applegate Trail crossed over Lost River on a natural stone bridge, just as Benjamin had said. Merrill was the first town in Oregon and farms surrounded it. Crops of wheat, oats, barley and rye were in abundance. They saw many fields of what they found out later were potatoes.

They made camp that night in a beautiful spot along the bank of the Klamath River. As they lay in bed listening to the sound of the running water, Farmer felt an incredible joy and peace.

"We climb over one more mountain pass an' then, oh, Emile, we air almost home." Farmer whispered.

"I'm so happy, " she murmured.

Farmer was up before the sun and by dawn the wagon started the climb into the mountains. The Applegates had named this portion Green Springs, and located somewhere past half way to the top they built a stop where spring water flowed from the side of the mountain. They formed three size tubs out of rocks to hold water for drinking. A sign marked it as Tub Springs. Walter and Clifton were pleased to find a baby size tub, just right for them.

The water was clear and so cold it hurt their teeth. Once they drank some, they wanted more and more. They filled all their containers with this cold fresh water.

Dropping down the other side they left the tall timber stands and now there were scattered small oak trees and brush. The trail was carved out of the side of steep slopes—

nearly straight down into deep canyons. Emile shivered as she peered down from her side of the wagon!

"Oh, do be careful!" Emile held tightly to the seat and then climbed back into the wagon. "I can't look anymore!" she exclaimed.

It was by light of a bright moon that they dropped out onto the floor of a shimmering valley. They made a hasty camp on the outskirts of a quiet little town named Ashland. They were exhausted from a long day's journey, but far too excited to sleep!

Next day, Farmer located a survey office and obtained a more detailed map of their property with the other sections of homestead land. Looking at the map he pointed out several things to Emile and the boys.

"Here's our land—er ranch. Shows a stream called Cold Creek runnin' right here. Ya reckon it be dry? Here's a town not ta far ta get ta it. It be called Douglas Landing."

Two more days of travel out of the Applegate Valley were required to reach their homestead, but nothing could have prepared them for what they would see.

They worked the wagon through groves of pine, fir and cedar trees. When the wagon could go no farther, they walked. They came upon deer grazing in sunlit, grassy meadows. They walked across juniper stands—plenty of grazing land for cattle. They were awe struck by the land's beauty.

Cold Creek was indeed that, tumbling clear and fast over rocks. They followed along the creek bank. The boys attempted to wade, but the water made their feet ache. Walking a ways in both directions, a place where the creek widened was discovered. A grass-covered meadow rising from the waters edge spreading out to tall stately pine captivated them. Wildflowers added a brush of color to the green. They both knew was the place!

Emile clapped her hands in childish glee!

"I reckon we'll build our house right here," Farmer declared, leaping into the air and planting his feet firmly on the spot! He threw his hat high in the air and went to whooping and hollering! Emile ran around behind him.

"The kitchen must be right here so the sunshine fills it in the mornings!"

"And our bedroom here—sheltered from the winter's cold!" Farmer was stepping out the shape. He stopped and looked towards the trees. "And over there, I'll build a barn fer the horses."

The two became so excited over their plans, running and pointing, bubbing over like the creek, finally collapsing in the grass. The boys piled on top, laughing and wrestling.

"Oh Farmer! I can't believe we are finally here," Emile sat up breathless. "It's almost heaven!"

CHAPTER 41

FIRST NIGHT IN THEIR OWN PLACE

Farmer went for the horses and wagon and immediately began to clear a trail into the home site so he could set up camp. A close study of the maps confirmed that the location Farmer and Emile had chosen was close to the north boundary of their section.

The main road from the Applegate Valley, which they had arrived on, followed the west bank of the Shanko River. The government had constructed a bridge across the river near the northern most section of the homesteads. There was a graded road from the bridge across government land that went north and south on the western sides of the homesteads.

The sections resembled stair steps on the map. Sections #1 and #2 were side by side at the top of the map. Below them and side-by-side were sections #3, 4 and 5. Below them side-by-side were #6, 7 and 8. The bottom or southern most sections were #9, the Trevors, #10, 11 and 12. This positioned section 9 near the Shanko River and the government road along its west side. Cold Creek flowing down from a higher elevation angled diagonally through section #8, crossed the northwest tip of #11, the width of #10, cut over the northeast corner of Farmer and Emile's property, the southwest corner of section #6 and dumped into the river. The town of Douglas Landing was a few miles north on the Shanko.

Farmer was able to work the wagon through timber. He cleared brush and some rock to reach the grassy rise on Cold Creek before nightfall. Emile and the boys had waited for him and had a campsite made and fire burning.

Walter ran to his father when the horses and wagon emerged from the trees.

"Pa! Pa! I near caught us some fish for supper!"

That night Farmer listened to the sounds of his wife's breathing next to him, the gentle wind in the trees in tune to the water rippling over rocks and the chirps of crickets. Contentment filled his entire being, as the reality of a dream come true settled into his thoughts. The years of restless yearning, gone. Feet that wanted to go west—stilled.

The Lord could not have given them a more wonderfully, perfect place, and Farmer admitted that the years of waiting—even the difficulties and dangers of the long trip were all worth it. Farmer whispered a simple, from the deepest part of his heart, "Thank you . ." to his Father somewhere out there beyond all the starry sky.

Sleep came sound and peaceful the first night in a place that was their home.

CHAPTER 42
PROGRESS

First thing in the morning, Farmer set about to make a more permanent shelter, and Emile set about to convert a campfire into a kitchen.

He located a large grove of pine—tall and straight, just right for making a log house. He took Sunset and Wind with him to drag logs back. By the end of the day he was so sore he could hardly move. Chopping with his axe was slow and hard work. He felt a time pressure to get a house built. It was August 21st, and Farmer sensed the first snow would not be all that far away.

There was a flurry of activity the next week. The walls of a two-room log cabin slowly took shape. Before Farmer laid the foundation logs, he caught Emile trying to clear brush and rock and smooth the ground where their home would stand.

"I'm not helpless, Farmer! I refuse to set around and watch you work!" Emile made herself understood in no uncertain terms when Farmer told her to 'quit'.

As the walls came up, she busied herself mixing mud to chink gaps between the logs.

"Am I doing this right? I've never done this before."

"Reckon so. I've never made a log house 'fore," he answered with a grin.

Farmer cropped down trees everyday, but progress was slow. He could cut only so many—then there was stripping limbs and dragging the logs to the home site. Farmer worked long hours, hoisting the logs into place by lantern light each night before crawling into bed.

By the end of their first week, necessity drove them to Douglas Landing. Farmer had worn holes in his one pair of gloves as well as his hands—and he sorely needed a good saw. Emile needed some items as well, and she was excited to go to town.

The trip took better than thirty minutes along a tree lined road that followed the bank of the Shanko River. The sun illuminated spots on the road ahead where it streaked through open spaces in the trees. When the timber opened up to a large meadow, they could see buildings ahead.

Douglas Landing was a logging camp that grew into a community. Farmer saw the burners of two lumber mills to his right, situated on the edge of the water. He had seen mills in the Applegate Valley, so he knew what they were. He saw logs in the water.

"Look, Emile, reckon I could get us some logs there fer our house," he laughed.

The town was small. A stand of fir trees grew between the mills and the main road. A gasoline station, café, post office, bank and a U.S. Forest Ranger building stood on the other side of the road.

Three short streets went due west off the main road, and Farmer drove the wagon down all three to see what was there also. The first street was Myrtlewood. Amidst the houses was one marked 'Doctor'. Emile was relieved to discover Douglas Landing had a doctor. The second street was Aspen. This one revealed a tavern and the town's school. Walter and Clifton saw swings near the building, so Farmer and Emile stopped to let the boys swing while they looked the school over. The third street was Peppertree, which was lined on both sides with small houses.

Farmer was pleasantly surprised that such a small town as Douglas Landing had a bank. He left Emile to shop while he went to the bank to open an account with Thomas Redkin's check. He became acquainted with the bank president, Mr. Rollin Graves.

"We have a branch office in Douglas Landing to facilitate the lumber mills. They have grown and their payroll became too large to transport, so—here we are." Mr. Graves responded to Farmer's surprise that he found a bank here. He remembered traveling through larger places that didn't have one.

"You becoming one of our citizens?" the banker asked.

Farmer showed him the official government letter. He described their journey in a chuck wagon, and they had arrived to claim their section of land.

"Ah yes, I have met some of your neighbors," Graves responded warmly. "Welcome to Douglas Landing. You came all that distance with a wife and two children in a wagon you say."

"Yes sir, actually three, as we is expectin' a third this year."

Rollin Graves studied Farmer for a moment as if trying to size him up.

"Well, Mr. Trevor, I must commend you for your courage and determination. That must count for something. Is there some way we can assist you and your family?"

Farmer squared up in his chair, holding his hat in hand.

"Yes sir, I reckon ta ask ya fer some loans against my land."

"The purpose of the loan?"

"We be needin' some buildin' supplies, some money ta get us through the winter, an' I would sure nuff like ta get me a car, er I met a fella with a pickup truck in New Mexico. Thet would be right handy. Next spring I aim ta start a herd of cattle."

"I see . . . You would pay the note from the cattle sales?"

"Yes, sir."

"The land will be deeded to you if you prove it in five years? Let me think on this Mr. Trevor. I have some ideas, but will need to make telephone calls. Come see me the next time you are in town."

Farmer stood up and extended his hand.

"Thank ya, Mister Graves."

"A Farmer who will be rancher," Rollin smiled, amazed at his own pun.

"Yes, sir!" Farmer answered enthusiastically.

Farmer met Emile and the boys in the General Store. There was a large sign across the front of the building that read, O'Malley's Merchandise."

"Farmer, I just made acquaintance of Molly O'Malley! She and her husband Michael own this store."

Molly came down an isle to shake Farmer's hand with a yank. She was a strong woman, a few years older than Emile, with a muscular, but still shapely body. Her hair was red that spilled down over a red-splotched face. There was no doubt she was of Irish decent.

"A hearty welcome to ye, Farmer. About time we get more families in Douglas Landing to help tame these rowdy lumberjacks. Me Mister would come out to be polite, but he's a wee bit—under the weather."

Molly covered her mouth and whispered loudly to Emile, "He likes to tip the bottle a wee bit, he does."

She smiled a pained smile that told Farmer her disclosing the information of her husband's drinking was a masked cry for help.

Farmer purchased a good saw, gloves and nails. He inquired about doors and windows. Molly told him they could be ordered—or found in the Applegate.

Next they opened a post office box and wrote hasty notes to family in Texas. Leaving there, Farmer insisted they meet the doctor.

"I wish Mrs. Riggs lived here!" Emile spoke, missing a friend.

"Me too." Farmer sighed, "But she don't."

The Trevors were shocked to be greeted by a dark skinned, black haired man. Farmer guessed he was from India. Something inside Farmer rebelled at the thought of this man examining his wife or children, or delivering their baby.

They introduced themselves, and he escorted them inside the house. The downstairs was made into a small hospital with two rooms for examination. The doctor lived upstairs.

"I am Doctor Sirikin Put," he spoke in a heavy accent.

"I was er—expecting an American," Farmer blurted out in a stammer.

The doctor smiled.

"I am an American. I served as an Army doctor in the great war."

"I don't understand! How did ya—get in a place like this?" Farmer asked bluntly.

"The lumber companies needed a doctor locally. This is dangerous business with many accidents. I was the only doctor they were able to retain." Then Sirikin's expression saddened. "And here was the only place to have me. Many of the families drive to the valley. I can give you a referral to several doctors there."

Farmer's heart burned within him, and he hated the way he thought and acted. Placing his hand on the doctor's shoulder and looking him in the eye, he spoke with humility, "Jesus Christ, whom I follow, surrounded His self with all kinds of different folks, and I reckon He loved 'em all. Would ya examine me first afore my wife Emile an' the baby, an' our sons, Walter and Clifton?"

The next Monday, August 31st, Farmer was sawing down trees when he was startled to hear a car moving through the woods towards their home site. He moved quickly to intercept the driver. He stepped onto the trail to halt a Model T Ford pickup.

"Are you a Mr. Trevor?" the man in the truck asked.

"Reckon I am."

"I'm Sammy Yukon, salesman for the Ford dealer in Applegate. Rollin Graves telephoned me that you are lookin' to buy a pick up. This Model T truck ain't new, but it ain't old neither. Only has four hundred miles on it. Rollin says if ya like it, meet me at the bank at 2:00 o'clock tomorrow, and he'll give you a loan."

Emile couldn't believe her ears when Farmer told her about it. He couldn't wait for tomorrow!

"When the Lord fixes things up, I reckon thet's fer real progress," he reflected.

CHAPTER 43

VISITORS

F armer was starting a fire in preparation to cook break-fast. Emile had just joined him.

"I hear a car—somewhere," he remarked, listening.

"Probably on the road," Emile replied looking in the direction of the sound.

"I think it's closer, on our land."

"Oh! And there it is!" Emile pointed as a car could be seen coming towards them through the trees. Closer, closer, stopping by the Trevors' pickup. The driver stuck his head out the window and shouted.

"Hello, neighbors! We are the Baltmans from Mississippi. We live on Section 6 just north of you. We heard you were here from the great state o' Texas. My misses has 'bout driven me crazy to come—she's been missin' some woman talk."

Farmer and Emile walked towards the car.

"We have salt cured bacon, fresh eggs too and hot baked biscuits. We came to fix breakfast for you and get acquainted." The man's ways were so genuine and honest that Farmer knew instantly this would be a long and loyal friend.

The Baltmans got out of their car. The woman came to Emile.

"I'm Sally; let me give you a welcome hug!" The women hugged each other, and Sally stepped back.

"I'm so glad you all are finally here! We were startin' to worry you wouldn't come."

"I'm Joe; welcome to Oregon!"

Joe grabbed Farmer in a bear hug the same way Benjamin would greet him.

"We air the Trevors. Emile my wife and I am Farmer."

Sally started laughing, "You are gonna have a baby, Emile—You must let me help. I can't wait! When?"

"Sally, for gosh sakes slow down. These good folks will think you haven't seen a soul the summer long."

"Seems as such."

"November, I think," Emile finally got her answer in.

Sally gathered her breakfast fixin's from their car, and she began preparing the bacon and eggs. Farmer noticed she kept glancing towards the car as she and Emile talked.

Joe went to look over the log house. He stepped through the door opening, walking around the inside. Farmer followed him. Joe touched the logs and mud chink. He was thinking.

"Doin' a good job, Farmer," Joe commented.

"Thank ya. It's slow gettin' built."

"Workin' alone, are you?"

"Mostly. Emile's muddin' the cracks."

"I hear the winters are hard here—cold and blowin' snow. Your house don't rightly seem big enough."

"I figure this is ta be 'bout all I can do 'fore the snows come."

It was still early morning when Sally and Emile called the men to come eat. The boys were still asleep so Emile used the opportunity to get to know her neighbor. She discovered the Baltmans had a little girl.

As breakfast waned Farmer thought to ask the Baltmans about the other homesteaders.

"Air we the last of the settlers ta arrive?" Farmer asked.

"No, the folks for Section 8, 11 and 12 are not yet on their land."

"Have you met the homesteaders that are here?" Emile wondered.

"Joe got the government to send a list of the home-steaders," Sally answered, "So we know a little 'bout all of them—and we've gone visitin' some—but we was most waitin' for you folks! Since these ranches are formed outa government lands, we have no way to identify them except by number. Later as we all get settled in, we'll become— The Trevor Ranch—The Baltman Place."

"Please tell us about our other neighbors," Emile's curiosity aroused her interest.

"Well," Joe began, "Section 1 is a man named Gardner Grubb. Not too sociable and lives alone. Section 2 is Junior and Mabelle Springfield from Alabama.

"A black family," Sally added.

"Section 3 is Scott and Catherine McQuirk—Hope I'm sayin' that right. They are Scottish from one of the Great Lakes states, but not sure which. Section 4 is Clarence and Locust-Tree Judd. I don't know where they come from."

"She's a Indian woman," Sally commented.

"Section 5 is Pendelton Green. He came from Chicago. Told me he had a woman there who would marry him in the spring, but she wrote and broke it off. We are Section 6 and in Section 7 are some people you will like—Gordon and Ella May Brooks from Oklahoma."

"They have a two year old son, almost same age as our Rachel," Sally piped up excitedly. "We're gonna have lots of children around here."

"Section 8 is not settled," Joe went on. "Suppose to be a family from New Jersey. You all are Section 9, and Section 10 are an older couple from a German settlement back east, Lyman and Helen Miller."

Sally grew serious. "Helen, poor dear, told me they can't have no young'ns, so she would be a grandmother to all of ours."

"Section 11 is not claimed yet by the Younger family out of Kansas. Olaf Anderson, a Swede is not on Section 12 yet."

Walter and Clifton came crawling out of the tent cover, sleepy eyed, curious about the people around the campfire, and hungry to eat. Sally went on over the boys for some time, talking to them, holding them, asking questions as she dished them up breakfast.

"Fellas, I have someone you will want to meet," Sally told them as she opened the back door of the car and went inside. She came out in a moment with a beautiful little sandy haired girl.

"This is Rachel, and she is almost three."

Rachel rubbed sleepy eyes, then looked at Clifton. "Who's that?" she pointed to him.

"That is Clifton Trevor," her mother told her, "and his older brother is Walter."

When the children played later, Farmer noticed that Walter was unimpressed with Rachel. It was like having two Clifton's around. But she was on Clifton's heels everywhere he went.

Later in the evening Farmer thought about the events of the day, especially their visitors. He thought a lot about Joe and Sally, and the children.

"Emile," he spoke thoughtfully as they worked on their house by the lantern light.

"Yes," she looked at him.

"Ya ever meet someone thet ya just know in yer heart is gonna be a powerful big part in yer life?"

She came over and warmly kissed him. "I felt that the first time I saw you in school, dear," she said softly.

Farmer smiled and took her in his arms.

"Well, I was thinkin' on the Baltmans, but I reckon I like yer thinkin' better."

CHAPTER 44

THE RAISING
OF A HOUSE

S aturday morning, the 19th of September 1925, Farmer
stood with a cup of coffee in his hand, looking at the
log house he was working on, wondering if he was
going to finish before the first snow.

It was a crisp, beautiful autumn morning. Mount
McLaughlin's bare jagged peak stood in the sun above the
surrounding mountains. All but a small patch of snow had
melted off in the summer warmth, but Farmer knew it was
only a matter of time until it would be white again.

Michael O'Malley told him one day that it was not
uncommon for the fall rains to turn to snow in October, so
Farmer felt driven to the point of exhaustion to protect his
family against the winter storms.

He had worked long, strenuous hours. The walls were
almost as high as needed, but the roof would still have to be
completed. He would have so liked a day for something else—
but dare not lose any more precious time. As he planned out
work for the day, it dawned on him there were many cars out
on the road. He was used to hearing logger traffic during the
week, but this was highly unusual for a Saturday.

The sounds became louder to deafening, and suddenly cars and trucks converged into the clearing where the Trevor house stood. Emile came running to him.

"Farmer! What do they want?"

"I have no idée!"

Joe Baltman got out of his car and came towards them, while Sally sat in the back of the car. Joe had a grin that filled his face.

"Been recruitin', Farmer!"

"Recruitin'?" Farmer was puzzled.

"Yep! Been spreadin' the word that we are gonna help you folks build a proper house. We're having an ol' fashioned house raisin'!" Joe spoke with a contagious enthusiasm. "The men will build, and the women folks are fixin' hot meals for lunch and supper. What don't get done today, we'll finish up tomorrow!"

Farmer and Emile were speechless. The pace picked up to a blur. People coming in that Farmer had never seen before.

Molly O'Malley, arms full of cooking pans followed right behind Sally. They both whisked Emile off to the campfire.

Joe took Farmer to the log house where another couple was studying what Farmer had accomplished so far.

Joe introduced them. "Farmer, meet Clarence and Locust-Tree Judd. Clarence told me last week in talkin' that he has built many a house. He can tell us how to build it bigger."

"Bigger?" Farmer questioned in a daze.

"Most certain. This is far too small. We aim to make a home to do you fer years."

"We can cut doors, erect walls from one side, go high enough for a attic room," Clarence pointed out.

"Tell us how to do it, Clarence," Joe responded.

Within minutes the campsite was filled with women and children, and men and some older boys surrounded Farmer at the house.

Joe started naming and pointing. "Here's Gordon Brooks," a dark tanned man in a straw hat reached out a hand. "There's Lyman Miller," a stern faced German waved. "By the corner there, Scott McQuirk and Pendleton Green," both men motioned a "hello."

"Michael O'Malley was gonna come but someone had to run the store."

"Why?" someone commented. "Everybody's gonna be here. They all laughed.

"Anyway," Joe continued, "Molly won out!"

Everyone laughed again, and Molly shouted from the campfire, "I'm a makin' sure ye get to workin'!"

Farmer saw a black couple walking from the trees to join them.

"Here come Junior and Mabelle Springfield," Joe acknowledged them. "Now we best get to work, as we have a lot of it to do."

Instantly Farmer's head cleared with a sense of what was right!

"Hold on—now hold on, I say!" Farmer shouted. Even the women folk grew quiet.

"I'm not sayin' we aren't grateful fer yer wantin' ta help—'cause I reckon we sure is. In fact, I'm so dumbfounded thet the words got stuck in my mouth."

A few laughed nervously and shuffled around.

"But sudden like it hit me what was right, an' there's this question I gotta ask—'cause I haven't been able ta visit ya all in yer places. I needs to know—air all yer homes fixed up as nice as mine will be?"

There was silence.

"Joe?" Farmer pressed.

"Ve gotten here sooner. Ve habben more time to maken our haus," Lyman spoke up.

"Reckon that didn't answer my question. What of the ones still comin'? Scott, did folks here'bouts help ya?"

Scott dropped his head.

"Junior? Gordon? Pendleton? Clarence?"

No one spoke a word.

"What ya all air doin' today is 'bout the kindest and most wonderful thing anybody ever did fer me an' my family—an' I'm right proud to have yer help, 'cause I'm powerful tired. But 'fore a axe or saw touches a tree, I needs yer solemn promise this won't stop today or tomorrow, but we will work together 'till everbodies' place is ever bit as big and fancy as this one will be. I need yer promise!"

After a moment of thought Gordon Brooks spoke up. "Farmer's right. We need to be fair, an' this is a good work we are doin' here. It shouldn't be the last but the first. You got my promise, Farmer."

One by one they pledged to work together to benefit all.

"Hey! Here come the lumberjacks," Joe shouted waving his hat in the air.

"Ye didn't inform me ye gave the loggers a invite," Scott McQuirk slapped Joe on the back.

"How quicker to get trees cut?" Joe laughed.

Two large trucks stopped at the trees, and men with axes and saws piled off. They wore knit hats on top of their heads, bright colored suspenders over plaid woolen shirts, jeans and logger boots. Farmer saw Joe talkin' to a young man, husky in build. Joe pointed to Farmer, and the young man walked towards him.

"You Mr. Trevor?"

Farmer nodded.

"Donald Parrigan." He shook Farmer's hand with a grip that made his eyes water.

"I'm right grateful fer yer help," Farmer said.

"He—er heck, we are as wild as a gunny sack full o' bobcats on the weekends. Gives something to do and stay outa trouble. 'Sides, Zeck won't have me throwin' someone through his front window!" Donald laughed, "Drinkin' and fightin' at Zeck's is mostly what we do—so we're the grateful ones, Mr. Trevor. Now, me an' the boys will only thin the tress so they can re-seed. We won't strip your land."

"Hey, Farmer, can those horses of yours pull logs?" Joe called.

The next two hours were like something happening in a dream. Farmer was amazed at how quickly the lumberjacks fell trees. He kept on the run dragging logs to the house. One trip, Farmer caught Emile watching him. Their eyes told each other without a spoken work how much this day meant to them both, and how pleased they were with what was taking place.

Clarence Judd instructed the laying of logs to line out the expansion of the house. The men shaped and notched logs, and set them in place. Log upon log the walls were raised.

Farmer saw something that bothered him. Locust-Tree Judd and Maybelle Springfield stayed near their husbands. They had spoken little to any of the other women, but did little jobs near where their men worked on the house. And the other women made no effort to approach these two. The more he watched this the more troubling to him it became. When he could stand it no more he went to Locust-Tree and Maybelle.

"Locust-Tree, ya been like a fly on a horses back, an' Maybelle, you're like a flower in yer man's hat, so I reckon I needs ta ask ya a question." Farmer motioned for them to follow him. When they caught up with him he turned to face them.

"Been noticin' ya ain't hed no talkin' ta the other women. Reckon ya don't care fer any o' their company?"

The two women appeared embarrassed.

"We can't fix anything ifen we don't know what ails us."

"I don't think they want my kind around," Maybelle spoke up.

"Well, Maybelle, wasn't any o' yer kind around the town I grew up in, but ya don't look ta be any different then other folks, 'cept ya been out in the sun more. An' ya, Locust-Tree, I met a Indian woman in New Mexico on the Rio Grande, a right polite and smart a women as I'd ever talked ta. Can't speak fer all the woman over there cookin' and fixin' and gabbin', but I never knew my Emile not wantin' anyone around—'cept if they was evil. Air ya evil?" Farmer asked with a twinkle in his eye.

Both women giggled, and answered, "No!"

Farmer grabbed their hands and drug them both into the middle of the other women. Everyone stopped short to see what Farmer was doing.

"We heve us two problems here thet I just can't heve on my ranch, an' I needs yer help."

Locust-Tree and Maybelle pulled back from Farmer shaking their heads in protest.

"These two fine women heve it figured in their heads thet ya all don't want their kind round ya."

Farmer didn't have to say another word. He saw the faces of the women soften and grow tender as they gathered around Maybelle and Locust-Tree and took them into their arms and their hearts.

While the incident with the women was taking place, crew of the Cascade Lumber Co. arrived with boards from their mill to lay floors, and line doors and windows. Farmer found out later the men had gathered money amongst themselves to buy the lumber.

The rest of Saturday and Sunday was filled with hard work, telling jokes, laughing, eating big meals, children underfoot and in mother's arms, the rings of axes from afar, rasp of saws, the cry "Timber", pounding of nails, voices— all these blended into one, and from the midst of the noise and activity rose a beautiful log home.

CHAPTER 45

HOUSEWARMING

B anker Rollin Graves drove out to inspect the house the next week. He was impressed, not only with the speed it was constructed, but also the size. The original two rooms that Farmer had started became the main bedroom and a room for the baby, off that was a large living room and kitchen. Clarence had the women gather stones, and he built a fireplace in the living room. Overhead was a big loft room for Walter and Clifton.

"Did all your neighbors help out?" Mister Graves asked.

"All but Gardner Grubb," Farmer answered.

"Joe told me about your house raising. I told him I could not come, but would try to help other ways. It would appear all of you did quite well without me."

Then turning to Emile, "Mrs. Trevor, I see no stove for cooking and you lack furniture."

Emile looked around, "No, sir, we don't. We are just thankful to the Lord for a roof over our heads—and for each other. I can cook at the fireplace."

Farmer's heart broke for Emile, and he wanted to cry for her. He wished to rush out that very minute and buy everyone of those things for her that Graves had mentioned.

"Farmer, I can increase the loan I gave you for the Model T. Stop by the bank and I'll have it ready—that is if you want it."

Emile was thrilled when Farmer took her into the Applegate Valley to pick out furnishings for their house. They found and bought the latest model wood cooking stove, beds and mats, table and chairs, sofa and extra chairs for the living room. It required three trips to bring all of it back to the house.

At the Post Office, they received their first letters from Texas. The Holts sent some money for the baby and promised a trip to Oregon to see them next summer.

Farmer received a letter from his mother. She wrote that Jacob married Dorothy Shipley and were living in Farmer and Emile's old farmhouse. William and Stella were fine, and they all missed them so very much. There was no mention of his Pa.

Emile kept herself busy now decorating the house, sewing curtains for the windows, which Farmer had installed. She was happy and radiant, and their home now took on a warmness that made it more than just a log house.

Farmer set to work building a corral and shed for the horses. He would have to store hay for the winter. He cut poles for the fences and worked at this several days. One morning, a week and a half after the house was built, Farmer decided to stop work and go see Joe.

Joe came out of a small shed when he heard Farmer drive up. He always seemed glad to see a visitor.

"I sure am glad to see you," Joe greeted him.

"I reckon ya'd welcome the devil his-self if he came callen'," Farmer teased.

"Only if he'd arm wrestle me at the table," Joe laughed, "but I am glad you came. I was planning on payin' you a call. Been thinkin'," Joe paused. "Been thinkin' you an' Emile need to have you a house warming party. Invite all the folks who helped you raise your house."

Farmer laughed! "I declare Joe, ya must dream up ways ta get people together."

"Only if we can eat like we did at your place!" Joe laughed deep from his heart—poking Farmer in fun.

"Well, reckon yer right, Joe. Thet would be a kindly gesture fer sure."

"Already have the day. Sunday, October 4th," Joe spoke straightfaced, then blew out of his mouth as he burst out laughing. "I'll start invitin'!"

"What a wonderful idea," Emile cried joyfully when Farmer told her Joe had figured they needed a house warming, and he'd already picked out the day.

"That gives us a whole three days to get ready." Emile reminded him.

The Saturday before the house warming, Farmer went to Douglas Landing with a list of supplies they needed. Emile was busy baking for the next day. Before he returned home he stopped by the doctor's house.

"Got me a question, doctor," Farmer said when Sirikin opened the door. "Was ya given an invite ta our house raisin'?"

"No."

"Then I'm a givin' ya one fer our house warmin' tomorrow. I'd be right proud ifen ya came."

When Farmer drove across the bridge on his way back home he saw a woman on the side of the road sitting on a suitcase. He stopped.

"Can I help ya get ta—somewhere, Ma'am?"

Farmer saw her wipe her eyes, and when she looked at him, he saw red eyes and wet face.

"I'm tired—and I'm lost—and—I don't know what to do." She broke down in sobs.

Farmer got out of his pickup.

"Let me take ya to my place; Emile can make something warm an' then ya can tell us were ya needs ta be."

Emile made some hot tea and the woman sat near the fire, starring into the flames, silent for a very long time. Finally she spoke slowly.

"My husband Morgan and I left Kansas early this year. We sold everything we had. He had this dream of us on a cattle ranch. We would take a train to San Francisco, then travel up the California Coast to Oregon to claim land we'd been given in a drawing of names. Morgan fell ill in California. We hoped, prayed he would get better. Weeks and weeks passed—he got weaker. He didn't get better."

She sat remembering for a while. Emile sat by her and put her arm around the woman's shoulder and held her tight.

"I ran out of money—had to catch rides—worked here and there. I don't know why I'm here. Yes, I do! It's for Morgan!"

She buried her face in her hands.

"How could he leave me alone? I have a piece of ground with trees on it. What am I going to do with that? I feel so lost!" she sobbed.

"Oh, you poor dear!" Emile cried with her. "You can stay here. Farmer, we can put her in the baby's room for now."

Sunday soon arrived, and the house filled up with guests. It was a time of celebration. Doctor Put also came and spoke politely to the few who spoke to him, mostly loggers. Joe, who usually kept everyone laughing, took second place to Donald Parrigan. It struck Farmer how many of these young men were far from homes and families. Their work was their family. When the afternoon was spent and folks were ready to start leaving, Junior Springfield stood up.

"Jus' wanna say thank ya, Mr. Farmer, fer helpin' my misses. She was sore unhappy and lonesome from leavin' all her family and friends back home. What ya did at yer home raisin' helped her to be happy once more."

"Hear! Hear!" Gordon exclaimed.

"Also wanna say," Junior went on, "Back home in Alabama when we did a house warmin', we asked the Lord to bless the house, an' the masser of the house said a little speech. Could you give us a little speech, Mr. Farmer?"

Everyone cheered and insisted Farmer make a speech. Finally he agreed, and started off slow as he thought of what he would say.

"Well, I reckon of families, the good Lord sure has blessed us, an' what Junior said is true. The Lord gave it an' we for sure want ta ask his blessings on this home and all who are in it an' shall come along later. Amen."

Farmer drew a breath. "I ain't much on talkin'. I try ta think a what ta say, then usually say what I'm a thinkin'—an' thet comes out all different. 'Fore I get ta thankin' ya good friends and neighbors fer yer hard work, I'm sure glad ya came along 'cause I reckon the snow woulda got here 'fore my roof got up. 'Fore I do thet, I want ta introduce ya ta a couple of folks. First is Doctor Sirikin Put, our Douglas Landing doctor. I learned thet he studied medicine in a fine school in England. He was a doctor in the British Army in World War I. He met some Americans who talked him into comin' ta our country ta be doctorin'! He loved our country and dang if he didn't become a citizen. Now when I first met Doctor Put, I had me some trouble with him 'cause he didn't believe things like me. But the Lord let me recall thet we met a doctor in Utah who wouldn't treat my wife 'cause we didn't believe things like him. Got ta thinkin', what's the difference? A doctor won't treat me 'cause I don't think like him, or I won't let a doctor treat me 'cause he don't think like me—reckon both are wrong. An' next, I want ya ta meet Mrs. Beth Younger."

Everyone started looking around.

"Can't see her. Found her on the side o the road yesterday. She be sleepin' from plumb exhaustion. She an' her husband came from Kansas ta homestead Section 11 next ta the Millers. Her husband took ill, and died. She showed up on the road, tired an' lost an' no money. Ta all ya comin' together ta build this house that will keep us warm an' dry in the cold winter, the words thank ya don't seem ta really tell ya what Emile and I feel 'bout what ya'll did—but we really mean it. Thank ya for helpin' us! Now, I'm askin' we all do what we pledged ta do, so Beth Younger can heve the next house warmin'."

CHAPTER 46

IT CAME UPON A MIDNIGHT CLEAR

A fierce winter storm hit the Oregon Mountains with wind and blowing snow before Beth Younger could have her house warming. The ranchers, town folks and lumberjacks gathered to raise her house the weekend before Halloween. Two days later the landscape turned a beautiful white.

The Trevors grew to love and appreciate Beth the short time she stayed with them. The young widow was a petite, attractive, light brown-haired woman. She had grown up on a farm in Kansas and certainly was not afraid of challenge or hard work. She and her late husband had planned to start their family in Oregon. One night she told how she wished she could have at least had Morgan's child, as she cried in Emile's arms.

"I feel so sorry for Beth in her house all thet alone," Emile spoke softly as she looked out the window at the blowing snow.

"Don't reckon she will be lonesome all that long," Farmer remarked. "Ya see how thet Chicago fella,

Pendelton had his eyes on her. Betcha there will be a weddin' next year hereabouts."

"I hope so—for her sake," Emile answered, reflecting, still looking out the window. "Oh Farmer, the snow is so pretty!"

"I'm a thinkin' we won't think so by next spring. I'm a prayin' this will melt off fer the baby comes."

But it didn't. By Halloween another storm followed on the heels of the first, and drifts were several feet high. Farmer became concerned as to how he would get Emile into Douglas Landing should her labor start.

"You may have to be Doctor Trevor and deliver the baby yourself," Emile teased him.

"Ain't no matter ta make fun at, Emile," Farmer snapped. He felt the weight of his wife and baby's health weighing heavy again upon his shoulders.

The first day of November, Emile told him she thought the baby had dropped lower and that she would give birth soon. Farmer started the pickup and tried to drive out to the main road. He got stuck in a snowdrift, which took two hours to dig out and return to the house.

"This will never do," he thought to himself.

November 2nd, Beth trudged through the snow from her house to the Trevors. She carried some of her things.

"I get frightened some times in that house all by myself. Anyway, I thought you could use some help as you get closer to your baby being born," Beth told Emile.

Farmer could tell Emile was relieved to have Beth stay.

Late that afternoon the sky grew gray and more snow set in. Clear blue sky, bright sun reflecting off a fresh layer of snow and cold crisp air greeted them the third morning of November.

Farmer crunched through the frozen drifts to the corral he built for the horses. He was thankful to have had enough time to erect a small shelter where the animals could stay warm and dry. He gave them feed and carried water from Cold Creek. Walter and Clifton came tumbling and laughing out of the door with Scout at their heels. Farmer threw snow at them as they ran towards him.

Farmer prayed that it would warm up enough to melt. The snow got a little watery, but when the sun went down, so did the temperature, and the snow turned to ice.

There was a commotion from Emile and Beth when Farmer came in that evening from checking the horses.

"Her water broke!" Beth exclaimed as she was frantically mopping the floor with a towel.

Emile sat at the kitchen table. Farmer was immediately by her side.

"Is it time?" he asked. "Do you have pains?"

"They started this afternoon, but I reckon—" she stopped to giggle. "I'm even starting to talk like you. I thought I had a stomach ache."

"Emile, you've had two babies!"

"I know—but I forgot what—oh!" she grabbed Farmer's hand tight and her face displayed pain.

Beth herded the two boys up to their loft bedroom. They wanted to know what was happening with Ma.

"The baby is coming!" she explained hurriedly.

Farmer's mind was racing! How could he get Emile to the Doctor! No, that was too risky! He would have to get Dr. Put and bring him to the house. Farmer grabbed his hat, coat and gloves. The pickup was slow to start and cold, but he finally got it going. He drove the trail that had become their road out to the bridge. He built as much speed as possible to plow through the drifts. The impact of some was so hard it jolted his teeth! Crossing an open meadow, he hit a drift so large it stopped the truck dead as though it had hit a wall. Farmer tried to back up, but the rear tire slid into a hole and just spun. Farmer attempted to rock the truck back and forth. In a few minutes it was buried.

Farmer felt his heart pounding as he tried to see in the dark. There was enough light from the stars and a partial moon to make out that the snow was over the axles.

"Dear God! Help me!" Farmer cried out in frustration.

He shut the Model T off and ran back to the house.

"Farmer, did you get the Doctor?" Emile called out to him from their bedroom when Farmer bolted into the house.

"I couldn't even get out ta the main road. The truck is stuck. I'm takin' the horses! Beth, heat water and Emile will direct ya ta cloths. Emile, ya gotta hold on 'till I get back! An' I be back as soon as I can." Farmer kissed her and was out the door.

He saddled Sunset and Dusty. He rode Sunset as fast as he could run in the snow, with Dusty trailing behind. The race into Douglas Landing seemed to take forever. As minutes added to minutes and mile after another mile passed, Farmer was keenly aware that babies wait for no one. Their baby would come whether Doctor Put was there or not!

"Sirikin! Sirikin!" Farmer yelled up at the upstairs window as he pounded on the door.

"Dr. Put! It's Emile's time!"

Soon a light came on—then the door opened.

"Doctor, it's time! I had ta bring the horses—the drifts air too high ta drive through! I got Dusty fer ya ta ride—he's the most sure-footed! Hurry—her water done broke!"

The doctor spoke not a word, but soon emerged with his bag and heavy coat. He was not familiar with horses so the ride back to Farmer's ranch was slow. Finally in exasperation, Farmer roughly instructed Doctor Put, "Jus' give Dusty his head. He knows the way home! He won't throw ya or fall down!"

Farmer had no idea what he would find when they at last saw the lights of the log house shining ahead through the trees. He heard Emile scream as they approached the house.

Both men ran inside, and Farmer led Doctor Put to the bedroom.

"Emile, we're here!"

"Oh thank God!" Beth spoke with relief. "The baby is almost born!"

Doctor Put took over and asked Beth to assist him. Farmer checked on Walter and Clifton, who were in their loft bedroom holding each other and scared.

"I want my ma," Clifton choked out.

Farmer sat with them and talked about a new baby brother or sister that would be born that night.

It was a few minutes after midnight on the fourth of November in the silence of a crisp, cold, clear night that the faint cries of baby Leah were heard on the Trevor's Ranch.

CHAPTER 47

THE LAST OF THE WAGON PIONEERS

After Farmer saw Emile and their daughter Leah, he ushered Walter and Clifton in to see their new baby sister, then sent them on to bed.

Doctor Put decided to stay the night to make sure there were no complications with Emile or the baby. He fell asleep on the sofa by the fire.

Eventually, Beth, who was awestruck by Leah's birth retired to the room where she stayed, leaving Farmer, Emile and their new baby alone.

"Emile, I'm right proud, an' my heart is mighty full tonight. I reckon Leah will be as pretty as her mother."

"Her first nine months was mostly traveling," Emile smiled weakly. "She will probably have your restless spirit."

Emile and Leah soon slept as Farmer kept watch.

Suddenly, he remembered he had left Sunset and Dusty standing by the house. He donned his coat and hat and trudged out into the snow to lead the horses to the corral and the shelter of a small barn.

After taking saddles and reins off, Farmer stood at the corral looking up into the starry sky. He remembered the night Emile told him she was with child. He thought of the births of Walter and Clifton. It was one thing to have sons—but a daughter! That was different, and already he felt the change.

"Lord, I'm mighty grateful fer the children Ya have given me," Farmer breathed a prayer. "I promise ta love 'em and raise 'em the best I can, but I'm gonna need a powerful lot o help. I promise ta live the best I can fer Ya."

About then, the horses came to him and nuzzled their noses against his hands. Farmer's thoughts went over the trip to Oregon as he rubbed each horse's face. For months and miles these faithful animals had pulled the chuck wagon in heat, rain and snow. He remembered the towns they passed through, the places they had seen, and the people they met. And tonight, they had carried the Doctor when the pickup failed.

"Sunset, Wind, Dusty," Farmer whispered. "I'm makin' ya a promise too. Ya will be fer my children, and I will never sell ya."

Farmer looked out into the trees, his trees, and listened to the wind moan through the branches, making a sound like a waterfall. The moon was bright and glistened on the snow. He could clearly make out the rushing water in Cold Creek through the holes in the ice. Then the wind stopped, a hush fell, and the whole world seemed at peace.

Farmer was overcome by the emotion of the evening and the scene spread out before him. His heart filled to overflowing.

"Lord," Farmer's voice conveyed the love and closeness he felt for his maker, "Don't reckon I know much 'bout heaven or the place Ya is a fixin' fer me an Emile. .," he paused as he broke down and wept. Wiping his face he finished. "Ifen the place Ya has fer us could look like this, Lord, I would be mighty pleased."

Farmer felt that he had concluded the first phase of his life and had only to look forward to the next. What if a man could look at this life from the end back to the beginning as God does? Would he make different decisions or would he live it the same? If Farmer could have seen the hardships of the trip—would he still have brought his family through that difficult and dangerous journey? Would that knowledge have frightened him enough to stay on the farm in Texas or would the satisfaction he knew now be over powering enough to cause him to risk the very lives of himself and his family? Then the bigger question! If it was revealed to him all that would befall them in this strange new land, would they still have made the move, would their choices remain the same, or would they keep the good times and try to correct the bad ones—wishing to spare themselves the heartaches. At what point would we put ourselves out of the path He has planned for our lives. Perhaps that is why God in His mercy doesn't tell us beforehand what our life will be or how and when it will end.

All Farmer knew that night as he gazed past the trees to the dim outline of the mountains, to the stars beyond, was that his restless spirit had been satisfied. An era had come to an end. He was the last of the wagon pioneers.

Printed in the United States
125668LV00003B/127/A